Here or There

Rebecca Strong

Legend  Press

Independent Book Publisher

Legend Press Ltd
13a Northwold Road, London, N16 7HL
info@legendpress.co.uk
www.legendpress.co.uk
www.myspace.com/legendpress

British Library Catologuing in Publication Data available.

ISBN 978-0-9551032-6-1

Set in Times
Printed by Gutenberg Press, Malta

Cover designed by Gudrun Jobst
www.yellowoftheegg.co.uk

Legend Press
Independent Book Publisher

To my father, the greatest storyteller I know.

'When you are sorrowful look again in your heart, and you shall see that in truth you are weeping for that which has been your delight.'

Kahlil Gibran, The Prophet

'Better is the sight of the eyes than the wandering of the desire.'

Ecclesiastes, 6:9

Prologue

Desire can always be split into two. The things you desire, by their very nature, are never the things you have. Although the things you have are still desired, still things you appreciate – when you take the time to remember. Desire will always disappoint you, in the end. For what you want is never as good as the wanting itself.

She had shown him this, in a way. He had to be grateful: without her he would have been lost, even unto himself, and at least for a while everything had had meaning, a purpose. She enlightened him, back then, and he drank her in until he was so intoxicated she controlled all his actions, a feeling he wholeheartedly embraced. Diminished responsibility, he'd like to claim, but he would be laughed at or, worse, despised.

"It was mutual; it was what we both wanted," she'd argue, "wasn't it?" she'd add, a little insecurity creeping through. Because, at the end of the day, she'd lost more than he had, sacrificed her whole world in search of one she could control, only to find herself wanting, again.

It had been on the news; he remembered the day she had gone to the front door as usual, picked up that day's national newspaper and retreated to the kitchen for a routine cup of coffee. He had been in the bedroom when he heard her exclaim and, thinking she had hurt herself, he rushed clumsily into the kitchen, almost tripping over the bags that at that time resided permanently on the bedroom floor. Instead she was seated, one hand over her mouth and the other clutching at the paper sheets, eyes rapidly scanning words that had by then become so familiar to them.

"What did you expect?" he had asked her. "It's no surprise they've covered it – there's a lot of interest in these sorts of things."

"'These sorts of things'?" she had responded defensively, immediately standing him alongside the media fiends and vicious critics. That's how it became, eventually; at one time the two of them had stood together, but now their own actions only served to pit them against each other.

"These sorts of things, as you refer to them, are our lives, our actions, our circumstances. How can you dismiss them like that? How can you offer them up to the media frenzy and sit back with satisfaction. How can you not care that more and more people are hearing about this? It's become a farce, not a consequence."

Her face crumpled and stained with tears, and he went to her and put his arms around her. Though he couldn't help thinking, yet again, how unattractive she looked when she was crying.

"I didn't offer anything, and I am not satisfied. It's just a small part of the course of events, that's all – one day it will be forgotten." She sobbed in his arms but was quiet for the rest of the day. He didn't know if he believed his own words. He wanted to agree with her, but he had to keep up his role as protector, had to sustain the meaning they'd once injected into their relationship in order to make it worthwhile.

Meaning was slipping as fast as time. Any chance of perspective had crumbled a long time ago, perhaps even the day she revealed her proposition, and the day he had complied, eager to please her and longing for an ideal that he foolishly believed was within their grasp.

He wondered if he had ever been a good person – certainly he didn't feel like one now – and if he had given up that side of him, sacrificed his integrity for the pursuit of pleasure. He was no longer capable of judging himself or her, though plenty of others were, and when he looked at her now, stared into her eyes, he saw a series of events, emotions, turmoil – several things, but no longer a person. She had transformed in his vision to embody all that they had been embroiled in, and in his eyes she was now the antithesis of her former self – suffocation rather than a means of escape.

He thought he still loved her and, despite events, he was not willing to let go of everything they had worked towards. They had deconstructed so much, painfully and ruthlessly, and there was no way he would give up before the reconstruction took place, wherever and however that may be. We owe it to ourselves, he told himself, otherwise we'll never know if we did the right thing. But the right thing is always wrong for someone, the good mirrored by bad, desire twinned with dissatisfaction.

He could remember that last night as clearly as if he were still experiencing it – in terms of senses rather than memory. The candles flickering across the room, casting eerie shadows on the walls and slowly dying away as the night passed. The smell of mint on her breath, the scent of which he caught from time-to-time as she whispered to him quietly. Jumbled words that he later forgot but nevertheless clung to, each one as poignant as the next. The light touch of her hand on the back of his neck.

They'd started the evening dancing cheek-to-cheek just like old times, and as the night went on he found himself reaching out to caress her face, as if trying to recreate the feeling of her smooth cheek against his. Then she'd slapped him, not once but twice, to remind him of the destruction that tainted them. The sting of her hand, her strength, the urge to be slapped again, if only she would touch him.

The warmth of her body against his, something he later sought on nights when his cool sheets would make him shiver and long for her. It hadn't been easy, and it hadn't been certain, and he couldn't even decide if it had been worth the torture he now felt. But he liked to think it was.

The infusion of coconut in her hair, its silky texture

underneath his chin, and the way she stretched to sweep it from her face.

In the dull light his mind twisted and burned, feverish with regret and longing. We were meant to find catharsis, he seethed, not play out this bitter endgame.

He realised that what once she had given him, only she could take away, and he loved and hated her all at the same time, resented her manipulation and impulsiveness, while also recognising those reprobate traits in himself. Their own desires had stung them, beaten them, switched the polarity so that, like two negative magnets, no amount of effort could keep them clinging together. Desire will always disappoint you, in the end.

At the close of the night, the harsh words and the emptiness he felt as she drew away, drifted almost, though not reluctantly, until she was gone. And the words on the small, white square of paper, written in pencil so as to render them finite:

'I don't want to be <u>here</u>'

Chapter 1

It was dark when she left the building and sloped off along the side alley, pulling her hat down over her head, all the while listening out for unfamiliar night sounds. The air was crisp and she could see her breath periodically materialising in front of her face. She was the last to leave, as was so often the case, and yet again she wished that her manager, Mr Busby, hadn't chosen to make an example of her, hadn't picked on her and pulled her up on her work in front of all the others, when so many of them were slipshod and apathetic.

"My boxes were all filled and complete, really they were!" she had protested, beginning to suspect that someone further down the line had been playing a cruel joke on her, but Busby insisted that each box could be traced back to its original workstation – something to do with the barcode or reference number.

So here she was, leaving an hour-and-a-half after everyone else, not even Busby staying to turn off the lights and lock up. He refused to believe in the quality of her work, yet he could entrust her with the security of the whole place – a lazy and vindictive man. The darkness smelled of stale flowers, precarious like the calm before the storm.

Each day began early at Taunton's Confectionary factory. A post-WW1 venture established in 1920, it started as a chocolate shop that expanded rapidly due to high demand and before long production had to be moved to a different site to facilitate adequate supply. It was a great time for confectionary: the lingering view of chocolates as a luxury made them all the more sought after, but ingredients were plentiful, and business thrived.

It was started by Mr A. Taunton, with ownership passing down the family line, and it was currently owned by Gregory Fellows, the son of Taunton's granddaughter, who had his finger in many pies and generally left the running of the factory to Busby. At five-minutes-to-seven in the morning, six-days-a-week, a cluster of weary but chattering women would gather at the front entrance, ready for Busby to unlock the doors. One-by-one they would traipse in, deposit their meagre belongings and packed lunches in the lockers provided, and take up their places along the production line.

There were a lucky few who worked in the two small factory offices: Busby and his personal assistant, Alice (an understandably nervous type), occupied one of them entirely, and the factory 'Supplies and Maintenance Office' vegetated in the other. But the Head Office was in a different location and the factory workers rarely saw the people who governed their working lives. Most of the processes were mechanical these days, but no machine could provide the checking services that each of the employees did. It was dull work but stable, and this seemed to keep most of the women happy. They chatted and joked, squabbled and gossiped, fretted and fussed, and whiled away the time with their petty grievances and latest tales. For her, it was different. The job was a means to an end, something she had to put up with in order to get where she wanted or, at the very least, in order not to slip back into the past.

She worked at the very end of one production line – the Belgian chocolates – each box complete with a small disclaimer stating that although some of the ingredients came from Belgium, the chocolates were not actually produced there. Her job was to inspect each box, once it had been filled by the great machine that stood in the middle of the line, making sure both trays were complete with one chocolate of each type. She had one colleague to her left inspecting the boxes before they were filled, and one to her right inspecting the plastic sheeting placed in between each tray and on the top.

"You're very lucky to be in charge of the chocolates, you know," Busby would sneer at her sometimes, sarcasm oozing from his tongue like the sweat from his pores. "Others only get to inspect the paper and plastic. Make sure you don't slip up; it's taxing work." His breath smelled of old fish and vinegary chips, causing those he addressed to slightly recoil. And with that, he would stride off to peer over the shoulder of another worker.

The best bit about the job was the samples or 'end-of-line' confectionary of which they were each allowed to take home a single box every week. This occasionally caused tussles and contention as the women pushed and shoved to get the best scoopfuls from the different tubs that stood in one corner of the main factory floor. Yet even this perk was tainted by the sickening chocolate smell that infused their working environment day-in, day-out, to the extent that she could no longer bring even a delectable Taunton's Truffle to her lips. Her flat was filled with unopened sample boxes just waiting for someone to consume them, but she had no one to give them to and was periodically forced to dispose of them.

In general, the days were tedious and dull, with lunchtime being the only reprieve. The workers seldom left the office during a break, aside from those who smoked, because there was nothing on the industrial estate other than stark, depressing buildings that were far from pleasant to look at. She would eat her lunch quietly in a corner of the canteen and listen to the other women harangue and chide each other, discovering whose husband was wayward, whose husband a drunk and whose children were causing trouble in the neighbourhood.

It was a welcome distraction, in a way, to immerse oneself in the idle chitchat and sometimes it was the only time of day when she could throw herself into another world (the third she had been party to, she supposed) and take her mind off her own concerns. Their combined lunches provided aromatic respite from the intensity of chocolate and she silently analysed each woman's circumstances from the contents of their lunch packs – tuna and mayonnaise here; ham and cheese there; some brought only a few cheap crackers with processed cheese spread and a packet of crisps. The scent of the food rose and mingled with the chatter, bringing the sparse factory cafeteria to life.

The workforce, apart from Busby and the two men who occupied the second office, was entirely female, and this was never questioned. It was not an environment that men could survive in – emotionally or socially – and the female workers would have ripped any man to shreds. It was their own union of solidarity and trust, which could not be penetrated by any male save Busby, and this, she was sure, made him all the more conceited. A lone dictator governing the *jejune* fairer sex, he prowled and sniped like a slothful lion with a pride of labourers. He wasn't married, unlike most of the workforce, and they never had any inkling of his life outside the factory. He would occasionally hover around a gossiping gaggle, clearly interested in their prattle but, the minute one of them spotted him, he would reprimand them for 'stealing company time' and verbally whip them back into shape. He didn't mind the occasional whisper or the rare conversation about work, but he despised any talk of which he was not within earshot.

He struck her as lonely, in some ways, but at other times she thought him so antagonistic to human company that he was better off by himself. The other women seemed to appreciate some kind of authority – they were set rules to abide by, even if they weren't always adhered to – but she hated his oppressive nature and the way he lurked around factory corners so you never knew when he would appear.

Strangely enough, it was Alice she thought about most during quieter days at the factory. For, as she had discovered, a female union excludes not only men but any woman unable to conform to its unspoken criteria. Like Alice, she revealed nothing of her past or circumstances, maintained a vague air of derision, rejected small talk, wore no perfume and, as a result, remained a mystery. Her clothes under the standard uniform were deliberately smartish but not trendy (these days, it was a relief to keep things simple, though on occasion she longed for the opportunity to don a skirt, heels and pussy-bowed shirt – clothes she had long ago discarded) and she privately struggled to coat her words in an unidentifiable accent, adopting grating colloquialisms from her colleagues in an attempt to ingratiate herself with them.

Two or three months into her employment, her social ranking at work was sealed; then she held herself back from her co-workers and they, in turn, were less than forthcoming. Alice, she came to realise, was ignored – none of the workers had any claims to the details of the private lives of senior staff. She, however, was silently snubbed, her mask mistaken for elitism, her mysteriousness for mistrust.

She had a fantasy, still, that one day she would end up in Busby's office, after he had gone home, for a *tête-à-tête* with Alice. She ran the scene through her mind almost daily, and each time her mind fudged the details until the point where she revealed her own history, Alice captivated and attentive. It always ended the same way – Alice would tell her that Busby was leaving and she would be recommended for the manager's position. As much as even Alice remained alien to her, she was the only fantasy audience she could find for the story she could never tell.

Sometimes she wondered if Busby knew, if someone had told him about her past, despite being reassured that nothing of the sort had happened. He seemed just the sort to take someone's weakness and manipulate it for his own amusement until they hit breaking point. She shivered at the memory of him approaching her earlier that afternoon, placing his hand on her shoulder and quietly tutting in her ear, the familiar smirks from her colleagues and the low chuckle he gave as he reminded her she'd have to stay late, again, and alone.

All the other women had left bang on five o'clock, most boarding the musty factory bus that fetched them daily and dropped them back to the nearest estate where the majority of them lived. It was seven o' clock and already dark by the time she'd locked all the doors, set the alarm and left. Striding round the curve of the alleyway leading from the factory car park to the main road where she could catch the No. 43 bus, her flat-soled shoes made a regular, dull thud. She walked briskly, occasionally looking around behind her, habit forcing her to stay alert and ignore the sound of her quickening heartbeat. She had trained herself so well that when she felt the hand grab her hair and jerk her backwards she didn't even scream; only a small gasp left her lips and disappeared into the darkness.

"Elisabeth Rowley?" a gruff voice growled. A waft of cheap aftershave mixed with cigarette smoke crept round her neck and tickled her nostrils. She turned and faced him, scanning desperately for familiar features that were not there. He was dressed all in black with a stern look in his eyes and he still held her hair with a firm grip.

"I used to be," she replied, knowing then that her time was up. A slight thrill shot into her bloodstream and she bit her bottom lip in disbelief.

She said no more and didn't resist as the man led her roughly along the alleyway, at the end of which was parked a dark blue car. He opened the rear door and placed his hand on the top of her head, guiding her into the vehicle. It was the first bit of gentility he had shown her and, despite her fright, she relaxed a little. She knew he wouldn't hurt her – he couldn't – and as she waited for him to walk round and get into the driver's seat, she set her mind to planning the best way to behave. Arguing would get her nowhere; these people wouldn't play games. She needed to work out where she was going and what they would do to her, how much she would tell them, and how much she would let them think they could manipulate her.

What she struggled with most was who to be; should she revert to her old habits, her old voice, her old accent? They were slowly fading from her mind, her training having been rigorous, yet a part of her welcomed the chance to reveal them once again. When you've deliberately reinvented yourself, erased the person you once were piece-by-piece, and convinced the world you're someone else, how do you begin to regress to your former self? In the quest for anonymity, there had been no police guidelines on the worst-case scenario.

He started the engine and the car roared to life, the hum of diesel piercing the silent evening. Contrary to the stereotypical profile she had already created of him in her mind, he was a careful and somewhat hesitant driver, the car jerking just once or twice. He stuck to back roads and after twenty minutes she had lost all perspective of where they were. The car was old and stagnant; a few discarded food wrappers lounging on the floor mats instinctively made her draw her legs towards her. At one point he reached for the radio but hesitated and drew his hand back. He remained silent, except for occasionally clearing his throat, and she herself dared not speak.

He had locked all the doors after he had entered the car, and she assumed that the green light glowing from the button on either back-seat door meant that the child lock was on. She slowly unzipped her handbag and reached into it for her mobile phone, wishing that she had been in the seat directly behind the driver and not on the opposite side where he would see anything she was doing the minute he turned his head.

Her hand trembled as she slowly lifted the phone out and tilted it to one side so that the light behind its façade would be hidden. The sound was on; if she pressed any of the keys he would hear it and, in order to turn the sound off, she would have to press at least three. She poised two fingers over the necessary keys and gave a loud cough as she pushed them. He turned round at the noise, just as she let her hand fall a little, and he noticed the phone.

"Don't even think about it," he warned, the first words he had uttered since getting into the car. "Who would you call, anyway?" He gave a flippant laugh, more cruel in light of the fact he was right – she had no one to call. What would she do? Explain the past five years to someone in a few sentences and convince them that she needed rescuing? She had lost her freedom so many years ago that she no longer mourned for it, no longer felt that acerbic taste in her mouth when she woke-up.

"Give it to me," he demanded, and for the second time in her life she handed over the last link she had to anyone she cared about.

He turned her phone off and threw it into the glove compartment. For a minute or so they continued, in silence, until again he spoke, "You might as well give me your handbag now; I'll need to take it off you anyway."

"But I've got things in here I need!" she protested. "Personal things, nothing that concerns you."

"I'll be the judge of that. Now hand it over and if there's anything you need later you may ask for it."

Hesitantly, she held it forward and he reached backwards and took the bag, placing it on his lap.

The next time they stopped at a traffic light he rummaged through it, finding her purse and driving licence, which he held up to the streetlight.

"Hannah Sampson, eh? Did you pick that?"

"No. You take what you're given – you must know that." She waited for a response, almost hoping to strike up a conversation or even glean any word from him that would give her a clue as to her fate, but he fell silent again, as unpredictable as the fresh wind that snuck in every now and then from a small gap at the top of his window.

They drove for another ten minutes or so, still skirting around back roads and unfamiliar terraced housing until the car slowed and turned into what appeared to be a car park with a closed repair garage at its head. He stopped the car and cleared his throat once more, before turning and staring her straight in the eyes. "We're here." He got out and walked around the car to her side, stopping first to open the boot and take something out.

Her heart beat faster and faster in its paranoia of what she was about to face, and when he opened the door for her she at first shrank away and then reluctantly tumbled out. He held out his hand to help her straighten up, but she chose to ignore it and leaned slightly against the car, willing herself to be strong. "This way," he said, pointing towards an enclave next to a 'M.O.T. While-U-Wait' sign.

He walked on ahead – obviously not the slightest bit concerned that she would not follow – swinging a black plastic bag. She breathed heavily through her mouth as she began to trace his path, lagging a good ten metres behind. She could detect a faint smell of chocolate on her own breath; perhaps her job had become part of her after all, not that she would be returning to it now. He stopped when he got to the enclave and turned around to wait for her, his patience perhaps a last-minute act of kindness.

Walking under the brick arch and looking to the right, she saw a door that he opened without a key, and he stepped inside into the darkness. She approached the door, squinting to make out shapes beyond the entrance, and took small steps inside. The door swung shut behind her and she realised another man had been waiting behind it; she had clearly been expected.

The man who had shut the door then grabbed her by the wrist and led her down a corridor, and she wondered where the first man had gone, almost longing for his now familiar presence. This second man was stocky but clean-shaven, dressed head-to-toe in dark colours. He led her to another door and opened it, gesturing for her to go ahead.

Light was spilling out from this room and as she entered she took a deep breath that her body instantaneously expelled when she saw who was standing before her. Her hands unclenched and her body slumped, as if the events of the past two hours had expended her entire spirit. She had always imagined this moment, too many times to believe it would ever really happen. Now that they were both here, in the same room again, she realised that every single moment of one's past dissolves into one's existence with the passing of each second; it is neither retrievable nor deniable.

"Elisabeth," he hissed, and she could not tell whether her name on his tongue was tinged with relief or regret.

She said nothing – there was nothing to say – but she held his gaze as he walked confidently up to her, past the black chair and dark, wooden desk that were the only objects in the room, and she stopped herself from flinching as he put both hands firmly upon her cheeks and brought his face close to hers. He had aged substantially, his skin rough and patchy, though his eyes remained youthful and inquisitive. His glistening temple creased and uncreased like a vexed slug. His warm breath smelled of whisky and his fingers were clammy as he ran them over her face and her lips. She closed her eyes and concentrated on breathing, but suddenly his hands left her face and cold air hit her once again. She flashed open her eyes to see him walk back to the desk and pick up a small shot glass that rested on one corner.

As he walked back towards her she slowly began to shake her head, glancing behind her only to find the door was firmly shut. She backed up but he was soon upon her, and in one swift move he reached up and held her nose as she instinctively opened her mouth to gasp.

"Drink this," he commanded, though the pungent liquid was already trickling down her throat as she swallowed, coughing in vain.

When she woke up with her wrists and ankles tied to a chair her scream echoed in her ears alone.

Chapter 2

Simon gulped down his morning coffee, feeling the caffeine buzz spread through his veins, and grabbed his jacket and keys. Looking in the hallway mirror, he realised he'd forgotten to slick back his hair in its usual trendy coiffeur.

"Hey, Amy," he called to the figure sleepily ascending the stairs, toast in hand, "what's the time?"

"Ummmmmmno," came the reply, as Amy turned her head lazily, glancing back at him. Simon continued to preen in vain, for now his hair was sticking up and fluffing at the sides.

"Ah, no porcupine today I see," quipped Amy, making a familiar reference to his usual hairdo. "Relax, I'm sure it'll survive without a whole tub of gel for one day!"

"Very funny," replied Simon, finally darting back to the living room to check the time and evaluate whether he had long enough to retrieve his gel. His face paled when he saw it was already gone half-past-eight – late again.

"Gotta go," he shouted back to Amy as he opened the front door, but once he had stepped outside and turned around he realised she was no longer standing there. He closed the door clumsily onto his finger and shrieked from the pain, silently glad that she hadn't still been there to hear his high-pitched squeal.

Still sucking on his finger, he started to jog, slowing only when he could see Mile End station in the distance. When he got there, huffing and puffing to allay a stomach cramp, he shuffled forward in the barrier queue, his face almost brushing against the coat of the person in front of him. When it was his turn, he stuck his ticket into the machine and automatically walked forward, his fingers reaching out to grab…nothing. He clutched at air as the barriers suddenly clamped down on him and he realised his ticket hadn't emerged. The ticket machine's loud beep nearly masked Simon's own exclaim, and caused those around him to tut in annoyance or snigger. He nudged his body this way and that but he was stuck fast. Soon the crowd about him parted like the sea, and a lone figure of rescue appeared, frowning condescendingly.

"Where's your ticket?" asked the London Underground employee.

"The machine swallowed it!" Simon insisted. "Look, can you please let me out of here?" The barriers were massaging his waist in a most unpleasant way, and he could almost feel his coffee swilling around inside him.

"We'd better open the machine," said the man, as if addressing a colleague, and Simon sagged with relief until he realised the he meant to retrieve Simon's ticket rather than to set him free. He waited, his cheeks reddening, as hundreds of commuters passed him by before his ticket was found. He tried to place his arms as if he were resting on the barriers instead of being trapped, but either way he looked ridiculous.

"Look, I have a valid ticket. I don't know why it was swallowed, but if you could just let me out…I'm late for w-"

"This the one?" said the man, holding up a slightly crumpled ticket.

"Yes, yes, that must be it. Now, can I go through?"

"Take your time in future," he instructed, as if explaining the laws of physics. "Don't put your ticket through for the person in front of you. No need to rush."

Simon muttered angrily as he was set free and made a dash for the escalator. He trotted as quickly as possible down the stairs, rushed across to the southbound platform, ran up to the train teasingly sitting there, before tripping on the carriage lip and flying head-first into the throng just as the 'beep beep beep' of the doors closing began to sound. They came together, sharply, onto Simon's legs, which had not quite managed to board with the rest of him.

"Oh dear," said a woman's voice, most likely the one looking down upon Simon's head. A few people tried to lift him up, but his feet were stuck and the best he could do was kneel sheepishly as if in prayer.

'Could whoever is obstructing the doors please move away? You're holding up a whole trainful of people,' came the announcement, just as the doors once again opened. Simon just had time to whip his feet in before they closed once more, and he managed to stand up, brushing down his suit.

"Sorry about that," he said to those around him.

"Are you alright?" asked the same female voice, a concerned middle-aged woman with wide eyes and mousy hair.

"I'm ok," replied Simon, then, on realising she was still staring, "I'm fine, really," and he turned slightly away to escape her gaze.

It was then that he realised he'd dropped his ticket somewhere in the rush, and he groaned at the thought of the hassle of explaining himself at the other end. But, even worse, he looked up to see Rose grinning at him from further along the carriage. Rose was easily the most attractive young woman at their office, and very much in demand.

As he smiled back, Simon noticed that today she was wearing a navy pin-stripe suit and blue…well, heels (aside from colour, how many different ways were there to describe high heels?). Her hair was neatly tied up and clipped together with a blue fabric flower that fanned out across the back of her head, perhaps a little too fancy. He'd previously considered it an advantage that they both lived near each other, using the fact as a topic of conversation whenever their paths crossed. But now he cringed at the thought of his fall and what she must have thought – hardly the suave, debonair type she surely would go for. That's why he never had much success with women – he was always the funny guy, game for a laugh, the *just a friend* guy they all liked to have around but not to date.

As he stepped off the train onto the seething platform at his stop, Simon glanced round for Rose and for once was relieved that she had disappeared. At the top of the escalator, he found the wheelchair access barrier open and slipped through it quickly, making a mental note to remember to buy another ticket at lunchtime. The station clock told him it was five-past-nine, and that he would surely incur the wrath of his boss, often referred to as 'Cold-Stance', once he reached the office. Finally, he turned left into Wood Street and made his way past the homogenous office buildings until he reached his own, the offices of Radison Consulting Ltd.

He plopped down onto his chair and stared vacantly at his desk. The voice of Jason, his colleague, jogged him out of his weary stupor, "You're late again."

"Stating the obvious, Jason." The two of them usually got on fine, but Simon sometimes resented the goody-two-shoes smugness that radiated from Jason. It wasn't his fault, Simon supposed, that women loved him, both at work and outside. He just wished that, occasionally, some of his colleague's good fortune would waft his own way.

"Well, she's not happy. She wants to see you in her office."

With a sigh, Simon stumbled over to Constance's door and braced himself for the reprimand. He had worked there for just about nine months, and it was the first serious job he'd ever had, although admittedly he could take it a fair bit more seriously. When he eventually slinked back to his desk, he made a joke of his telling-off to Jason, who kindly indulged him.

Later that day, Dan phoned. Dan was one of Simon's housemates, a teacher employed at an inner city school through one of those government schemes that aimed to entice bright young things to mould younger not-so-bright things into first-class British nationals (diversity welcomed, of course), with the bribe that they would subsequently be placed in top jobs that might never materialise. Dan was shouting unintelligibly about Bill and Amy, and it took Simon a while to decipher what he was saying. It was only when he got home that evening that he got the whole story.

Dan had returned that day at lunchtime, feeling the onslaught of a sore throat and not wanting to pass it onto the pupils – the perfect excuse for leaving early. He'd stopped at a chemist on the way back to pick up sachets of a honey and lemon drink and some throat sweets, and hurried back to the house. He thought about phoning Amy, who had the day off, but decided he was feeling too sorry for himself to do anything but vegetate, and he was hardly in a state to trek to her flat. For a good few minutes after he entered the house he heard nothing but silence, and it was only after he had fixed himself a cheese sandwich, retrieved the quilt from his bedroom and positioned himself on the sofa that he heard muffled voices and stifled laughter. His hand paused on the remote control, and he heard them again (male? female?) so he eased himself up and out of his cocoon, and wandered back up the stairs.

"All the doors were open apart from Bill's," he told Simon. "I could hear a female voice, and I even chuckled to myself because I thought Bill had a girlfriend!" Bill was trying to make it as an actor – and, to his credit, had been in one television advert for a hardware retail chain, which he talked about so much that the others frequently joked about his name being in 'halogen lights' – and worked in a pub most evenings and weekends. His arrogance and deluded aspirations usually put women off so Simon could understand why Dan had been amused and surprised.

"So, I was just about to creep back downstairs when I heard the woman say, 'Good thing I had the day off.' I turned round again and pressed my ear to Bill's door, and that's when I heard her! Amy! Then I even heard Bill say, 'Hey, I wouldn't worry – he thinks I don't like you' with a real smirk in his voice, the idiot."

"Oh gosh," said Simon, wondering what was coming next. "So, what did you do?"

"Well, I flung open the door and caught them in bed together!

Bill and Amy! I can't believe her especially; I mean, Bill really took his chance, but Amy! I thought she had better taste…well, I mean, she was with me, and…" He put his head in his hands, and Simon patted him on the arm, suddenly worried that Dan might be crying. But then his flatmate raised his head and his face was only flushed with anger.

"I don't ever want to see her again. And he'd better stay out of my way."

"Hey," said Simon, desperate to offer some words of consolation, "she wasn't that pretty anyway. She did have a nose a bit like a horse, and she was kind of squat." He gesticulated in front of Dan, until he realised his friend was staring at him incredulously.

"Neeeiiigh!" he imitated, trying to provoke a laugh. But then Dan got up, shouting, "What's wrong with you?" before declaring him an idiot too and storming out.

"Bit too soon for the ribbing then," he mumbled after he'd left, marvelling at just how often he managed to put his foot in it. Dan's bedroom door slammed shut.

The house they lived in had four-and-a-half bedrooms, a living/dining room, a bathroom and separate toilet, and a constantly messy kitchen. Tim, a P.E. teacher and fitness-freak, had the biggest room which was cluttered with gym equipment. Simon and Dan had average-sized rooms next-door to each other, close enough so that they each heard more than enough of what was going on in the other's room. Garth (an unfortunate name bestowed upon him by a mother with a passion for country music) had the ground floor room by the front door and was trying to become an estate agent though he had worked for, and been fired from, three different agencies for lack of sales technique – which he claimed was actually a lack of innovation and vision on the part of the agents.

Bill had happily taken the box room, partly for the lower rent and partly because he upheld the ridiculous notion that one day, when he was accepting his Oscar, he would look back with fondness on his humble beginnings and memories of the house and his room would keep him grounded – a real joke considering he was hardly grounded to begin with, let alone if he ever made it big. Occasionally, one of them would become so fed-up with the mess, he would go through the motions of tidying up, only to discover more clutter hidden under the visible clutter and give up.

For a long time, Simon's parents had been trying to convince their first-born to move back home, though their pleas ceased once he got his job at Radison – a reputable company he knew they'd love to tell friends and neighbours their son worked for. The day he was offered the job, he jumped on a train to tell them in person, grabbing a bunch of flowers for his mother on the way. He spent the afternoon with his mum in quiet contemplation of her imminent joy at his announcement, which he kept to himself until his little sister had returned from school and his father from work.

He told them over dinner, watching their growing smiles as his words sank in, and blushing with anticipated pleasure as his mother jumped up to embrace and commend him. His sister, too young to be aware of career challenge but old enough to understand their parents' expectations, smiled graciously and also congratulated him, as happy at her parents' delight as at her brother's news. He reiterated that it was just an assistant's job, that he had a three-month trial period, that he wasn't quite sure yet what the job would entail, but his contractions fell on deaf ears, and he revelled in the long-awaited glory.

His father's reaction was the one that elated Simon the most – he visibly beamed and immediately proffered a proud toast to "his son, the Management Consultant", which struck Simon as so poignant, so longed-for on his part, that he wholeheartedly overlooked the inaccuracy of the statement and didn't even joke about it later.

From his first day at Radison, Simon enjoyed his job because it had transformed him into the son his parents had always wanted, which, as trite as it seemed, made it a job worth hanging onto with all the potential he possessed. He cherished the independence of living in a house with friends, despite its melodrama, and the freedom to be who he really wanted. Even though he was still a joker, he now commanded a degree of respect, and the feeling of failure that had plagued him for many months after he graduated had now dissipated. In his parents' minds, he had gone from being 'Simon-who-is-perpetually-looking-at-his-career-options' to 'Simon, our son, in Management Consultancy training at Radison', and this, he knew, was gold dust he couldn't afford to let blow away in a gust of complacency.

Chapter 3

When there's something you want more than anything in the world, something you yearn to have at any cost, something you would do anything – and sacrifice everything – for, it consumes your existence like an acidic obsession that churns in your stomach and mind, day and night. It's the first thing you think about when you wake-up, but not the last thought of your day as it pervades your dreams, making you toss and turn and thrash in a deep sweat throughout the night.

For Johnny Miller, the worst thing about his ultimate desire was that he had absolutely no control over the situation and, no matter how hard he tried, he never felt closer to his goal. For what Johnny wanted more than anything in the world was for his alcoholic, good-for-nothing, pseudo-sole guardian, joke of a father to stop drinking. Whisky, vodka, beer, gin – anything he could get his hands on. Johnny had once caught him drinking white spirit from the (now empty) bottle that sat on a dusty shelf in the garage.

In a bizarre twist, his father's drinking made Johnny feel as sick as if he consumed the same daily quota of toxicity. He worried about his father constantly, tried to take care of him at all hours and sacrificed any semblance of a social life in order to keep an eye on him. His father, in return, cursed, burped and swigged his way through life.

"Get up, Dad," Johnny would say every Friday, "we don't have any food in the house. Go and get the dole, will you?

C'mon Dad."

"I've told you," his father would slur back, "I'm not getting the dole. We don't need other people's money. We're fine." And then he would rise up from the sag of the sofa, leaning heavily on the arm, and lumber into the kitchen, shouting in triumph as he discovered hidden treasures.

"See, we've got plenty," he'd shout with a disoriented grin, waving a can of beer at Johnny.

"You'd never be like this if Mum were still here!" Johnny would shout, before storming off to school. He meant that line to be painful, but he'd said it so often it had lost its sting. He knew that, eventually, his father would wander to the Post Office to collect the money, as they had no other income. But his state of denial had progressed so far that he couldn't even admit to taking benefits to himself, least of all to his own son. Recently, they'd managed to buy some time by re-mortgaging part of the house, and this money had been set aside to meet the endless stream of bills, taxes and direct debits. Still, this didn't alter the fact that Johnny's main motivation for attending school each day was the constant embarrassment he felt at being around his own father.

Johnny's mother had died when he was twelve-years-old, a pubescent cub with what seemed to be a promising future and the world at his fingertips. Soon after, he had become the antithesis of his former self: an emotionally-scarred, cynical young man whose daily struggle to maintain a hopeful existence was rewarded with further struggles and challenges.

It had been good, Johnny often thought, when his mother was alive. His parents were both smokers, starting as schoolchildren in the seventies and smoking their way right through the eighties, with the exception of his mother giving up while she was pregnant – a sacrifice that many would take for granted but that, looking back, Johnny recognised as no mean feat.

When she was diagnosed with lung cancer, she finally quit smoking for good and lost the tense anxiety that plagues every smoker killing time between cigarettes. She remained shrewd and falsely chirpy for Johnny's sake and, being an inquisitive but trusting eleven-year-old, for a long time Johnny thought not to question her reassurances that she was going to be fine. She never hid her illness from him, but neither did she elaborate on her condition and the constant trips to the hospital were, in Johnny's mind, connected to the recovery process.

"Why do you have to go to the hospital so often, Mum?" he'd once asked her, a slight suspicion niggling at the back of his mind.

"Doctors are there to help people darling," she'd answered, "so the more I go, the quicker I'll get better."

Thus he was satisfied, perhaps even wanting her to go more frequently so that she would receive more treatment. One time he found medical notes she had left lying on her dressing table – 'TREATMENT SCHEDULE FOR MRS FLORA MILLER' written boldly at the top – and scanned them quickly, but he didn't understand most of it and couldn't find anything untoward.

His mother told him about radiotherapy, and much later chemotherapy, and had explained that it would leave her temporarily feeling worse, but better in the long-run because it was zapping the cancer inside her. She simplified the procedures for him and, although he didn't understand any of the medical jargon, he found the complicated machinery, the names of the seven pills she had to take twice-a-day, and the progress updates somewhat comforting, as if anything that was unknown to a young boy must be bigger and better than he could comprehend at that age. Sometimes, when he played his computer games, he pretended he was holding a radiology machine – he had no idea what one looked like but envisaged it to be like a laser gun – that he pointed and fired at cancer, swiftly eradicating all cells until none were left to multiply.

His father, on the other hand, was increasingly absent during this testing time. Daniel worked long hours, leaving the house at 6.30am and usually returning around 9pm, in time for dinner and the ten o' clock news before retiring to bed. He worked as a car salesman, attending auctions and striking up deals with large enterprises that wanted to sell ex-company cars in bulk. He had left school at eighteen, two years later than most of his friends, after taking a vocational course in auto-mechanics and basic vehicle engineering.

He began an apprenticeship at the local garage he had been helping at every weekend since he was sixteen, and gradually worked his way up to starting his own business. He was dedicated and mildly ambitious, and the extra hours he put in during his wife's illness turned him into a successful and well-respected salesman. As his wife grew more sick, business became healthier and, unable to face the reality of impending loss, he invested all his time and energy into the one area of his life that wasn't being torn apart.

He employed two 'day nurses' to look after Flora, one from eight o'clock in the morning to midday and the other from five o'clock until nine o'clock, and in the middle she would read, watch television or sleep. They gave her breakfast, lunch and dinner, and, on the rare occasion that she was still hungry, Daniel would prepare her a snack when he came home, if Johnny had not done so already. They had once been so close, convinced that together they could handle anything, but they were a *team* and without her he shrank away, unwilling to contemplate a family without all of its components. Daniel was present just enough to play the caring husband, but absent enough to render it a lie.

Johnny heard his mother every night, coughing and wheezing, sometimes hacking until she threw up, and he pulled the edges of his pillow up to cover his ears. All part of the healing process, he told himself – she was coughing out the cancer. He felt defensive on his mother's behalf, often jumping in to reply when family friends or relatives inquired after her health and repeating the terms he had overheard her using, becoming confused and frustrated when they smiled kindly at him in return. Several times his mother would send him to play in his room, or fetch some drinks, and he would later catch her murmuring to them intensely, their faces showing no trace of a smile and their eyes conveying pity.

His father's parents were long deceased – Johnny had been told he'd met his paternal grandmother as a baby just two months before she'd died of a stroke – but his mother's frail parents, who lived a two-hour drive away, phoned Flora constantly until she could no longer maintain a conversation and visited now and then to see her. He didn't like his maternal grandparents; they were cold and unfeeling, and had an air of disapproval about them, almost as if they blamed his father for his mother's illness. Johnny had always instinctively known that his grandparents did not like his father, but a thought at the back of his immature mind made him resent them for letting that come between them and their sick daughter, for he could see that his mother perked up whenever they appeared.

At these times, he would observe her regress to the vulnerability of a small child, needy and weak, and it made his stomach churn to think that she was something other than his mother, his provider, that she needed looking after too. At each visit, his grandparents would ask Johnny if he was doing well at school, and he would look down and nod to their satisfaction. The only good part was when his grandmother pressed a crisp £5 note into his hand before they left. She would then tilt his chin upwards so she could stare into his eyes, perhaps to suck some of the spirit out of him, he thought – mentally bestowing supernatural powers upon her. Sometimes he would save the money in the back of a notebook under his bed, but more often than not he would use it to buy chocolate and comics on his way home from school.

Johnny trusted his mother, doted on her, and knew that she would not lie to him. Eventually, however, the hospital visits became more and more frequent, the medications stronger, and his mother appeared more pallid and weak by the day, an oxygen mask attached permanently to her face. He knew then – had known for a while without having to be told – that the treatments were doing nothing and, by the time she stopped going to the hospital at all, he had resigned himself to spending every minute he could with her; in those last two weeks nobody insisted that he went to school.

He was allowed to sit with her and sometimes read to her from his latest Alex Rider book, continuing while she slept. He told her about his friends, about the weather, about the fox that had been seen in the area which had upset Mr Gregory's bins, and made up plans for the future – holidays they could take and places they would see. His face alone brought a tiny smile to her face and, as he talked to her, day-after-day, tears would slip down her face. Even when sleeping she would gasp for breath, the sheer effort of breathing making her perspire and gently clench her fist, and seeing her like that he almost wished it were over. One evening he went to say goodnight, as he always did, and her eyes briefly fluttered open.

"I'm sorry," she mouthed on seeing him, and, for the first time since she had become ill, he allowed himself to cry in front of her, a small boy wishing for the arms of his mother yet only able to bury his head gently in her stomach. She raised one hand slowly and placed it on the back of his head attempting to ruffle his hair, but he stood up and moved away, not wanting to look at her again. He recalled the memory of a healthy mother who laughed and scolded and brimmed with energy, rejecting the unbearable image in front of him.

His father woke him early the next morning, red-eyed and robotic, to tell him she was gone, and Johnny pulled the duvet over his head and remained there for hours, listening to the bustle of the house, undertakers arriving and people interfering. He realised that he had been too shy to tell her that he loved her and berated himself cruelly, for the first time experiencing the bitter taste of failure.

On the day of his wife's death, Daniel stopped smoking and took up drinking. It began with a whisky the day she died, just to get him through the day, and one afterwards to help him act the grieving husband. Then he had one before he went to bed, which led him to shed a few tears and, feeling grateful at the conventional release of emotion, he repeated the imbibition the next day. He stoically went through the motions of organising the funeral and burial, informing all those concerned as well as those who weren't, and making sure that his son wanted for nothing, aside from the comfort of his mother.

Neither he nor Flora had any siblings, so the funeral attendees consisted of older aunts and uncles and a few old friends, most of whom had been religiously visiting Flora since she fell ill. Flora's heartbroken parents attended too, but Daniel knew that, now Johnny was a little older and Flora was gone, so too were their reasons for visiting. He also knew that they saw Flora every time they looked at Johnny, for he did too, and that despite the boy's innocence it was painful. He closed the office for two weeks and by the time he re-opened it he was dependent on drink, the future of the business hanging precariously on the edge.

The house they had lived in for as long as Johnny could feasibly remember was a post-WWII, semi-detached, brick building on a quiet, residential street of similar abodes. Most garages were white, nobody painted their front doors garish colours and gardens were kept neat but simple. His parents had picked out the house when Johnny was still a baby and at a time when business was thriving. They had never missed a mortgage payment, always found the neighbours quiet but amicable, and had never taken their good fortune for granted, though they aspired to one day having more.

The house had four bedrooms: his parents' room; a spare and immaculate bedroom for guests that Johnny thought smelt perpetually of his grandmother's flowery old-woman perfume; Johnny's room (decorated blue with a football border at the top of each wall and a small wooden desk, chair and CD player in one corner); and a small fourth bedroom that was hardly ever used, but was the only part of the house to make Johnny feel the lack of a sibling, as if its nursery potential had been wasted.

To the world at large, there was no change to the house after Flora's death; the grass at the front grew a little untidy, yes, but the general exterior belied little of what was really going on behind closed doors. Inside, it suffered for the disappearance of its primary caretaker, deteriorating as rapidly as familial communication. At first, the changes were not immediately noticeable: surfaces became dusty, clutter lingered in corners, and smears decorated windows and mirrors.

Neither Johnny nor his father had any idea of the maintenance and housekeeping required and, in an effort to deny the void that Flora had left, neither was keen to assume her prior duties. Before long their abode was dirty and messy, the sour smell of loneliness and alcohol pervading each room, and the house became as unfamiliar to them as once it had been homely.

In the early days after his mother died, Johnny could not be left at home alone, so most days after school he headed over to the car warehouse. His father would give him £2 for every car he washed or £8 if he washed three, so usually, after rushing through his homework, Johnny picked up a sponge and a bucket and got stuck in. During the day, at school, he was distracted and aloof, but in the evenings, working alongside his father, he was focused and renewed.

He often hung around the office at weekends too, contented with the silence, and ignoring the warm incense of liquor that wafted from his father's breath like a whispered secret. At times like these he had felt close to his father, as if their family unit had not been fragmented but had shifted to another level. They ate takeaways at the office and got home late, barely communicating for anything other than practicalities, and his father's regular customers continued to call, though few new ones emerged.

Johnny was a nervous twelve-year-old, introvert but impulsive, who didn't make friends but remained loyal to the few he had. His closest friends were boys he had known since primary school, had grown up with, fought with, explored and laughed with, but even they had receded during his mother's illness, not understanding in their childish minds how to cope with someone whose mother was dying. When he had returned to school after two weeks' bereavement absence, Rufus, a classmate, had come up to him and asked, "Is it true? Is your mother dead?"

Unfazed by his directness, Johnny had simply nodded, wondering why they were questioning what had become his universal truth. By now, a group of boys and girls had gathered around him, some his age, some from other years.

"Why aren't you crying then?" a girl's voice rang out, and Johnny looked up, astonished.

They stared at him blankly, waiting for an answer to an inquisition mirrored on all their faces. He opened his mouth to answer but realised that he didn't know what to say, couldn't put into words the feeling of being completely and utterly lost. He shrugged. His fellow pupils gave him puzzled looks, searching for signs of emotion in his body language, and then one-by-one began to drift away as if the buzz of melodrama had fallen to ashes.

One girl remained, a girl he recognised as Sabrina Sandhurst from Class 7C, and she sifted through the crowd until she stood right before him, promptly throwing her arms around him in a tight squeeze. He squirmed, pleasantly surprised at the physical contact but aware of the sniggering boys turning to stare at them. After a few seconds he flung her arms away with a dazed look on his face but, unperturbed by his hostility, she turned and ran off towards a group of girls chatting on a bench in the corner.

Feeling exposed and blushing slightly, Johnny was relieved when the bell rang and he could scurry into the classroom with his head down. Some of the boys whispered as he walked in, as if he were a ghost or an impostor, and he was reassured to find his usual desk and possessions in order, though there was no reason why they wouldn't be.

It was only when the teacher entered and hushed them up, and looked straight at him, saying, "We were all terribly sorry to hear about your mother, Jonathan," that he looked around at his wide-eyed classmates, all of them with mothers at home, and to his distress found himself welling up.

He burst into tears, burying his face in his arms and didn't flinch when he felt the strong arms of Mrs Nayler around him. From then onwards, there were no whispers or staring; in the minds of his peers, his show of emotion converted the news of his mother's death from fiction to reality and, according to an inexplicable social code, this earned Johnny a certain respect.

It was at this time, when life had changed beyond recognition, that Johnny came to know his first girlfriend and the first person in a long time he could act his own age with. Aside from her spontaneous contact that first day back at school, Johnny knew Sabrina from the year-wide Current Affairs classes they had every fortnight, but he had never really taken any notice of her.

The classes were boring – a radio was put on in time for the news and afterwards pupils had to discuss everything from ASBOs and arson to the tired old subject of the war in Iraq, which none of them really understood or followed anyway (apart from Smoky Allen, a crazed know-it-all with an opinion on everything under the sun, and so monikered due to his penchant for pilfering his father's fags and selling them for thirty pence a stick). Most of the class would spend the hour-long session passing notes, whispering until they were reproached or, as in Johnny's case, staring blankly around while in their minds devising a new superhero with super-human capabilities.

It was one Thursday, when the monotone newsreader was droning on about oil reserves, that Johnny absent-mindedly caught Sabrina's eye. She was seated to his left and one row in front of him in the large music room, where the Current Affairs classes were held in order to accommodate a quarter of the 198 students that made up Year 7. He noticed her smiling at him and he quickly looked away, his heart jumping with the sudden realisation that he may well have been staring in her direction for quite a while without being conscious of it.

Thereafter, he rapidly descended into a Catch-22 situation: if he stared straight ahead for the rest of the lesson he would become fantastically bored and might possibly nod off to sleep, which would no doubt result in 100 lines as a punishment and the condemnation of sitting in the front row for the rest of the year; or, if he continued to let his mind wander and his eyes drift aimlessly like a feather in water, they would no doubt land upon Sabrina again and she would think he was deliberately trying to get her attention. He couldn't resist trying to peek at her through the corner of his eye though, and he was horrified to see that, although she looked towards the front, she had turned slightly in her chair and sat sideways so that her body was addressing him.

As he stared helplessly at her childish, white ankle socks, rolled down slightly to create a small cuff, his left-hand neighbour Biff (a.k.a. Richard Biffey) turned his head and stared at Johnny, his gaze inquiring why on earth Johnny kept looking his way. Johnny gave a wry smile, for Biff was not one to mess with, and turned back towards the front – the risk of becoming drowsy not being as threatening as an altercation with Biff or, worse still, some sort of communication with a girl like Sabrina.

At the end of the half-hour news programme, they all had to get into groups and discuss the state of the world before presenting communal decisions and statements to the rest of the class. Johnny was grouped with Biff and two other male classmates. For the rest of the session Johnny completely forgot about Sabrina, until he heard a voice ring out and, on turning, noticed that she had appointed herself spokesperson for her group. He couldn't remember if it was the first time he had heard her speak but his befuddled mind somehow recognised that she was becoming more significant with the passing of each second. Now that he had noticed her, he wondered, would he ever be able to 'un-notice' her?

He remained distracted as one of his classmates read out their group's conclusions, simultaneously thinking about Sabrina and trying *not* to think about her. He was relieved when the bell rang and he gathered up his books, stumbling along with the others to escape the educational cage. He had almost dodged his way to the door when Biff shoved past him and his notebook fell to the floor. Bending down to pick it up, he noticed a rolled-down, white sock in close proximity to his hand and he snapped straight up again, only to face Sabrina, who was eyeing him quizzically.

"You alright?" she asked. Her slightly superior tone, coupled with the awareness that he must be blushing, irked him greatly.

"Yes, fine." He shifted from one foot to the other, wanting to leave but unsure how to proceed now that Sabrina had planted herself between him and the doorway.

"Boring, isn't it? I don't know why they make us sit through these lessons."

"Um…yeah." He was confused by her self-assuredness, which seemed laced with something less tangible…nerves, perhaps. He had the vague idea that she might have planned what she was saying – there was something rehearsed about her tone.

"I almost wish we had to take notes in the class – at least it would be something to do."

"Um…yeah," he repeated, aware that he was sounding like an utter moron. He had no idea what she was trying to achieve – the conversation was clearly going nowhere – and from outside the cries and shouts of others chasing, fighting, and colluding echoed through the corridors and bounced into the music room.

"Are you coming out?"

"Maybe." He mentally kicked himself; what did he say that for? Of course he was going outside – everyone had to unless they were ill. He had been trying to shake off the air of mystery that had surrounded him like a dark cloud ever since his mother had died, and this wasn't helping. He smiled wanly to make up for his unfriendliness and, although Sabrina beamed back at him, he wondered if her emotion was also forced. It was the first time it occurred to him that they might have something in common – were they both putting on an act? If so, what was her motive? He understood his own well enough as it preyed on his mind, but he couldn't quite work out how and why the two of them had come to be standing there, alone, having a bizarre and pointless conversation.

Sabrina took his smile as a signal to move (though not before time, he thought) and turned left out of the room and down the corridor. He followed reluctantly; never before had he felt so unfamiliar with such a familiar environment. They walked in silence for a whole minute, round three corners and along to their respective classrooms. To his ensuing apprehension, instead of entering her classroom to leave her books on her desk, she reached around the doorway and dumped her books on a ledge, turning back and following him to his room. He took his time, shuffling to his desk and fiddling around with his bag on the floor, as Sabrina waiting patiently by the door for him. Eventually Miss Nutley, one of the language assistants, walked by the classroom and shooed them outside, giving Johnny no option but to traipse after Sabrina, who was still turning round to smile at him now and again.

When they got to the playground outside, Johnny finally got what he had been yearning for for – a bit of breathing space. Sabrina slipped away to join a group of girls from her class, glancing back once to indicate goodbye, and Johnny trotted off towards some boys playing football. He was slightly relieved, yet unsettled and confused at what had just happened, if anything. And although his day immediately shifted back to normal, something in his mind recognised that he had just shared something with someone he hardly knew, someone he might perhaps think was alright (and vice versa?), and someone he might like to share something with again. He suppressed the thought but, although he joined in the game, his hazy mood ensured he stayed on the sidelines for the rest of the day.

Chapter 4

In a vain attempt to make herself feel better, Constance Romijn ran a bath and sank into it, feeling the steaming hot water massage her bruised ego. She picked up the glass of red wine she had placed on the side of the tub and took a large gulp, the soothing aroma of the dry Rioja juxtaposed with her trembling hand. She put the glass down again with a clumsy 'clink' and her lungs spewed forth a large sigh.

The clock in the downstairs hallway chimed eleven times as Constance sank further into the tub, immersing her entire head under the surface until the sound of hot, rushing molecules enveloped her brain. She exchanged her onerous world for that of a virtual submarine; the physical change of environment tossed her into a parallel state of awareness. 'One…two… three…' She counted the seconds passing, her inner voice increasing in volume with each moment, and reached twenty-six before, gasping and spluttering, her body threw her head above the water and drew in great pockets of air.

When it was appeased and once again at rest, she rewarded it with another slosh of wine and reached down to massage her aching calves. As she did so, her thoughts flashed back to last night when Jason had run his warm hands up and down her leg, giving her shivers and making her face flush with anticipation. He was good, Jason, the best she'd ever had in fact, but she was loathe ever to admit this to him; his narcissism needed no encouragement. It was precisely what had drawn them together

– mutual recognition of a hidden spirit, but she had since realised that what he lacked in humility, she made up for in insecurity.

She knew that he still saw her as the archetypal older career woman: single, confident, domineering in the office and a pussycat in the bedroom and, as much as she hated to admit it, she wanted to live up to his every fantasy. He was young, only twenty-six, and easily excitable, with a refreshing lack of experience in responsibility and consequence.

The previous night, he had been waiting outside her flat when she got home, seated on the stone steps in the light drizzle and looking all the more attractive for the raindrops that caressed his hair and ran down his cheeks. He knew it would turn her on to find him adjusting to her schedule, waiting patiently for her attention until she deigned to bestow it. For all she knew, though, he might have arrived five minutes before she had and positioned himself to his advantage. That was why it worked – the unspoken words, the silent lies, making their relationship all the more potent.

She had led him inside and threw her coat on the floor, unzipping his immediately. Combing her fingers through his damp hair, her skin absorbing the moisture that had touched his skin, the cold had made her tingle. He had run his hands up and down her arms before reaching under her shirt, making her flinch with nervousness despite his familiarity – her body was no longer as it had once been. She had shifted away slightly, but not before he had stroked her breasts, and she had reached for his collar, unfastening his top button and loosening the metallic-blue tie as he snagged the bottom of her shirt and tugged at it, the poppers bursting open. She had unbuttoned his shirt, slowly, both of them staring each other in the eyes in what would have appeared to a third-party to be a hostile gaze. In the spirit of his stare, once his shirt was off she had run her hands briefly over his torso before turning him around and aggressively shoving him over to the sofa. They had made love urgently, but with fragility, as if at any moment it would end and, in truth, any moment it could have.

This might be the last touch, the last scent, the last consumption of him, she had thought, and her ecstasy was bittersweet, an urge of longing overcoming her. As she cried out, he mistook it for satisfaction and something deep inside her had thought him a fool. He has none of these thoughts, she realised, and embraced him tighter for his ignorance, almost wanting to protect him.

In the morning when she awoke, he was gone. It was to be expected. She shifted onto his side of the bed and drank in his scent on the pillow, suffocating in his shadow. She would see him later that day, at work. No one must find out about them, she iterated to herself; it had practically become her mantra. No one at work must discover that one of her young assistants was giving her more pleasure than she had ever imagined – all she had worked for was at stake.

She rose and wandered over to the en-suite bathroom, inspecting her figure in the floor-length mirror as she passed it. Her flat, on the second floor of a converted town house in South Kensington, was peaceful and minimalist: large enough to feel spacious, yet small enough to be cosy. It had two bedrooms, side-by-side, with an en-suite accompanying the main one, and another bathroom down the corridor. Walking away from the bedrooms, the bathroom on the right, the corridor opened into a spacious living room, with a large kitchen to the right and a dining room through a graceful arch. The left side of the living room had floor-to-ceiling windows, either side of which long crème velvet curtains hung, and in the middle of the living room two French doors opened out onto a balcony overlooking a communal garden, which was perfect for languid summer drinks and cocktail sunsets.

Constance had entertained as and when she felt like it – thrown the odd dinner party, invited people round for drinks – and each room was filled with the shadows of those times, although nothing diminished the pride she felt at the fact it was hers, and hers alone. Not even Jason could leave his mark on the place; her sheets smelled of him, but she could wipe out his trace whenever she felt like it. She had invited him into her enclave and could emotionally banish him as and when it pleased her, or so she convinced herself.

As she rifled through her wardrobe that morning, selecting one of the dozens of crisply-ironed shirts hanging uniformly inside, she wondered whether Jason had told any of his friends about her. They were bound to have guessed that he was seeing someone – she would never expect a young man like Jason to remain unattached for long, and neither would his friends. For the hundredth time she questioned just how much 'attachment' Jason had to her, but pushed the nagging doubts of his infidelity to the back of her mind; she liked to think she could make a claim to him but, never having spoken about it, she feared that he wouldn't see it in the same way. Still, he must have some affiliation to her or he would have ended it a long time ago.

They had been seeing each other on and off for almost six months and she prided herself on the fact that nobody else in the office knew. Occasionally, at office parties, someone would jokingly ask about her love life and, blushing slightly, she would retort with a quip about being married to her job. She knew they thought her pathetic and standoffish (once she had overheard another manager referring to her as 'Cold-Stance') but she consoled herself with the knowledge that her love life was far more exciting than any of theirs and, if they ever found out, they would be shocked by their underestimation of her.

She never sat near Jason at office functions; as was the norm, she sat with the other managers and he sat with the young assistants, laughing and joking in a raucous manner. But at the last quarterly office dinner, Jason had joined their section of the table to converse with Anna, one of the Partners, who had called him over with a drunken giggle and patted him on the back. He sat down, politely, and from the corner of her gaze Constance could see that he was uncomfortable, longing to escape back to the social epicentre of the party. Anna was slightly slurring her words, occasionally touching Jason's arm, and Constance couldn't help but sneer slightly in disgust, partly at Anna's coquettishness and partly through envy at her public display of desire.

Peter, a kind but ever-so-dull manager, was trying to engage her in a conversation about garden vegetables, but she had switched off as soon as Jason appeared, keeping her eyes on Peter and her ears across the table. Which is why, when she heard her name called, she jumped in surprise and forgot all about Peter's rhubarb. Worse, it was Anna that had called her name and she and Jason were staring at her intently.

"Huh?" she replied ineloquently.

"I was just saying to Jason, Constance – you and Peter look so engrossed in conversation that, if I didn't know better, I'd say there was something going on between the two of you. You can't take your eyes of each other!" she tinkled, followed by an irritating giggle. Anna turned and winked at Jason, who gave Constance a tight smile.

"Don't be ridiculous Anna, Peter was just telling me about his…um…rhubarb," she said, turning to find Peter beaming inanely, no sound of protest on his lips.

"I bet he was!" declared Anna, guffawing into Jason's shoulder before becoming distracted by a passing waiter from whom she ordered another glass of wine. Jason took this opportunity to extricate himself, though not before offering Constance an apologetic shrug.

"I have to go," she said, half-heartedly turning to Peter, only to find that finally his attention too had been diverted. Constance pushed her chair back subtly and slipped away, for it was getting late and her enjoyment of such forced social endeavours diminished with the acidity of the passing years.

She hadn't seen Jason that night and had no idea where he had gone after the meal, but the rumour in the office the following week was that some of the younger men had ended up in a well-known but seedy strip club; despite the inclination, Constance didn't have the courage to ask Jason if he was one of them.

When she arrived at work, having stopped at the coffee shop around the corner for her morning pick-me-up, she was one of the first there. It was 8.15am and Jason would not arrive for a while yet – no doubt he had slipped back to his flat to shower and change before work. She passed his desk and entered her office, subconsciously keeping a look out for him. She went through her emails, replying to a few, and made a list of duties for her two assistants to complete that day.

When Jason eventually arrived just before nine o'clock, she waited for him to hang his coat up and turn his computer on before leaving her office and casually strolling to his desk.

"Morning Jason," she said coolly.

"Morning Constance," he replied, nonchalant as ever.

"I've sent you a list of things I want the two of you to do today. And make sure you get that parcel out first thing," she instructed, tapping the brown package on his desk.

"Sure," replied Jason, tilting his head upwards and looking her straight in the eyes. There was an intense moment of silence, witnessed by no one but them. After a few seconds she spoke, collected and confident, "One more thing – when that tardy colleague of yours finally makes it into work, tell him I want a word with him." And with that, she strode back to her office, a faint smile gracing her lips.

She saw Simon arrive a little later, dishevelled and trying not to attract too much attention. Most people were at their desks, silently checking emails or hurrying around the office with hot cups of coffee. The mornings were usually intense – everyone would have their eyes glued to the screens in preparation for afternoon meetings (the general company rule, for some reason that escaped Constance, was that meetings should always be scheduled for the afternoon unless absolutely necessary) and Reception fielded most of the calls so that the telephones rarely rang.

The office telephone system was such that an external call would ring aloud immediately, but an internal transfer (usually from Reception) would make the phone vibrate twice before it sounded, and most people picked up within that timeframe. The result was an extraordinarily quiet office that alluded to hard work and, although it barely affected the managers, who each had their own office, Constance knew that many of the more junior staff resented the tense atmosphere that the hush provoked. Some – but not her two assistants – were permitted to listen to music on headphones, although the irony of this isolation in relation to the joys of music sharing made it a scarce practice.

As Simon set his bag down and removed his coat – another distinction between the two of them: Jason wore a long, fitted overcoat and Simon wore a short, hooded, military-style jacket with mesh pockets – out of the corner of her eye she could see Jason whispering to him and gesturing towards her office. Simon nodded and headed over, knocking on the glass door even though it was slightly ajar.

"Simon. Come in," she said in a tone glimmering with displeasure. He walked in and sat on one of the heavy black chairs that were placed in front of the desk like loyal bodyguards. There was an awkward silence before Simon piped up.

"Morning. Um…sorry I'm a bit late, problems on the Tube, you know." He smiled apologetically, his uplifting cheeks only serving to highlight the bags under his eyes. His 'just got out of bed' hair waved mockingly at Constance.

"Simon, how many times do we have to have this conversation?"

"I know, look, I'm sorry, it won't happen again."

"You are consistently late at least two days out of five each week and plenty of people get the Tube. And I have to say that your appearance recently suggests to me that your personal life is affecting your professional one…"

"Well, there've been a couple of late nights, but nothing-"

"…Not to mention your recent inability to finish tasks promptly as required. I really haven't been very impressed with your general conduct."

"I'm sorry Constance, I'll focus more." He looked suitably regretful, yet Constance's urge to milk the situation caused her to transmogrify into a schoolteacher.

"You need to buck up your ideas young man, or you'll run into problems later in life."

"Um…yeah, sorry." His face displayed a touch of incredulity; he was repentant for his undeniable failings, but his happy-go-lucky nature would not permit him to take her words to heart.

"From now on, I expect you to be in on time. You're old enough, and familiar enough with the transport system, to leave sufficient time for your journey. And I think your general attire could do with a little attention as well."

Simon looked down and immediately adjusted his shirt, squirming as he attempted to tuck the lagging tails into his trousers. He stood up and reversed a little as he did so, knocking the chair into the wall with a loud clink, both of them cringing at the noise. It was at that point Constance felt her phone vibrate and she managed a quick nod at Simon, who scurried out and closed the door behind him, before she picked up the handset and heard the familiar voice of Peter asking if she would like to join him for lunch. She accepted out of politeness, and for want of something better to do, but regretted it as soon as she hung up, given that doing nothing was infinitely more exciting than listening to a dull, middle-aged man drone on about his broken antique record player or his unsuccessful attempt at playing golf.

She could see Jason and Simon with their heads together, Simon no doubt relaying their conversation, and Jason visibly broke out into laughter. Paranoia pierced her chest and, not for the first time, she wished she were their peer rather than their manager; something told her she would have more influence over them that way than as the apparent figure of control that she had trained herself to be.

The distinction between her two assistants was significant. She was aware – though not ashamed – of the poignancy of having hired two males to do what was traditionally viewed as a woman's job, but she relished the prospect of moulding their careers, commandeering them in a professional manner that would never cultivate a female mind.

She saw herself as a role model, a mother figure in fact, and despite her intimacy with Jason, Simon was the one that benefited most from her nurturing. He was hopeless at many things, not least timekeeping, but his willingness to please and his somewhat forlorn demeanour appealed to her maternal instincts. When he first came for an interview, he was just on time but slightly dishevelled, his mumble about the public transport system was accompanied by a flush of distress. He had smoothed down his hair, throwing her a sheepish grin, and, although she responded with a prim smile, inside she had wanted to reach out and adjust his attire for him.

First impressions were not his strong point, but the irony was that this actually left a great impression on Constance. Simon wasn't shy, but those who knew him well realised that his lack of confidence manifested itself through verbal labyrinths. At his first interview, he had answered all of her questions adequately, but garnished them with several tales of wisdom and woe, clearly playing up his life experience and virtually declaring himself the man for the job – an attitude that usually put Constance off. But there was an underlying tone of self-deprecation that made her think there was potential for growth, a hesitance – but not reluctance – to admit his weaknesses when prompted (impatience he claimed) and something in the way he listened intently, whenever she managed to get a word in, endeared him to her.

He'd had a further interview with Constance and a more senior manager and was offered the job at the end of it, accepting straightaway and beaming like a child with a good report card. She'd shown him around the office that day, she remembered, even though he would not be starting until the following week. When she introduced him to Jason the two of them shook hands with an immediate sense of camaraderie, and she couldn't help but feel a sense of pride in her 'new brood'.

That had been back before anything had developed between her and Jason, and she felt protective of the two of them, wanting them to be united in their 'support role'. Jason had been there five months by the time Simon started and no doubt filled him in on all Constance's idiosyncrasies, likes and dislikes. Before long, she found that she couldn't recall her working life without them.

The two of them were well liked in the office and complemented each other: Jason was confident, stubborn and a little arrogant, whereas Simon was eager to please, humorous, and boyish. She even suspected that they both preferred working for an authoritative woman. They could dispel tension by dismissing the female psyche as whimsical, but knew that any praise was genuine and well-deserved.

Most of the other assistants in the office were female, and no other department had two male assistants working so closely together. She had once overheard Simon in the kitchen joking about her cracking the whip on young men and, rather than tense up as she would if she heard anyone else commenting on her position, she smiled to herself before cruelly sweeping into the room at that pertinent moment, trying to disguise her smile with a curt, "Hello Simon", as she picked up a glass and then exited, pursued by loud guffaws and an "Oh heck" from Simon, confirming the desired effect.

Constance tried to remain professional and objective at all times despite her magnetism to both employees in discrete ways. As time went on, however, they all became more familiar with each other (two in more ways than the other) and the pressures of the job required her to spend more and more time with them in the office. She couldn't help but think of her team as a ready-made family without any of the social responsibility – she had found in these two young men, in effect, a lover and a son, and this thought instilled in her both fear and desire on a daily basis.

Chapter 5

There are temporary goodbyes and more permanent farewells, but Elisabeth – as she was then called – came to the realisation in her late-teens that the former could easily be as painful as the latter. In fact, the temporary goodbyes she faced over the years, due to the uncertainty of time, amounted to a more painful imposition than the absolute goodbye she was to make in her mid-twenties, which, she discovered to her slight consternation, was ultimately not that difficult at all.

There was the time when she was sixteen and her sister fourteen, when their mother dragged them from their bedroom in the middle of the night, tears sweeping down her face like razors, to stand them in the living room to say goodbye to their father, who was leaving them to run away with a woman he'd met at a sales conference. In the preceding commotion, her mother had knocked over a glass of warm milk and, afterwards, whenever Elisabeth caught a whiff of the previously comforting smell, she was ruefully reminded of that unsettling night.

The 'other woman', a bulimic power-dressing hotel manageress who stank of overripe fruit, had three teenage sons, two Chihuahuas and a faux-beehive hairstyle – a terrible package that she knew made her mother feel even more rejected. Their family was torn apart: her mother very nearly had a breakdown and took two months' unpaid leave from work, her sister took up smoking, and Elisabeth herself missed many days of school in an important year. Neither of the girls ever recovered the academic prowess they had formerly maintained, and this, more than anything, influenced their futures.

She knew she would see her father again, probably quite often, yet the idea of saying goodbye to her previously tranquil family life, for even a short period, filled her with anguish. The adulterous pair took off on an exotic holiday to Bali, returned to face the thunderous music of the woman's menagerie, and as a result their relationship dissolved as quickly as sugar in hot tea.

He came crawling of course, barely six months after he had left, and eventually their mother took him back, though not before he had grovelled, pleaded and promised that things would be different. Life was different, in that none of them ever quite forgave him (a household of angry women seeking emotional retribution is not a content one) and because he forevermore felt he had to appease them. However, within a year, things had returned as close as possible to normal and no one spoke of the terrible six months of gloom. Only the lingering residue of spilt milk served as a melancholic reminder of the closed chapter.

There had also been her first boyfriend, at seventeen, or at least the first one she really cared about, who doted on her throughout the school year – bought her perfume, followed her around, chose to spend time with her over his friends (which at the time she mistook for maturity, but she later realised his inability to integrate the two hinted at the exact opposite). Then, at the end of the academic year, he had declared that he was going to spend the summer in California with two wayward cousins. She hoped, as she saw him off at the airport, that things would be the same when he returned, but three months under foreign skies can be life-changing at any age, let alone to an impressionable seventeen-year-old.

They kept in touch from time-to-time while he was away – she was working most days in a local 'greasy spoon' café and had precious little time for tales of his gallivanting – and she tired of the endless girls' names he dropped deliberately into telephone conversations. When he returned, he was boastful and brash, his tan topped up with an odour of misogyny, and, although he tried to mould her to fit his new façade, the two drifted apart.

Then there was her sister, Genevieve, who at the age of eighteen decided she wanted to make a difference in the shantytowns of Brazil, and went over there for a year to help the poor. A worthy cause indeed, but for a short time Elisabeth, who was then working long hours in a local Italian restaurant, lost the only ally she had taken for granted over the years, the only person who had walked in her shoes. At the end of the year, Genevieve flew back to England, but soon decided to move to a different area of the world, eventually becoming a perpetual flying philanthropist. Elisabeth could do nothing but encourage her, though secretly she wanted to beg her sister to come home, to provide support and to lavish her charity on her own family. By this time their parents were emotionally pallid, devoid of excitement and going through the matrimonial motions, though they never separated again.

She visited her sister, once, during a two-week break from her legal secretary training. At the time, Genevieve was making her way around India with Voluntary Services Overseas, stopping off in villages around the country to build modest homes and water purification systems. Mistakenly, Elisabeth had believed that by closing the physical distance between them she'd be simultaneously increasing their sisterly proximity; not so, she discovered to her chagrin.

The two villages they stayed in during her time there were basic to say the least, though what they lacked in amenities they made up for in graciousness. The pungent toilets consisting of holes in the ground made Elisabeth feel embarrassed and unclean; the food was spicy and unfamiliar; the sunshine turned her skin red and tender; the water was unsafe for foreigners to drink unless boiled on a basic stove, which was shared by many. The villagers were delighted at their presence, eager to chatter in a language she could not interpret, to have their photograph taken, and to wonder unashamedly at her pale, peeling skin. Elisabeth tried to help as much as possible, following

Genevieve's instructions, but she was bumbling and clueless. Despite the villagers' dependence on the kindness of strangers, Elisabeth couldn't help feeling that it was they, not she, who were better off.

During the two days she and her sister went to visit the nearest large city, the gap between them only widened. In contrast to the villages, the city was thrumming with technology, people and commerce – incense, traffic fumes and humidity filled the air. Genevieve moved seamlessly through the crowds while Elisabeth was caught-up, cajoled by street vendors and frequently left behind. This alien culture made her unintentionally xenophobic, unconsciously snobbish, and made her long for home. Whether Genevieve was aware of it or not, the continents constantly separating them had made them lost to each other.

Elisabeth noted that these opportunities changed those around her, whereas she remained the same as ever. She longed for developments in her own life, to initiate an adventure, to metamorphose; little did she realise at the time that she was soon to pave her own path of adventure.

Tied to this chair, in the dank, cold room, her screams eventually summoned footsteps. She ceased to cry out and instead sat upright, listening to the 'thud, thud, thud' of approaching menace. As the door swung open her chest constricted in sympathy with her limbs, and she stared, wide-eyed, at the man who walked in, balancing a small white tray in his right hand. On it was perched a glass full of clear liquid, and a plate holding some kind of food. It was him again. She kept her eyes on him as he placed the tray on the desk a few metres away from her, and then wheeled the black chair over, sitting down on it so his face was a few inches from hers.

"You're awake." He grinned, his breath laced with nicotine. Her own mouth felt dry, stale like old chewing gum. She wondered how long she had been unconscious, and what else they might have done to her.

"Untie me, please," she pleaded weakly, knowing he was not about to do as she asked. Neither her hands nor her feet were numb, but her limbs felt stiff and she longed to move and stretch them. The more she contemplated her restrictions, the more she became aware of the panic rising from her stomach to her throat.

"No can do Elisabeth. Not until I get some answers."

"Please, I…what could I possibly tell you? It was such a long time ago; I've moved on – I don't have any information." She sobbed a little before steeling herself and looking him in the eyes. "What do you want with me?"

"Well, firstly," he said, rising from the chair and retrieving the tray from the desk, "I want you to have this."

"What is it?" she asked, eyeing it with suspicion. She was dying for a drink, but, after the last concoction he had forced on her, she wasn't about to accept another readily.

"Relax, it's just water. And some bread and cheese. I'll feed them to you."

He held the glass to her lips and she took a small sip, welcoming a further tilt of the glass once her tongue confirmed it was as he said. When she had almost finished the water, he broke off some bread and cheese and fed it to her, watching her take small bites. The cheese was odourless, probably processed. She felt humiliated but grateful for the provisions, and something in his behaviour towards her reassured her that his intention was not to harm. She kept her eyes down as she ate – her only degree of privacy.

"I had to bring the food myself," he said, as she chewed intently. "I've waited so long to see you again that I wanted to talk to you straightaway."

She swallowed the food in her mouth and raised her eyes. "What do you want?" she said, knowing his question but simultaneously hoping she was wrong.

"Where are they?"

She was right then. She had always thought that one day he might find her, her one consolation being that she was the go-between, the middle-women – it was not her he was after. And that alone would surely mean he would let her go, if she could give him the right answers.

"I don't know exactly. I've been away a long time. It's been five years and I lost track of everyone when I left – I had to, those were the rules." Her stomach cramped at the thought of the limbo she was perpetually in – caught between the decayed scent of a past long buried and the thick, chocolate mud she had buried her head in.

"Some rules you live by. We've been tracking you for months. These programmes aren't foolproof, you know. What's your name now – Hannah? Did you know that the Superintendent named you after his daughter's pet rabbit? He felt sorry for you, that's why. And Sampson was the Detective's mother's maiden name. We hacked into their computer files.

"Of course, the whole thing was encoded, but we narrowed it down to nine women and tracked them for a few months. Most of them I ruled out as soon as I saw them – they were nothing like you and some of them were abroad. I had a feeling you'd have stayed in this country, plus, you were lower risk than some of the others. There was one woman in Wales, working as a secretary. She had an English accent and looked a little like you; I thought maybe they'd performed some surgery. I went as far as to bump into her one day on the street to see if she'd recognise me. My heart was beating fast – I had been anticipating the moment for so long – but she looked straight into my eyes and apologised before hurrying on. I was angry then and it spurred me on to find you. We didn't even get to the end of the list – you were the penultimate one.

"Working in that pathetic factory – you really let them sell you out, didn't you? Still, good disguise; I thought you'd be totally different. One of my guys approached the Manager one day, told him he was a private investigator and offered him cash in exchange for information on you. The weasel took the bait; he provided us with your employment files, copies of your identification, information on your working times, your home address and your behaviour. The dates of your employment, his description of the way you acted around others, and the sad life you led all matched our expectations – I knew we'd found you. So, you don't want to let me down now, do you?" His tone changed, his expression mottled with anger. He rose and walked towards her chair, reaching out for the straps wound around her wrists and tugging hard at the ends. She cried out and he said, one more time, "Tell me where they are."

"Please, I don't know. I…I don't even know if they're together anymore. They moved away after the trial, all of them, just after you went…" She stopped, exasperated, tears now leaking from her eyes as she squirmed with the pain, unable to flex her fingers.

"Oh come on. You *must* have some information. By which I mean for your own good, you must have some information to impart." He tugged once more on the wrist straps and she screamed, squeezing her eyes shut with the pain and feeling the meagre food she had just consumed rising back up into her throat. A metallic taste rose in her mouth. Think, she must think.

"Please, stop. I'll tell you what I know – it said in the papers after the trial that they moved out of London, the two of them, north slightly. I can't remember the name of the town. They had to go on their own; there was a lot of bad press. Somewhere in Buckinghamshire I think, name began with C…no, G…oh, I don't know, please, loosen the straps; I feel faint." She willed herself to focus, to stay conscious – she would be in more danger if she gave in to the nausea.

To her relief he loosened the straps a little, and brought the glass of water with a few drops remaining once again to her lips. She clenched her fists, her fingertips infused with pain as the blood flowed back into them.

"That's a start, I suppose," he conceded. "See how much you remember when you really make the effort. You'd better remember more – I want to know exactly what happened." She remained silent, realising it was better to at least feign compliance. He placed the plate and glass on the tray, which he picked up before walking towards the door, turning the handle and opening it. But just before he disappeared, he turned back and spoke.

"I won't let you go until I've found out everything I need to," he vowed. "And even then, I'm still not sure I'll want to." He closed the door behind him.

Elisabeth thought again of all the goodbyes she'd said, all the things she'd let go of, all the excitement she'd witnessed and never been part of, and the inconspicuousness that had surrounded her all her life. She smiled; it seemed that, finally, the spotlight was on her. Yet just as soon as the light shone, it began to flicker and fade away.

Chapter 6

There are two types of fear. There's the fear that creeps up on you slowly, from the bottom of your stomach, through your chest and up to your throat, compressing your lungs. This fear is like a fresh injection of nausea every time it springs to mind, and it eats away at you until you develop a nervous exhaustion, either resolving to attack the source of panic or crumbling into a heap of hysteria.

The other fear is the type that hits suddenly, a slap of reality that brings about a knee-jerk reaction, except that more often than not it causes you to freeze. Such is the reaction Éric had that autumn morning when his eyes locked with those of the uniformed gentleman standing diagonally to his left, at the exact same moment as the small yappy dog at his feet started to bark.

For a few seconds his body froze, before realising that his right hand was still poised in mid-air, hovering above the lady's coat pocket. Éric retracted it swiftly and tucked it snugly into his jacket, while shuffling his feet and tilting his head away from the policeman's stern gaze and onto a pile of second-hand books resting on the edge of the table. He picked up one or two, allowing the lady time to move away, dragging the still protesting dog with her, and made sure he moved around the table so that a few other perusing customers could slip between himself and the *gendarme*. Éric then waited until he was sure that the policeman had lost interest, and glanced round, eventually heading away from the Quai des Gesvres and onto the rue d'Arcole.

The roads were busy, or as busy as they ever became. Tourists in bright clothes chatted loudly as they inspected paintings on the bridge, nudging each other in wonderment and marvelling at the river, as green and polluted as it actually was. French *mesdames* shuffled through the crowds, clutching at their purses and muttering under their breath as they pushed through the *étrangers*. Young men strode through the streets, greeting other young men with exuberant embraces and refusing to move aside to let others pass. All-in-all, Paris was thriving and Éric knew it was the perfect day for business.

Midday was fast approaching and so far he had acquired three wallets, a packet of chewing gum and a supermarket advertisement including a voucher for €1.50 off vegetable soup. Two of the wallets contained MasterCards and a combined total of €20 in cash, and the third contained €400. Not bad for a morning, thought Éric, and he stopped in his favourite Salon de Thé for a celebration beer. *Hold the beer*, he suddenly decided, *a glass of red wine would be better, might as well push the boat out.*

"*Salut Édouard, du vin rouge, s'il vous plaît.*"

"*Eh voilà Michel, ça va?*" the usual from the landlord. Éric used his pseudonym on the slightest social occasion, and he sensed that the locals more readily accepted those among them with familiar-sounding names. Not that names were crucial in a place such as this – he had a suspicion that the landlord was actually called Jean, but he always responded to Édouard and thus the name sufficed.

"*Ouais, ça va bien.*" Éric nodded to the other regulars at the bar before claiming his usual table in the corner, the prime spot for people-watching. It was his last day in Paris; his train was due to leave from the Gare du Nord in a couple of hours.

He had been considering leaving France on and off for a while and one day, surprising even to his own contemplation, he decided he did want to move away permanently. His mother was English, so the blood coursed through his veins, and, although he had questioned whether he could ever be at home under a dank, English sky, the longer he thought about it the more he realised it wasn't so different from his home in France.

After all, he thought, to deny a part of oneself is to deny the whole, for a rotten apple with rotten parts removed may no longer be an apple. His mind had always been disparaging of England – few of his friends back home even knew he was part English – but his opinions were based on nothing but a few tedious childhood visits and drunken, teenage forays in youth hostels with Northern '*rosbifs*' who hadn't particularly warmed to Éric or his confrontational skank friends.

On the Eurostar, on his way to London's Waterloo station, Éric made the most of the isolated luggage racks by pilfering a few electronic items as well as a small black case with wheels to put the horde in. He hopped off as soon as the train pulled into the platform, new acquisitions in hand, to embrace – for the second time in his life – the sights and sounds of the English capital.

He wanted to settle in before getting to work, so he caught the Tube to Piccadilly and navigated his way to a small Bed & Breakfast he had found on the internet. It was two grotty streets away from Piccadilly station – perfect for the tourist trap, and cheap and obscure enough to grant him anonymity. He checked in under his usual alias of Michel Verlaine (a tribute to his two favourite writers: Michel Montaigne and Paul Verlaine), paid a deposit and sidled away, inconspicuous as ever. The sleepy receptionist barely glanced up, didn't ask for a copy of his passport, and merely grunted when Éric asked if the bathrooms were communal. His English was rusty, as his mother – the only person with whom he conversed in English – had died a few years previously, but years of feigned Anglophilia at home had given him more than enough to manage on.

His mother had always declared London a depressing and heathen place. Once when they had visited, they stayed for one night in his great-aunt's one-bedroom council flat near Euston, with metal stairways that clanked well into the night and voices that echoed like lost souls, unfocused and random, searching for acknowledgement. He had huddled with his mother on the sagging sofa with a thin blanket and a crumbling armrest for a pillow. In the morning, no water came out of the taps, and the old lady with a face as wrinkled and delicate as tissue paper had sighed and explained that sometimes this occurred and it would no doubt come back by midday. Not wanting to hang around long enough for confirmation of this, his mother left her aunt with some money and whisked Éric away, murmuring about poor conditions and government apathy.

He knew even then that there were similar places in France, even if he had never seen them, for he had watched the riots on television, but in Brive, Dordogne, where they lived at that time, home comforts were undiscriminating, nature was abundant, and poverty was an alien concept reserved for strange people in distant lands.

His mother was a proud lady, and proud of Britain, though he wondered why she always seemed so displeased with it when she went back. She would criticise small things – the lack of interesting cheeses, the glum disposition of the natives, the waste, the unemployment – griping so much that anyone would think she came from an incomparably better place, instead of neighbouring France.

She never spoke much of her childhood, and his grandparents had died when he was little, but the impression she gave was that the England of her childhood was vastly different from the country she returned to, though Éric suspected that it was his mother, not the country, that had changed. By the time Éric was in his late-teens, his mother had lived more of her life in France than in England and, although she would never consciously renounce her heritage, it was clear she had voluntarily become more French than brie.

After a small sandwich he picked up in a corner-shop on the way, Éric headed for the tourist hotspot and got to work. The sky hung low, dripping on ruffled heads and fragile umbrellas, the raindrops suffused with smog. The distraction of rain always served his purpose well. Within half-an-hour he had successfully purloined two wallets and a mobile phone, and he used his ill-gotten gains to treat himself to a proper English pub lunch, although he kept his head down as he ate, not in the mood to converse.

After his meal, he discreetly flicked through the wallets, transferring any cash and cards to his own after leaving enough money on the table to pay for his meal with a 15% tip. He had strange morals for a thief – he never tipped less than 15% and never neglected to pay a bill. Such, he believed, was the way to avoid getting into more trouble than he already risked. There was £110 left after his meal, and he had barely begun. He smirked but then stopped himself, looking up to check no one was watching, and immediately placed his own wallet back in his inside coat pocket. He would dump the empty wallets once he left the pub, after wiping his fingerprints off them with a soft handkerchief he always carried with him. He had 'unlocked' the mobile phone and kept it tucked into his back pocket, planning to wait a week before acquiring a Sim card for personal use.

It was just as he was putting the second wallet away that he noticed it was still rigid, despite having apparently emptied it. He flexed it uncertainly and, yes, there was definitely something still inside. He turned it around a couple of times, before noticing a small slit along one side. He ran his untrimmed nail along it, expanding it until he could slip two fingers in and extract the treasure. It was a white card with a blue strip, and a big logo on one side. Indulging in a grin, Éric mouthed a silent 'thank you' to one Mr Newman, and headed back to the Bed & Breakfast to check out.

The walk to Mayfair would have been a short one but, feeling extravagant, Éric jumped on the Tube with his case and grabbed the vacant seat nearest to the door. He watched the tourist couple seated opposite him arguing about the Underground lines, a large backpack balanced on the man's feet. A teenager got on at the next station, engrossed in a Playstation Portable frothing football jargon as his fingers tapped wildly on the buttons. Éric coughed and cleared his throat loudly, causing a prim middle-aged woman to glance up from her paperback romance novel and purse her lips at him. From his position, he could just about see the couple on the front cover of the book, a tanned man with his hand on the arm of a young woman who was twisting away from him, and only part of the title, 'Traded to…' The woman noticed him looking in her direction, and turned the front of the book away, her caged mind repelling intrusion. He'd forgotten how standoffish the English could be.

At his stop, Éric jumped up and skirted around the tall man in the doorway to exit the carriage and wound his way down the platform to the exit. He placed his case on the escalator and swung his light jacket over his shoulders, pushing his arms up and through the sleeves, as if in a yawn. As the barriers swallowed his ticket he broke through into the daylight, feeling fulfilled with his day's work but slightly nervous of what he was about to do. He took small steps along the street, constructing a plan as he went, his case dipping and rising in accordance with the uneven pavement.

As he approached London's exclusive Mayfair Hotel, his pulse raced with excitement. The thrill of the game was what kept him motivated, kept him dishonest – a 'chancer' some would call him. One of the doormen greeted Éric with a suspicious nod as he approached – after all, most of the guests arrived by taxi, not on foot. The other doorman had become distracted by a pigeon boldly pecking around his feet and was attempting to gracefully shoo it away, but the first man furrowed his brow as he noticed Éric's small travel case and his less-than-pristine garb. Éric smiled confidently at him, having encountered several such men before with their stifling uniforms and bloated egos. He breezed through the revolving doors and was immediately confronted by so great a mass of luxurious marble that he very nearly gasped at the exquisite world he had just entered. Maintaining a stiff façade, he strode up to the Reception desk and immediately attracted the attention of one of the staff, hoping that she would not question his identity.

"Can I help you, sir?" She was a young woman, probably in her twenties, with a generous smile and immaculate makeup spoiled only by the red lipstick decorating one front tooth.

"Yes. I'm not happy with my room. I want to move," Éric declared in his most authentic English accent, his heart beating slightly faster as he teetered on the cusp of his game plan. Would it work? Would he be caught out?

"I'm sorry to hear that, sir. Which room are you unhappy with?" This is where his genius plan came into effect.

"Here's my room card," said Éric, handing over the small, plastic rectangle he had extracted from the ill-gotten wallet earlier that day. The young woman, whose badge read 'CARA', scanned his room card into the slot at the top of her keyboard and peered at her computer screen.

"Room 302. May I ask what you're unhappy about, sir? Perhaps we can solve the problem without moving you."

Éric had foreseen this reply, and had his excuse all ready. "It's the view. I don't like it. I'd like to be moved to a room on the other side of the hotel. And on a different floor." He kept his tone firm and sure, allowing no room for negotiation.

"I see. But you are happy with the room itself, sir? You just want an identical room on the other side of the building?"

"Yes, as I said."

"I just need to see your credit card again, sir, so that I can change the reservation." He was also ready for this; he opened his wallet and slid out the most prestigious-looking American Express gold card that belonged to Mr Newman – surely the one he would have used for a booking at such an exclusive hotel.

Cara turned the card over, checking the numbers, and typed a few digits into the computer. "Ok, that's fine, sir. I just have to check what's available – we don't have that many triple rooms and this is a busy period."

Éric was momentarily stumped.

"Triple rooms?"

"Yes, sir, it says here that you have two children with you, in a triple room. I'll see what we can do." She turned back to the computer and began to type, earnestly.

Children. The man had children with him. Éric rubbed his forehead as he considered the complication. The Reception phone began to ring and was left unanswered. He glanced along the desk to the other member of staff, a well-dressed man in a waistcoat and bowtie, attending to a short woman awkwardly clutching several shopping bags while standing on tiptoes to sign an invoice on the counter-top. The phone continued to ring, a piercing noise, and Éric wished she would answer it. He suddenly realised what he should have said a few minutes ago.

"Actually, excuse me," he bumbled, causing Cara to look up in surprise. "The children won't be staying here anymore. I just need a single room."

"Oh. I see." Cara stared at him for a few seconds, perplexed, before catching herself and turning back to the screen. He knew that she wanted to question him about the children, that his behaviour seemed odd, so he attempted to clarify the situation, not wanting to remain as memorable to her as he no doubt already was.

"Their mother has taken them home. I have some business to do. You know what kids are like, always demanding attention," and, realising he was sounding uncaring as she looked up again, he continued, "I mean, I love having them with me, but I really have to get a lot of work done." He gave her a beaming smile and, to his relief, she smiled back, unquestioning.

"Well, that makes it easier, sir – we do have a few single rooms free." She reached under the desk and pulled out a new room card, swiping it before handing it to him. "Here you are. Room 519. It's on the other side of the building, sir, and I hope the view is more satisfactory for you. And you're booked in for…let me see…another week, yes?" Éric nodded, making a mental note of the dates. "Would you like some help moving your things?"

"No, thank you, I'll move them myself. Haven't got too much now that the children have gone," he added for effect, just as it struck him – the children's things, what on earth would he do with them?

"In that case, here is your old key card, sir, so you can clear out the room; it's effective for another hour, so please return it to Reception after that so we can ensure you're checked out of the original room." She smiled again, displaying the rosy tooth, and he returned her warmth.

"Thank you very much." He picked up the old card and retreated, furtively glancing round for the lifts, trying to appear as if he knew his way around the hotel. He spotted them to his left and strolled over, the first wave of success only hitting him as the lift doors closed around him and he was alone to contemplate his achievement.

On the third floor, he wandered along the corridor until he came to room 302, and slipped the key card into the slot by the door handle. He pushed it down and entered, wondering what he would find inside. The lights and the television came on automatically, and a chaotic scene was revealed – bed linen and towels strewn haphazardly around, clothes occupying the chairs and desk, bags left in the middle of the floor. He turned the television off quickly, not wanting to attract attention, and took a look around. He picked up the occasional item, inspecting things here and there, and it was soon evident that Mr Newman had two young children – a boy and a girl perhaps.

Wary of time, Éric threw the large suitcase open on the floor and, after searching it for valuables and pocketing a digital camera, he began to pick items of clothing up from around the room and throw them into the suitcase. Once it was full, he perched awkwardly on top and pulled the zip round before wheeling it to the room door. He surveyed the scene. All that was left were a few children's toys on the bed, a couple of books in the bathroom and some cosmetics by the sink. He opened the cupboards to check they were empty, and in them he found a small child's pink suitcase and a *Star Wars* backpack.

He felt a pang of regret as he pulled them out and stuffed the last remaining toys, books and cosmetics into them before placing them next to the large case.

He stood for a moment, wondering if the soft toys had names and if they were precious, but, noticing the time, forced himself to snap out of his reverie and attend to matters at hand. He balanced his own bag on top of the large suitcase and the rucksack on top of the pink case, clumsily managing to open the room door and wheel everything out. He closed the door behind him after double-checking that he had both key cards and all personal belongings. He glanced down the silent corridor and wondered what he should do with the cases. The big one he should take with him for now, he decided, otherwise someone might trace where it had come from and who it belonged to, especially as Mr Newman would no doubt come looking for it. The children's bags were the problem – he almost wished he could leave them for the children to retrieve, though he didn't want the cleaning staff to find them and return them to Reception.

As he rounded the corner on the third floor, he spotted the answer – a big silver panel on the wall by his feet. He pulled the heavy flap open, no doubt heavy so that small children couldn't fall into it, and peered down what must have been a laundry chute. The hole was just big enough to swallow both the rucksack and the pink suitcase, and he winced as they clanked and rattled their way down, landing with a thud at the bottom. At least this way they may not be found immediately and would not be traceable back to the room. Satisfied with his actions, he hurried back round to the lift, lugging the large suitcase and his adopted bag that looked modest in comparison.

When he got to room 519, which was indeed on the other side of the building, he tucked the big suitcase into a corner behind the curtain, delved into the mini-bar for a beer, and made a silent, solitary toast to his sponsor, the wonderful Mr Newman.

Little did Éric realise the complexity of the world he had just thrust himself into.

Chapter 7

Amelia held tightly onto Luke's hand and pulled him along behind her. He resisted and whined, tugging the opposite way and making some protest against the trolley she was trying to steer with her spare hand. She was suddenly reminded of the anti-war protesters she had seen on the news the previous day, and remarked to herself just how much priorities widen and grow with age: one day you've lost your favourite coloured pencil, the next it's your exam notes and, before you know it, you've lost all sense of who you are, why anything matters, and your priorities are determined for you. Oh, to go back to the days of coloured pencils and notebooks, she thought, and stopped suddenly in the vegetable aisle, her teary son staring up at her with blank confusion.

"Why do we have to do this every time, Luke?"

He fell silent, his objections invalid now that he had her attention, and pouted instead, screwing up his face and wiping his nose on his sleeve.

"Wait, I've told you not to do that," she instructed as so often before, foraging in her handbag for the wad of tissues that she never went anywhere without. She reached out to wipe his face, but he recoiled, so she dutifully handed him the tissue and watched as he gave his nose one quick wipe and pocketed the sheet, immediately skipping off to inspect the cucumbers.

As she made her weekly way around the supermarket, Amelia switched on her autopilot mechanism. In the fruit and vegetable aisle Luke would be bored; at the delicatessen he would be fascinated; in the cheese and fish section he would wrinkle his nose and declare that things were 'yucky'; in the washing and cleaning products aisle he would struggle to put bulky items she didn't want into the trolley; and in the chocolate, sweet and biscuit section they would always have an argument about how much he could have, usually resulting in her compromising much more than she should just to keep him quiet.

Other customers would stare at her for the slightest tantrum from Luke and, depending on her energy levels, she would either ignore them, look pleadingly willing them to empathise, or stare straight back at them until they uncomfortably swept their trolleys into a different aisle. At least Luke was now seven-years-old and at a whining, rather than screaming, stage. She wanted him to appreciate just how lenient she was with him, but he was too young to understand that he had moulded her into the mother she was, with his incessant crying, wheedling and demands.

Amelia had a strict rule – an hour in the supermarket for the weekly shop, and then to the checkout. If they were in the middle of a biscuit/ice-cream/pizza debate when time was up, more often than not, the item was thrown into the trolley and Luke, triumphant, was marched to the till, where he would dart in between Amelia's legs, singing nursery rhymes and prattling inexhaustibly.

"That's a lively one you've got there," the checkout lady would sometimes say.

"Don't I know it?" Amelia would retort, making the interlocutor chuckle. "I should leave him here to help you out!" And thus with a wry joke she appeased her disparaging public, desperate to cloud the judgement that she was a *bad mother*.

Today, she was in more of a hurry, because they had been stuck in traffic on the way from Luke's school to the supermarket. She had just 45 minutes before they had to leave and head to the local kindergarten to pick up Lydia, who attended for afternoons only, from 1pm to 5pm, and finished an hour-and-a-half after Luke did. At the checkout, packing frantically, Amelia handed over her card, entered her pin number quickly, and grabbed her receipt before herding the trolley through the back entrance, calling for Luke at the same time. He trotted up and walked alongside her for a few seconds, before dashing ahead into the car park, almost darting out behind a reversing car.

"Luke!" she screeched, but he was already too far ahead, continuing on in a bid to get to their car before her. When she reached him, she grabbed his arm before he could run around to the other side.

"How many times have I-"

"...told you not to do that?" he sang back at her mockingly, a vainglorious grin on his face.

She let the trolley slide a little and reached behind him with her right arm, smacking him firmly on his bottom. Luke barely flinched, but looked straight at her, sulking. She noticed a woman in the car parked opposite staring at her in the rear-view mirror.

"Don't be cheeky," she said weakly, with a sigh, dropping Luke's arm so that he ran to the left and jumped into the back of the car without a word. She unloaded the shopping into the boot and left the trolley in the empty space next to her, furtively looking round to make sure nobody had seen her. And with that, she too jumped into the car and started it, after checking that Luke was wearing his seatbelt.

Amelia was 28-years-old when she married Ian, a lawyer four years older than her. When she met him, she was working as a legal secretary in a prominent law firm, and he had just completed his training. She was confident, attractive and diligent, and barely paid him any attention – he was just another of the bigwigs around the office, and she had far more fun socialising with the other secretaries and enjoying the perks of the job. She had left school at eighteen and worked as a secretary, taking a legal secretary course in her spare time. She was first employed at the law firm to cover maternity leave but, when her predecessor decided not to return, Amelia was immediately made permanent and continued to fare well.

Ian arrived with an in-take of approximately fifty trainees, all of them cocky and assertive until they realised how demanding the job would be from the outset. Amelia admired the women in the group, dedicating themselves to such a career, but never envied their positions. She knew that it was not a case of intelligence – she too could have been a lawyer if she had wanted – but it was a matter of priorities, of a life-changing decision she'd made at an early age not to pursue an all-consuming career.

She had seen Ian in meetings and presentations, but he never stood out from the rest; in a whole firm of suits, another young lawyer was like a drop of water in the ocean. Amelia dated various men, none of them seriously, but never dated a lawyer, as appealing as they sometimes were. The secretaries exchanged gossip about their bosses, their bosses' bosses, their bosses' assistants, the trainees and the other secretaries – according to the grapevine, there was a whole world of scandal taking place behind those glass doors. Amelia enjoyed her work immensely, dabbled in the office politics, socialised, harmonised and clocked off by 6pm everyday, though nobody could have accused her of not being dedicated to her job.

It was when Ian's secretary was fired one day for an undisclosed reason, that Amelia found out he had noticed her. Her boss at the time, Mr Ryan, called her into his office and told her that Ian had inquired whether Amelia would like to switch to working for him. It was a strange request – secretaries did occasionally get passed from one lawyer to another, but Mr Ryan was very senior and everyone knew it would be laughable for a secretary to move from a powerful lawyer to a novice. Mr Ryan valued her and was confident she would not move, but had been obliged to pass on the offer as he was soon to retire and knew that she would need to think of her own future. She duly turned it down and, the next time she saw Ian at a corporate function, she noticed him looking wistfully at her before turning away.

Over the next couple of years, they encountered each other more and more, albeit only in passing. He would come into her office with a trivial question he could have asked anyone, would attend meetings that she was taking minutes at, and she would often catch him staring at her from across the canteen. She liked the way he dressed – not boring or fusty, but in well-cut suits, trendy shirts and matching ties, with polished shoes and his hair slightly too long.

Mr Ryan eventually retired and Amelia was transferred to a different department, working for another senior lawyer who was brash and disrespectful. She had been in her new position for just three months when Ian approached her one day and informed her that he was leaving to set-up his own practice and he offered her a legal assistant's position for very good money. She accepted without asking too many questions, eager for a fresh start and excited that he had noticed her potential. He had great plans for setting-up his own firm and, over two or three months, she helped him realise them – by which time neither of them could deny they had fallen in love. He loved her mind, he said, the way she viewed the world, her laugh, her body, her vision, her passion. He couldn't get enough of her, and she herself became obsessed with his addiction.

By the time the practice was set-up and ready to go, they made the mutual decision that it was no longer appropriate for Amelia to work there, and she happily took a 'career break', planning to go back to work just as soon as she desired. Within a year, they were married and she never went back to work, though she was kept very busy at home, supporting him while he worked long hours, and running the household. He was nearly always at the practice but, when he did come home, he gave her everything he could – his mind, his heart, his emotions – and she grabbed at his attention greedily.

The house they lived in was a modest detached property on the suburban outskirts of North London. They had a fair-sized garden, flowerbeds that Amelia regularly tended to, and elderly neighbours who sometimes popped round for a cup of tea. It was a big house for the two of them, and Ian would often tease her that they had to 'make more use of the space'. They both wanted children, and each secretly thought the other would make a great parent, though they never overtly made plans for them. The thought of children excited and frightened them both, an odd combination that in the early days of their marriage led them to mutual procrastination.

When Amelia fell unexpectedly pregnant at the age of 29 – Ian was nearing 34 – she was apprehensive yet relieved; it could be a fresh start for them, a new injection of interest in their lives. Ian had continued to work long hours and the 'honeymoon' period of their marriage seemed increasingly distant. Having a child was the next obvious step, an experience other than work that they could share.

They chose not to find out the sex of the baby in advance, it being their first, and Amelia spent much of her time at home reading about pregnancy, motherhood, what to do and what not to do, how to do it, when to do it and how much. She read so many theories, made notes, talked to friends with babies, the doctor, family members, that she drove herself crazy trying to organise all the information in her head. She wanted to organise the baby itself, when it was born, file it, tidy it and nourish it like a project, but Ian didn't seem to understand – he remained undaunted, reassuring and dismissive of her fears. (Would she make a good mother? "Yes, of course," he said, "stop worrying so much.")

When the baby was finally born, one sunny June day, she was relieved that it was a boy. She couldn't pinpoint why, and she kept her feelings to herself, but boys she was unfamiliar with; she wasn't quite ready, she decided, to bring up a little girl, wasn't quite ready for the self-examination and comparison that would inevitably ensue from raising a child of the same sex. She named him Luke after her grandfather, and Ian, happy with his wife's visible joy after months of angst, was content to be a bystander as motherhood took its course. Luke was a happy, contented baby who grew into a confident child, and Amelia found that her collected theories flew out of the window.

When Lydia was due, three years later, Amelia was relaxed and happy. She knew what to expect this time, had her own rules, and had a healthy three-year-old to prove her success as a mother. It was good to have a girl – one of each 'completed the set' – and she never imagined that her previous worries, instead of being dispelled, would be projected onto her young daughter. Lydia was a fretful baby who cried for hours and slept lightly, waking for the slightest change in atmosphere. She would be fed, changed, rested, and, still tearful, Amelia became exhausted and depressed.

Ian distanced himself by spending more and more time at the office, and taking on the easy duties when he was home – playing with Luke, making food, and generally avoiding any of his new daughter's distress. If he carried her and she began to cry, he would pass her over to Amelia, saying, "Here, she wants you," which they both knew would not appease the baby. Still, there were happy times: the four of them, together on a Saturday night, their home occasionally tidy, nobody thinking about work. Amelia strived for these times, held onto them, and convinced herself that one day, when the children were older, the hard times would be behind them and it would all have been worth it.

Turning into the kindergarten car park, Amelia checked the clock and noted with relief that she was right on time. Lydia had grown into a sensitive four-year-old and would almost certainly be screaming at the top of her voice if Amelia was more than five minutes late, because all the other super-efficient mothers would have arrived early and whisked their children away as soon as they stepped out of the kindergarten. If she was ever late for Luke, on the other hand, he would sulk – her son seemed to have been born with a 'guilt trip' mechanism. Amelia couldn't decide which method was worse, but she did love her children, despite their dreadful idiosyncrasies. She often questioned whether she had bestowed their behaviour upon them (wasn't it always the parents' fault?) or whether, as she hoped, they had been born with some sort of preconceived personalities (because then it wouldn't cast any reflection on the type of mother she'd turned out to be).

At home, Amelia let the children turn the television on as she prepared dinner. Usually Ian would be home around 7pm, bringing work with him, and they would sit down together at the table. It was a little late for Lydia to be eating, but it was the only way they could dine together as a family and, however selfish, Amelia couldn't bear to let these times go.

Ian and she would share a bottle of wine, Lydia would complain that she didn't like any of the food (or that she would only eat certain colours) and Amelia tried to make her eat a little until she eventually gave up trying, and Luke would eat a bare minimum and then claim he was too full for any more. Amelia was continually tempted to prepare less food, seeing as so much of it went to waste, except that she wouldn't want anyone to be able to accuse her of starving her children.

After dinner, the children would be escorted up to the bathroom, occasionally by Ian but more often by Amelia, and then Amelia would clear the plates away while Ian got on with work. She would spend the evening doing chores, watching television or sometimes would catch-up with phone calls, determined not to disturb Ian. At around 10pm, he would finish his work and come and join her, and for a short while each night they would be alone together.

These were the times that Amelia dreaded most in the day, because they never lived up to her hopes and expectations. When she was feeling indulgent, she imagined that Ian would throw his work aside, take her in his arms and insist on making love to her wherever they were in the house, not caring if the children stirred or how late it was getting. He would cherish her because she was a fantastic wife, a great mother, the only person he could imagine standing by his side in every way and the only thing penetrating his thoughts for those few glorious minutes each day. There would be a spark between them, they would whisper to each other like schoolchildren, giggling and awkward, their heartbeats quickening and synchronised. And, afterwards, he wouldn't let her go, would hold her tight to himself as if clutching desperately at time.

It was the small things she missed, the little things that had consumed her and made her high: the light pressure of an unfamiliar hand on her waist, making her skin prickle and her body tense; looking into someone's eyes and being pleasantly surprised at the reflection, the whole world melting into one look; a first touch, a first kiss, the whole body fragmented into parts that meet – eyes, lips, hands that touch and caress, all other parts futile, evanescent, meaningless without connection.

They had had this and lost it, too soon she felt, before she'd even recognised it and realised how much it cemented their mutual existence. She fantasised about others, strangers and acquaintances, secretly allowing her thoughts to take her back to those feelings, those irretrievable moments she had sacrificed with a few vows and replaced with two new lives. She caressed her own body when no one was around, willing her hands to be alien, to invoke the power of elsewhere, another time, the memories that once were truth. She remembered how easy it was when they first started seeing each other, first made love – so effortless, exhilarating, intense. She was different then: carefree, eager, seeking opportunities and grabbing every second. Now things felt tainted with time, with paths chosen and overused.

These days, Ian was distracted and tired, rarely focusing entirely on her, as she tried to do on him. The end of their evenings would be spent in front of the television – on a good day they would exchange mundane conversation but on most days they would watch something, anything, in silence, until one of them decided they were tired and would go to bed. The worst thing of all was that Ian didn't seem to mind, didn't seem to want to change the situation or connect with her more. Amelia longed for this connection, longed to communicate with her entire being and feel her longing reciprocated.

She sometimes thought of reaching over to slap him, punch him, anything, not in order to hurt him but to see if he would react, though she was fearful he wouldn't. He was full of kindness, hard work, loyalty, yes – but devoid of passion, interest, feeling even. Was love made of loyalty, stability and duty still love if it was without fire and urgency and lust and spirit? Is there such a thing as half a love and, if so, where does the other half go?

Amelia was on the verge of finding out. For months now she had been tired of the routine, the lack of spontaneity, the emptiness she felt that never seemed to end. She had changed as a person, gone from being attractive and extrovert to being sullen and dismayed, though she could not justify marriage and motherhood as the catalysts to her depression. They were meant to bring happiness, fulfilment; she had chosen them, invested time and effort in them, and she was meant to be reaping the rewards, not biding her time. She had made mistakes, she knew, but she would not let herself wallow in them, would not sit back until she was nothing but pieces: a shell of a wife, a hollow mother. Tomorrow night Ian was looking after the children because he thought Amelia was attending a local council meeting. She wasn't.

Chapter 8

Daniel sat at one end of the bar tracing the edge of the glass with his finger. He hadn't had a drink all day, the first day in...he couldn't remember...more than a year, that was for sure. His hands were trembling and his mind wandered in all directions, like an ant not sure of which way to go. He glanced at his watch; it was 7.10pm. He had deliberately arrived early so he could get at least one drink in before she arrived.

Yet now that this whisky was in front of him, he wasn't sure what to do with it. His mind told him to knock it back – he couldn't remain trembling and anxious the whole evening – but his organs protested. His heart was sluggish these days, devoid of feeling and ardour, and his liver was well on its way to giving up. His business had been flushed away and his son was estranged – even the blood ties had been polluted by ethanol. He didn't have much to keep him going, except the drink. But all that had changed, last week.

He had made a rare trip to the supermarket, in search of a few more bottles and some ready-made food. He always made an effort with his appearance when he went out – brushed his teeth, put on some decent clothes, combed his hair – as he didn't want society to see him as he couldn't even bear to see himself: a lonely, pathetic alcoholic. Plus, if he stank of booze, as Johnny so often complained, and he went to the supermarket to buy some, he might be denied; they might even call the manager, as had happened to him once. He thought he'd get the boy a treat too, something to show he still thought of him, appreciated his presence if nothing else.

It was while he was perusing the racks of sweets (for he still thought of his son as a young child, the alcoholic haze having shielded his eyes from Johnny's enforced maturity) that he noticed the small boy next to him, trying in vain to reach a packet that was above his height. Daniel reached out and lifted the desired sweets off their rail and handed them to him.

"Thanks." The child grinned and, promptly turning to depart, spotted a woman whom Daniel presumed must be his mother. "Uh-oh," the boy declared, before spinning around to run off in the other direction, unfortunately forgetting that Daniel was in his way.

"Oomph," Daniel exclaimed as the boy ran into him, doubling over slightly and then reaching out to pick the child up. The boy was scrabbling on the floor to get to the sweets that had rolled down the aisle.

"Luke!" the woman called, jogging slightly behind a full trolley. She seemed flustered and, blushing, turned towards Daniel.

"Sorry," she said, giving him a wan smile. He noticed how pretty she was, her hair a natural chestnut colour and her lips thinly veiled with lipstick. She left the trolley next to him and trotted a few steps to scoop up the young boy who had just reached the sweets on the floor but had become distracted by some on another shelf.

"I've told you, you can't have those. Now stop wasting my time and come on. We have to go in a minute." She held the boy's hand and dragged him back to the trolley. "Now hold onto this," she said, placing his hand on the side, "and don't let go or you'll be in serious trouble, young man." She smiled apologetically again at Daniel.

"Oh, don't worry," he said. "I've got one myself, I know what they're like. In fact, I was just getting him some sweets, you know, as a treat."

"How old's your son?" she asked, trying to make conversation. Perhaps, like him, she was devoid of adult company, Daniel thought.

"Oh, uh, just fourteen actually, but they never grow out of sweets, do they?" Daniel looked down at his empty basket, grateful that he hadn't yet visited the drinks aisle.

"True. Or trouble – they never seem to grow out of that." Amelia smiled warmly but then frowned as Luke broke free and dashed away. "Actually," she went on, apparently deciding to ignore him, "he's not mine – I'm just looking after him for a friend."

"Oh, ok. Well, you're lucky you can give him back later, eh?!"

"Yes. I'm Amelia by the way. Nice to meet you." She stepped forward and held out her hand but, after grasping it politely, Daniel stepped back a little, keen to maintain the distance.

"I'm Daniel. So, do you come here often…I mean, are you local?" He blushed slightly and looked down. Why was this so awkward, he thought? We're just two people in a supermarket making conversation. But already, by that point, he knew – he hoped – it was more than that.

"Yes, I live about a five-minute drive away. This is the nearest big supermarket. Feels like everyone in a ten-mile radius shops here."

"Yes, it does. I live a few minutes' walk away actually. It's quite convenient." He cringed internally at the suggestion it might appear he was making. But then she brought him back to his senses.

"Oh, gosh…I mean, Luke, I have to find him!" She realised that they must have been talking for enough time for Luke to have done anything, for anyone to have…

Without saying another word, she turned and rushed to the middle of the supermarket, sweeping along the centre and scanning the aisles on either side. Daniel followed closely behind, keen to help. They found Luke by the deli, holding a box of eggs and poking at one that had cracked.

"Luke, what did I tell you?" Amelia scolded. "No television tonight; you'll be going straight to your room!" Luke began to whine, and she grabbed his arm and whisked him around to head towards the checkout. It struck Daniel as a strange threat, given that the boy was not her son.

"You found him then. Anything I can give you a hand with?"

He ended up carrying her shopping to the car and, once she had seat-belted the boy into the back, she turned and began to fumble in her handbag. He wondered what she was doing, if he should simply say goodbye and retreat. Just as he was about to speak, she pulled out a piece of paper and a child's crayon, which made him laugh. She scribbled something down awkwardly and handed it to him, saying softly, "Any day before 7pm." He waited until she had driven away before looking at it, and smiled with glee on seeing her phone number and the words 'Call me'.

He rang her the next afternoon, nervous but excited, not knowing what to expect. If she really was single – unattached without children – and if she really was interested in him, he had struck gold. His one fear was that nobody but him and his son knew that he was an alcoholic, and he wanted it to stay that way. He had squandered most of Flora's life insurance money on alcohol (insurance that, ironically, he had insisted they both get, back in the days when they'd felt invincible) but there was a small amount left, and he had promised himself that he would clean-up his act and get a job before it ran out. He'd even taken to drawing the dole, something he'd never imagined himself doing, just to fund his habit. He had never even considered another woman since his wife died – for one thing he knew he wasn't fit to be in a relationship – but perhaps this was the sign he had been passively waiting for, a reason to start again.

It was Amelia who answered the phone and she sounded pleased to hear his voice. They chatted, that first time, for almost an hour before he heard a child crying in the background and she said she had to go, mumbling something about looking after children as a favour.

He told her a bit about himself and was mostly honest – admitted that he used to run his own business but eventually he'd had to close it down, and that he was looking for a new opportunity. He talked a bit about his son and revealed that his wife had died some time ago. Their conversation was comfortable, mutual, refreshing. Before she went, she asked him if he wanted to meet, and he readily agreed.

"No strings attached," she said. "It would just be nice to carry on this conversation in person. Say next Tuesday at 7.30pm?" She was confident in taking the lead, and he immediately liked that about her. She named a bar that they both knew in the town centre, and he hung up the phone, elated.

As he waited in the bar the following week, he pulled at his collar nervously. Glancing at his watch every few minutes, he decided just before 7.30pm that he could no longer wait, and he downed his drink in one quick gulp. *Just one to steady my nerves,* he thought. *I've done so well to not drink all day.* That familiar warm glow enveloped him straightaway, and he relaxed back on his stool.

He was wearing his best shirt and suit, without a tie (didn't want to appear too keen), and polished shoes. His trousers were loose – he'd lost a lot of weight since he'd last worn them, to work, and he hadn't been able to find a belt. He had some money in his wallet and he hoped it would be enough; all these worries circulated in his mind, making him feel anxious.

Amelia walked into the bar at 7.35pm, wearing a beautiful summer dress and modest heels. Her face lit-up with a smile when she spotted him at the bar, and she wandered over, slid onto the stool next to him and leant over to kiss him on the cheek.

"Hi," she said, and it was enough to make him feel like he was on a film set, as if at any moment someone was going to shout 'Cut!' and he would find himself back on his sofa, a can of lager in his hand.

He got them both a drink, and they began to talk. He forced himself to drink slowly, matching her pace, not wanting her to get a true impression of him. She was engaging, lively, intelligent and very attractive, and before long he realised he could fall in love with this woman. But it was too easy, too ideal, and it was only much later that he realised what a fool he had been; you can't drink from a glass that's in shards.

Chapter 9

Johnny raised his head and watched as the clumsy, slightly chubby profile in the regulation navy swimsuit and light-blue swimming cap lifted its arms, wobbled a little, and then plunged *almost* cleanly into the water below, the splayed legs causing a small splash as they connected with the surface and disappeared underneath into temporary oblivion. He stared at the rippled water, waiting for her to emerge so he could grin, perhaps even wave, but he was distracted by someone calling his name.

"Johnny! Hey, Johnny! It's your turn."

He turned his head sharply to see his best friend, Will, gesturing wildly towards the water. Looking beyond him, Johnny could see Mrs Dartford, the sports teacher, standing at the side of the pool, both hands on her hips and the whistle in her mouth.

"If you paid as much attention to your swimming technique as you do to the girls, Jonathan, you'd be swimming the English Channel by now," she declared, her booming voice echoing around the room like that of an almighty being.

The other boys sniggered, and it was then that Johnny noticed several of them already in the pool and ready to go. The rest of them – those that had finished their turn – sat impatiently on the bench behind, dripping and fidgeting until the next time they were summoned.

As he shuffled to the edge, Johnny turned to look at the other end of the pool where the girls were practising their diving. He hoped they hadn't all heard Mrs Dartford's comment as well. He sat momentarily with his legs in the water and saw Sabrina give him a small wave from the left side of the pool where she'd surfaced but, feeling the eyes of his peers boring into various parts of his body, he dropped into the water quickly, without giving her so much as a nod.

After the lesson, which Johnny endured each week without enjoyment due to the unpredictable wrath of Mrs Dartford and her penchant for anti-favouritism (there was a rumour that she made her own children get up at 5am and run ten miles every day before they could have breakfast), the boys retreated to the teasing/alienation/camaraderie of the changing room (depending on which 'group' you were in) and the girls traipsed off to theirs, before all meeting to get the coach back to school. Sabrina was dawdling outside the bus doors as Johnny approached, rummaging around in her bag and conveniently finding whatever she was looking for just as Johnny stood in front of her. She looked up and smiled.

"Hi," she said.

"Hey," he mumbled, before shifting in between two other boys and climbing onto the coach. He knew she would follow soon after and duly take a seat among the girls. A few of their classmates knew something was going on between them – in fact, a few had 'things' of their own going on – but at the tender age of fourteen, none were entirely comfortable with displays of affection. Especially not in confined public places.

Over the past couple of weeks, however, when it came to Sabrina, a growing awareness that it was not enough had been niggling at Johnny. The quick 'hellos' in passing, a sneaky kiss or two behind the corners of school buildings in break time, a public grin and wave in the cafeteria; once these had been the highlight of his day – of their day, he imagined – but now it was no longer as exciting as it had been almost six months ago.

When they had discovered at the beginning of the school year that the customary reorganisations had placed them in the same form, they had both been happy. The year prior to that, ever since Sabrina first spoke to/cornered him, had been filled with awkward conversations, strange attempts on Sabrina's part to sit or work with him in shared lessons, and eventual concession on Johnny's part to indulge her attempts at friendship, seeing as he'd come to the conclusion that this girl was *not* going to go away. And once he got to know her better, he discovered that the undefined nerves he was harbouring were dispelled and she was actually quite nice. When they'd ended up in the same form that year, Johnny found himself separated not only from Will, but from a significant number of familiars, and he was thrust almost brutally into a sea of faces whose names, as yet, had no connections to personalities. It was then that he began to really value the unceasing efforts of an eager Sabrina, and a firm friendship developed.

Nearly six months ago, after a St. George's Day disco thrown on a whim by the Headmistress at which boys and girls were encouraged to barn dance and do-si-do with each other at a strict distance of one metre), Johnny had finally taken the initiative and whisked Sabrina outside under the guise of not feeling very well and needing some fresh air. Before she had acknowledged what was happening, he had leaned over somewhat abruptly and pecked her on the lips before standing back, blushing ferociously and staring at his shoes. Delighted, she had stepped towards him, kissing him again and parting her mouth slightly as the evening breeze rushed through his ears and into his mind, there forming a mist that hung over him for days and kept him from concentrating. By the end of the evening he was feeling mildly giddy, and he also couldn't stop thinking about the budding breast he'd felt through the blue velvet dress she was wearing.

But that had been a while ago now, and things hadn't progressed much further since. He wasn't even sure if – and how – they should have progressed anyway. They were still good friends, paid each other the requisite amount of attention, and exchanged the odd, awkward kiss, but lately Johnny had noticed a slightly wistful look on Sabrina's face each time he saw her. As a result, he was beginning to think that she shared the same frustrations.

As he sat on the coach back to school next to Will, who was hanging over the head of the seat in front and exchanging terrible jokes with its occupant, Johnny, painfully aware of Sabrina's presence a few rows ahead, vowed to do something about it. As they pulled into the school driveway and got down from the coach, Johnny rushed to catch up with her, interrupting her conversation with another girl, and whispered in her ear, "Come to my house for dinner tomorrow evening?" – a part-demand, part-question that nonetheless caused Sabrina's eyes to widen with excitement, and this time he reciprocated with a warm smile before jogging casually back to Will and slapping him on the back gleefully. This, he thought, would be the beginning of the next stage, whatever that was, and he felt proud of himself for having initiated it. Now all he had to do was tell his Dad that evening, and brace the inevitable barrage of questions.

There was another reason why Johnny now felt comfortable inviting Sabrina over for dinner: a few weeks ago, the miraculous had happened – his dad had stopped drinking. At first, Johnny hadn't noticed. Caught-up in teenage angst, he supposed it must have been a day or two before he'd realised his dad was no longer in permanent residency on the sofa, glass or can in hand, and was instead up and about, shuffling around the house, making pathetic attempts to find something useful to do after all the wasted time.

They had taken to largely ignoring each other and going about their routines (or lack thereof) almost as if the other were invisible, each as predictable and consistent in his habits. Then one day, just before he left for school, Johnny rounded the corner to the kitchen and bumped, smack, into a small plastic bag that was hovering magically in the air. He looked up, befuddled, to see his father's hand and above it, who was looking down on him with a sheepish smile.

"I've made you lunch," he stated in a reconciliatory tone.

"Ham sandwiches. You always liked ham."

Johnny glared back at him, his uncertainty causing him to fall back on hostility. Later, he managed to fathom the sensation he'd experienced at that moment – the moment his antithesis of a father transformed with one small gesture into a parental figure with *potential* – and that feeling was of fragility, that their mutual existence had come to a fork in the road, and Johnny had the power to make it go either way. He was in control; his father was looking to find a purpose in him, a reason to get himself together. He felt resentment and compassion all at once, a small sense of triumph juxtaposed with grief at past failures. But there was no part of him that questioned the significance of the moment or doubted that his father was on the cusp of metamorphosis; the miracle of change need not be a big one.

And as he stood there, staring up at his father as he once had in adoration and noticing that the dark patches under his eyes had faded a little, Johnny felt his legs move slightly and knew that he was going to walk away. He took one silent step backwards, never taking his eyes from the matching set that blinked and buckled under the pressure of huge disappointment. But as he took a second step away and saw his father's hand drop, the bag rustling dejectedly as it fell to his side, Johnny felt a pang of fear in his stomach. He suddenly realised that he didn't want to spend the rest of his life with *what if*, and stepped forward again and reached out for the bag, looking downward to avoid the shameful onrush of pity that he felt for his father.

As both hands met and the bag was transferred, Johnny mumbled, "Thanks," and stuffed it into his open backpack, turning to rush into the hallway, through the front door and into a haze of relief. He heard a feeble and almost unfamiliar voice call after him as he left, "There's an apple and a drink in there too," but he didn't turn round to acknowledge it.

Now, a few weeks later, their home life – and his father – had made a remarkable turnaround. Granted, they were still two males shuffling round a home and grappling with domesticity, but the house was cleaner than it had ever been – surfaces had been scrubbed, papers tidied, rubbish bins emptied and the carpet vacuumed – and there was once again an air of humanity lingering about the rooms. More surprisingly, all the glass bottles (green, red, yellow, blue, clear), cans, mixers, tonics, strange juices and sodas had been removed, the vast majority of the latter items still full as his father had long ago rejected any 'impurities' that would dilute the bittersweet grip alcohol held over him. The house smelled fresher, looked more homely, and sunlight highlighted the worn furniture.

As soon as they were once again keeping up appearances, their biggest challenge was communication. Having lived as silent shadows for so long, they now found themselves ready to converse, but about what neither could establish. They began by having short conversations about practicalities, nothing personal or familiar, but before long they had progressed to asking how each other's day was, sharing anecdotes or information, eventually drawing enough courage to ask questions about the other's intentions or schedule. They were not father and son in a familiar, affectionate sense – perhaps they never would be – but they bonded through the acknowledgement of their mutual boundaries and the resulting respect. There was generosity in the mundane, kindness in practical discussions, and hope in the contents of the fridge. For the first time since Flora's death, they were two people in a home forming a family comfortable with itself.

Before long, the only remnants of the dark period were on his father's ageing face, in his slow-gaited movements and exhausted, aching muscles. Johnny could see the struggle his father was facing: the mammoth hangover of several years' solid drinking, the way his limbs cried out as the numbness faded, the headaches, the last of the blurred vision clinging to his retinas, the bones that creaked and ached for want of the poison.

He had to lie down a lot, he occasionally rushed to the bathroom to vomit, and had to reintroduce himself to a lot of foods that his body had been trained to sacrifice. His organs were revived – his liver praised the Lord – and slowly, slowly, his body accepted that it had passed through hell and was now edging back up to earth. And once the worst had passed – minimal shaking, stamina rebuilt, alertness restored – Johnny began to recognise and remember something of the father he once had, the father he had always wanted and, as it emerged, the father he had always had. He had returned the alcoholic's costume to the fancy dress shop and resumed a normal fatherly outfit. He became clean-shaven, more articulate (he now spoke instead of grunting) and even went out and, presumably, talked to other people. Johnny had what he had wanted for so long – a fully-functioning parent – but the trouble was that by now other issues preyed on his mind.

That day, when he got home from school, his father wasn't at home. He looked in the food cupboards, which were fairly well stocked, and settled down in front of the television. By seven o'clock, his father still hadn't returned, and Johnny was slightly anxious. Just the previous week, his dad had acquired a part-time job, three-days-a-week, at the Nissan showroom about four miles away. On Mondays, Wednesdays and Saturdays, he would catch the bus (the rusty old Renault still sat in the garage but he said it felt refreshing not to drive) and work all day from 8.30am until 5pm, returning always by 6pm. Johnny absent-mindedly kept one eye on the television and one eye darting every so often to the window while rehearsing his planned speech.

He was going to tell his father in an understated manner about Sabrina, that she was a friend from school and she would be coming over for dinner tomorrow, and he had answers prepared to all possible questions, including the ones his dad would never ask. He would tell him that he could join them for a bit but not cling to them all evening, and that her parents would pick her up later on. He even had some potential recipes in mind, though nothing fancy, and he would suggest that maybe his dad and he could prepare some of the food that evening. At quarter-past-seven, Johnny went into the kitchen to get a drink, and that was when he heard the key in the door.

"Hi," he called, picking the fruit juice up in order to put it back. "You're a bit late; where've you been?" he asked into the fridge.

Aware of his father shuffling about in the hallway, putting down his keys, taking off his coat, Johnny went over his lines one more time – Sabrina, dinner, friend from school – and closed the fridge door as he heard footsteps approaching. He turned round with a smile, one hand ruffling his gelled-back hair. Two people stood before him: his father and an overly made-up woman with an ample bosom. The smile dropped off Johnny's face with a thud, like a rotten apple from a tree.

"There's someone I'd like you to meet," said his father. "This is Amelia."

Chapter 10

Ian Newman strides into the hotel lobby and immediately looks around to check how many staff are ready to aid arriving guests attentively. He can see three in smart brown trousers, cream shirts and yellow waistcoats – a ghastly uniform, but nonetheless pristine on each of them. He nods at the one he passes and heads towards the lifts, satisfied.

This is how he judges a hotel – the number of waiting staff (there should be at least two ready and waiting in the lobby at all times, not counting the concierge), the speed and quality of service in the restaurant, the number of times a day the room is cleaned (two, at least), complementary internet access in all rooms, being greeted by name by regular staff and the general flexibility of a hotel to cater to a guest's every whim. He isn't bothered about the cosmetics left in the bathroom, the number of mirrors, the presence of a swimming pool (though frankly, these days, it was a given in any good hotel), the number of channels on the television or how often they changed the numerous towels; these were small details to excite the infrequent traveller. It is the more unusual features that make a good hotel great, he thinks, that *extra* attention to detail and service that make a guest's stay pleasant. Oh, and a children's activity centre of course, for when the children are with him. Like now – he'd almost forgotten.

Luke and Lydia traipse into the lift after their father and fight for a few seconds over who should press the button, before their father reaches over and presses number 3. The children stop fighting in their mutual irritation and look up, whining "Daddy!" which falls on deaf ears. Lydia is dressed in a pink skirt that comes down to her knees but doesn't quite hide the angry, maroon scab she has from falling over in the playground last week, and a pink t-shirt with a purple, winged 'My Little Pony' emblazoned on it. She clutches a small doll with long brown hair and a bizarre patchwork outfit that her mother bought her just before the trip. One of her short white cotton socks, which are patterned with little cut-out hearts, has rolled down slightly towards her pink jelly shoes. Luke chews on his fingernails until he is chided, and then begins to walk up and down on the spot so that the back of his trainers flash small red lights each time he puts a foot down. When the lift arrives at the third floor they exit in a line and walk – Lydia skips – right, then left, until they get to their room. Ian reaches into the back pocket of his corduroy trousers and pulls out…nothing.

He swears loudly. The children look up at him, wide-eyed and frightened, because Daddy told them never to say bad words. He reaches into his other pockets and swears again. "Daddy, what's wrong?" asks Luke, already afraid of the answer because he realises it doesn't look good.

"My wallet's gone. You didn't take it, did you? Either of you?"

"No!" they chorus, indignantly. Lydia lets out a small nervous giggle, wondering if they're playing a game.

"Lydia! Did you take it? It's NOT funny. Give it back to me please or you'll be in serious trouble," he booms, hoping the loss of the wallet is her mistake, not his.

Lydia's face crumples though she doesn't cry. She is often like this – on the verge of tears in case she needs the emotional defence, yet superbly in control until she feels it's necessary to appear vulnerable. "No Daddy, I don't have it."

Another swearword. So far, two different swearwords that Luke has heard before. Lydia has only ever heard one of them before, once, on the television in the evening before her mother sent her promptly to bed.

They follow their father back down the corridor, left then right, back to the lifts. Ian presses the button that says 'R' and they are all sucked downwards in silence. Lydia strokes her doll's hair gently and Luke keeps his feet still. They walk quickly to the Reception desk and the look on Ian's face causes both members of staff to immediately glance up at him. One of them promptly puts down the phone and comes over.

"How can I help you, sir?" he asks, his eyes showing concern at Ian's anxious face while his mouth smiles at the children.

"Well, uh, it appears that I have lost my wallet. That is to say, I think it's been stolen. Pick-pocketed or something."

"How awful sir," says the man, his frozen expression conveying little sympathy. "Would you like to use the telephone? Perhaps call your bank?"

"Yes, uh, I'll need to do that. And I'm afraid I've lost the key card to our room."

"No problem sir, I'll get you another one. What's the name please?"

"Newman. Mr Ian Newman. Room 302."

"Right, well, you go ahead and use the phone while I sort this out for you." He passes a telephone across the desk and smiles at the children again. Luke ignores the faux warmth, but Lydia smiles back though she's decided she doesn't like him – or his outfit. Yellow is for girls, she thinks, though her favourite colour is pink.

Ian dials an operator and asks for the customer services number of his bank. After being transferred, he presses five different option buttons, keys in his sort code, account number, date-of-birth, two numbers from his pin code and finally gets through to someone in India who asks him for his sort code, account number, date-of-birth, the first line of his address and the third and sixth letters of his mother's maiden name. Finally, he is able to inform them that all his three cards have been stolen. The customer services representative with a thick Indian accent is called 'John' (pronounced 'Jaan') and reveals Ian's current account balance and recent spending on his cards, which to Ian's relief seems as it should be. All his cards are promptly cancelled and he is informed that it will take up to ten working days to send him new ones.

"That could be two weeks!" he protests, to no avail.

"Banking policy, sir," says John, with the strong intonation that doesn't help the situation. "You can get money out by taking some identification into your account holding branch, sir."

"My account holding branch? But that's nowhere near where I live now. You mean I can't get money out at any branch except that one?"

"Banking policy, sir," replies John, as if he's quoting a universal law. Ian notices the Reception staff staring at him sympathetically and feels more annoyed. The children have wandered off and are now running around the revolving doors.

"Right, thank you, goodbye," he says, and hangs up quickly in case 'Jaan' felt the need to tell him to "*Have a nice day!*"

He calls American Express and cancels that credit card as well, this time swiftly and easily, before dialling one more number. He knows what he has to do; they can't possibly stay here for a whole week without any means to pay. He phones Amelia and gets the answer machine. He leaves a message explaining what has happened and informs her that they will be returning home later that day; fortunately, their open-ended train tickets are in his bag in the room.

He fetches and scolds the children – several people have been tutting at them running around – and makes them sit quietly on the red armchairs. Then he returns to the desk and collects his key card. The room has been paid in advance and they have not incurred any extra charges, but he informs the receptionist that they will be collecting their things and checking out that day. He is told that he'll still have to pay for the next two nights in full, and thereafter will be refunded 85% of the room charge for every night he is cancelling.

Slightly outraged but not wishing to prolong his misery, Ian agrees to phone the hotel to obtain the refund once he has received his new cards and, once more, he gathers the children and ascends to the third floor. It's only when they reach room 302, slide the keycard into the slot and see the red light, that Luke and Lydia both hear a swearword escape their father's lips that neither of them have ever heard before.

They take the lift down to Reception again, their father muttering under his breath. At the desk, the receptionist he spoke to a few minutes ago has disappeared, and in his place is a shortish, blonde-haired girl who smiles a little too enthusiastically and holds two sweets from the dish on the counter, waving them in Luke and Lydia's direction. Neither of them accepts, and they watch as she retracts her hand, her eyes squinting, and drops the sweets back into the dish.

Ian ignores the gesture and proceeds to explain the situation in a short, sharp tone, his eyebrows juggling angrily up and down. The receptionist re-programs the keycard and beckons a bellboy over to "accompany this gentleman and his children up to the room, as they've been having some trouble accessing it." Ian protests that he does not need accompaniment, merely a card that works, but by then she has already become distracted by a gaggle of schoolchildren wielding hefty instrument cases that has just planted itself in the middle of the lobby. Ian sighs and follows the bellboy to the lifts, knowing that the children will follow, vowing that he would not give the bellboy a tip. Then he remembers that he has no money anyway. Back at Room 302, the bellboy tries the card in the door. The red light flashes again like an angry boil and Ian erupts. The children cower slightly, not accustomed to this irate stranger who displays no hint of kindness.

The bellboy, wondering how he has managed to get himself caught up in such fury, apologises profusely and tells them to wait right there. As he crosses from the lifts to Reception, he sees Muriel at the information desk look up and smile at him. In response, he holds up his two forefingers in the shape of an 'X', the sign for a difficult guest. Unable to converse in front of customers, the hotel staff has developed its own sign language, which makes the day go faster and allows them to convey events without the knowledge of the guests: a thumbs up means that everything is fine; a slight pat of the pocket means 'I've been paid and the first drink later is on me'; a tug on either ear means that Gallows (the Manager) is on the warpath; forming the mouth into a small, round 'O' means 'join me for a cigarette break out the back'; a slight wave of the hand means 'I'm extremely busy'; a gentle stamp of the foot means 'I'm entirely bored.' Some staff members have even developed a sub-language between themselves, like Derek the chef and Ina the barmaid who have recently started a relationship and often use empty hotel rooms to 'get their end away'. If either of them blows the other a subtle kiss, all the others, unbeknownst to them, are aware of exactly what they'll soon be up to.

At Reception, they finally realise what the problem is – they have been trying to access Room 302 with a card programmed for Room 519, which the computer tells them is occupied by Mr Newman. The bellboy is confused but returns to meet the guest with a card for each of the rooms. Ian is insistent – they were staying in Room 302 and, to his knowledge, there had been no change. They open the door but, to his horror, the room is clean, tidy and completely empty. He curses again and wonders if he is going mad. But no – the children too are confused and remember this room as theirs, in the quaint way that children take ownership of even the most temporary home.

Before frustration finds its voice, the bellboy suggests trying room 519, and Ian follows incredulously, wondering what on earth is happening. They open room 519, all three Newmans now worried about their things (Ian about the camera and expensive clothes in his case, Luke about the Harry Potter wizarding cards he'd recently been given, and Lydia about 'Nippo', her favourite stuffed hippopotamus she slept with and who, she thought, might be scared on his own). Room 519 is also empty, with no possessions though clearly recently occupied as the bed is unmade and towels are strewn across the bathroom.

"There must have been some mistake," says the bellboy, now immersed in the same twilight zone as the Newmans.

"Where the hell are our things?" asks Ian, a rhetorical question that he wishes weren't so.

Back in the lift for the seventh time, and at Reception for the third (where the bellboy abandons them swiftly after giving the latest receptionist the low-down), the mystery is only partially unearthed. Mr Newman's name is removed from Room 519 ("Terribly sorry, sir, must have been a staff error") but nobody has any clue as to the whereabouts of their things. Checking the computer again, the new receptionist, an older, matronly woman with dyed red hair and dark roots, informs Ian that it says he checked out of Room 302 that day so he must have taken his things with him. Ian's blood boils and he spits slightly as he speaks, in long, slow 'I'm talking to an utter imbecile' diction.

"We-have-not-checked-out-and-went-back-to-the-room-to-collect-our-things-at-which-point-the-card-didn't-work-and-then-I-was-informed-that-we-had-apparently-been-occupying-a-different-room-so-we-tried-there-too-but-our-things-are-not-in-either-room-and-I-don't-know-where-they-are-which-is-why-I-want-you-to-find-them. Immediately."

His tone must work, because she has a brainwave and Ian is relieved to find someone taking some action. She retreats to a back room and returns holding Luke's blue *Star Wars* backpack, and Lydia's pink 'Roller Girl' wheely case. They look bashed about and grubby, though the children eagerly come forward from the sofas, where they have been waiting patiently, to grab them. Lydia pulls Nippo out and hugs him tightly, dropping the second-choice brown-haired doll carelessly into the case. Ian looks on tensely, and waits for the receptionist to disappear again and fetch his case. Instead she stands, gormlessly, staring back at him.

"Before we even get onto the subject of what our things are doing down here, where on earth is *my* case?" he asks sharply.

"We found these in the laundry room, sir. We didn't know how they got here or who they belonged to, but when you told me you'd misplaced your things it rang a bell."

"For the love of cod, I did not misplace our things. They were missing." Even in his anger, the old phrase slips out and jogs his subconscious, recalling Amelia's laughter. "For the love of cod, where's my dinner, woman?" he used to say, and she would roar with amusement.

"I'm sorry sir, this is all we found. We can try and find out what happened to your room, but no one else had access to it and I'm afraid we don't accept any liability for personal belongings that aren't secured once you've checked out. And seeing as you're reporting this problem after you've checked out…" Her words trail away and Ian knows he will make no further progress. He makes a mental inventory of the contents of the case, and their value, and assures the receptionist that he will be in touch about compensation and will not be staying there again. She doesn't seem to care, but she does want this awkward man to leave as other guests are now eavesdropping. She offers them a complementary car to the train station, which Ian accepts after calling Amelia, who is now home and who manages to phone the station with her credit card details and purchase three single tickets for them to pick-up when they get there. At the station, they march to the platform to wait for the train, Luke hauling his backpack on his shoulder, and Lydia tripping over her case as her rushing feet get in the way of the wheels. Ian, bitter and empty-handed, heads the line.

Two weeks later, Ian phones the hotel to arrange his refund, and is promptly informed that no money will be returned seeing as he occupied Room 519 for the entire length of his original stay. As his family witnesses him cursing and shouting, threatening and raging, Amelia realises just how much she has come to loathe her husband. But she will not be leaving him.

An idea begins to form in her mind and before long she knows just how Ian will be sealing the death of their marriage.

Chapter 11

"Sorry, could you repeat that?"

Constance turned her head and gave Jason what some would class as a glare. She began her statement again.

"As I was saying, the Bartholomew Müsen Trust is not in trouble – yet. Its economies of scale are poorly managed, efficiency is being compromised and staff turnover is high. Quantity, rather than quality, has been the emphasis; profitable in the short-term, but in the long-term detrimental to the extent of damaging profit potential. I have put together the following list of measures for us to present to the client." She gestured towards the projector screen behind her. It was blank. Turning to her left, she realised that Jason was still furiously scribbling and was yet to place the first slide on the projector.

"Jason," she called in a stern voice, "please turn the projector on to the correct slide."

From one side of the table Anna, seated with the other Partners, tutted at him, which irritated Constance even more.

Jason mumbled quietly as he finished whatever sentence he was trying to capture and jumped up to hit the projector switch, simultaneously turning it slightly so that it was centred on the screen. Constance was relieved to see that he had set-up the slides in order and had already adjusted the focus. She felt a little guilty for her mental criticism of him, her mind constantly wanting to find fault in a bid to avoid bestowing any sense of perfection upon him. She could not afford any sort of addiction to Jason or, worse, adoration, though she realised the fact she was fighting it confirmed its very existence.

Radison was auditing a well-known private medical organisation, The Bartholomew Müsen Trust, named after a pioneering surgeon who had allegedly discovered new techniques for keyhole foetal surgery and set precedents for saving the lives of extremely premature babies. He had come to England in his thirties to reveal his ideas to the NHS, only to become disillusioned with its bureaucracy and limitations. He returned to his native Germany for a short while to find investors and eventually returned to England to open his own private hospital. When he died at the age of sixty-eight, he bequeathed a substantial amount of his fortune to what became the Trust, which soon expanded.

For the seven years since his death, the BMT had thrived, but in recent times the management had become too greedy, sacrificing patient satisfaction by squeezing in as many operations as possible and sending people home too quickly in order to free up bed space. The BMT operated on three different sites: a mother and baby unit that had a renowned antenatal ward and welcomed those willing to shell out a large amount of money for a private birthing and maternity suite; a children's hospital that specialised in the ever more prolific so-called 'behavioural disorders' such as hyperactivity, anxiety, food, and phobias; and a more recent general hospital for various adult surgeries.

The Trust once had a reputation as high as its prices, but standards had slipped. Unfortunately, this occurred at the same time a journalist from a broadsheet newspaper checked in for heart surgery, and he was appalled at the service and lack of care before he was 'turfed out'. In his subsequent newspaper report on the BMT, he exposed its shortcomings, on which the rest of the media pounced. Mistakes were exaggerated, the staff were disgruntled and patient numbers significantly decreased. Of course, the media was ruthless in its evaluations and the British Medical Council was called in to investigate. It found no evidence of foul play, though the Trust was ordered to commission a full practice audit and adopt any recommended measures.

Naturally, Radison was its first choice – the firm was known for being thorough and trustworthy while tailoring results to the client's needs and maintaining their integrity. There was no consultancy better suited to such a high-profile case. Constance had been appointed to manage the project and had led a team of six people to complete the task. Their findings and recommendations had to be presented to – and approved by – the Partners before being revealed to the client. Constance was quietly confident that they would agree with her presentation, but nerves still greatly affected her whenever she had to present her work, defend her management style or expose her thought-processes to the most senior people at the firm – people she hoped, one day, to replace.

Jason managed to keep up for the rest of the presentation, switching the slides when appropriate and taking down notes at the same time. She had especially instructed him to note down the Partners' comments, and any significant facial expressions or gestures they made as she spoke – people's body language often revealed more than their words.

There was a brief discussion between the Partners at the end of the presentation before they looked up, and Constance was relieved to see that three out of the four present were smiling; a blank expression was glued to Anna's face, but this was to be expected. The others – all men – congratulated Constance and whole-heartedly agreed with her proposal, giving her free reign to present her findings to the client. Anna merely nodded slightly, and then they were all filing out.

Constance left Jason to tidy up the room and retreated to her office. It had been a long day, and her preoccupation with the presentation had led to a backlog of work. She closed her office door and got stuck into it, barely noticing as one-by-one her colleagues left to go home. An hour-and-a-half later, she finally looked up from her computer and surveyed the empty office floor. It was both peaceful and lonely at the same time. She decided to stretch her legs and wander the long way round the offices to the kitchen. The building was shaped like a squashed ring doughnut – if you kept walking round the long corridor, you would come full circle, but not without a couple of twists and turns along the way. It was only as she approached Anna's office that she heard raised voices puncturing the silence.

Straight away, she could tell that it was a battle of egos. The two voices escalated to the age-old struggle of one sex against the other in the quest for recognition. Yet they were unequal in the most fundamental of ways, genetics ensuring that striving for any kind of equality would have flaws, exceptions and inconsistencies. They must have been at it for a while, their points-of-view as diametrically opposed as chalk and cheese.

"Leave me alone," the familiar male voice demanded.

"Why? Why should I, just because you've said your piece and you've had enough? You can't have things your way all the time." The female voice sounded desperate and stubborn.

"Why not? I've got no ties, no obligations. I don't owe you anything."

"As true as that may be, you seem to think everyone else owes you whatever *you* want. I don't owe you anything either, don't forget. And I have the ability to make things very difficult for you."

This poor threat was laughed off. "You're pathetic! I'm the only thing you have to cling on to and when I don't bow down to you, you seek some sort of revenge. Do you really think you could affect me like that?"

"I'm fully aware that any influence I've had on you has been purely libidinous; it's ridiculous that you should ever think I had a real need for you in order to fulfil something I lacked."

"There's a lot you lack – I don't think I could make up for that."

The provocation works.

"How dare you! You think you understand the whole world, in all your twenty-six years of experience."

"You have to come back to that, don't you? It always comes back to that: age, experience, knowledge – you're a stuck record. Time clearly does not breed wisdom. I've had enough; there's no point even talking about this."

"I agree." Talking was clearly not their strong point.

"Well then, let's just walk away and forget about it. I've got better things to be doing."

"And people?" A small insecurity is exposed, like a banana ripped from its skin.

A scornful laugh is the only retort, followed by heavy footsteps.

Constance ducked behind a corner and took a few deep breaths. So now she knew.

She peered back out and watched as Jason swept out of Anna's office, stopped for a couple of seconds to compose himself, and then strolled down the corridor, his back to her. It was almost 7pm and most people in the office would have left. She knew, anyway, that his conduct and expression would reveal nothing of the verbal altercation she had just overheard – clearly, he was a master of deceit. She was almost tempted to walk into Anna's office herself and find out exactly what had been going on, but she knew she couldn't and her mind boggled with the newfound information.

Jason had been sleeping with Anna. And with her. With both of them. But for how long, and just how much of a fool had she been? Anna, who was almost ten years older than her, with her stifling old woman's musk, her Louis Vuitton bag collection, her dated belts that pinched her just above the waist, her arrogance, her two divorces, her cackle of a laugh and her deepening crow's feet; what on earth had he seen in her? And how long had it been going on – which of them had been first? Was it better to have been first – a 'new venture' – or was it better to be the second, seeing as the first clearly hadn't been enough? Had he sometimes seen them both on the same night? And suddenly she was stabbed with horror; did Anna know about Jason's relationship with her and, if so, had she told anyone?

Feeling sick and in shock, Constance turned back the way she had come, her stomach cramping in waves, and trotted weakly to the Ladies' where she attempted to be sick and failed. She threw some water over her face and looked at herself in the mirror, watching her reflection's trembling hands. She had never felt such a fool in her life. And then, as she stared her physical image in the face, her kindred spirit walked in.

"Hi," said Anna. In that one word, her voice shook slightly, though perhaps only because Constance was expecting it. She studied Anna's face intently, looking for signs of tears or frustration and found none. To her relief, neither was there a flicker of recognition at their mutual stupidity; Anna did not know.

"Hi, how are you?" Constance asked, aware that of the two of them, she appeared the more flustered, though by rights it should have been Anna. Why couldn't she be as composed?

"Fine. Are you alright – you look a little…ill?" Anna's tone conveyed slight disdain, rather than concern.

"Must have been something I ate. I'm fine now."

"Hmm," remarked Anna, and passed behind her to enter a stall. Constance dried her hands, ran them through her hair to tame it, and left the bathroom, hoping that by the time she got back to her desk, Jason would have gone home. She didn't even actually know where he lived.

The roots of Constance's steely determination came from her paternal grandmother. Married to a Dutchman she had met at the tender age of nineteen, Imogen Romijn had embarked on life as one of a pair before she'd even had the chance to live as an individual. Her husband, Onne, left school in Amsterdam to take up an internship at a local newspaper, soon becoming a purveyor of local current affairs. He became well-known in his local community, and before long people were phoning him with news stories, requesting that he personally interview them and wanting guarantees that he would pay special attention to their tales of woe (for even in those days, it was the woe that brought in the money).

By the time he was eighteen, he was full of journalistic promise and, as a result of exploiting every networking opportunity in the industry that he could, he was offered a junior job researching articles for a national newspaper. He remained there for five years, working his way up to writing features and finally to sub-editing a small section of the paper. At the age of 24, he decided he needed to see more of the world and, having heard about the media industry in London, left for the 'Big Smoke' without so much as a sniff of a job there. For a few weeks he freelanced, at first unsuccessfully sending his CV and sample articles off to national newspapers, until a national broadsheet caught onto his talent and commissioned him as a regular writer.

He met Imogen in a bar on the day the paper had given him the good news. By this time, he had been in London for five months and had made friends among the small Dutch community that hovered around Hackney in East London. He celebrated with three of them that night, clinking glasses and supping English beer as though it were sweet nectar. They became good-naturedly raucous and the man sitting behind them asked them to keep the noise down. Onne turned around and stared at him, racking his brain for an amusing retort, when he noticed the beautiful young girl with him who was looking at him with a sassy smile. He quietened down unexpectedly, and the irritated man paid him no more attention.

For the rest of the evening, Onne stole glances at the girl and before long she too was sneaking looks back at him. She found him interesting, this brash, good-looking fellow who had been dancing and singing loudly as if the world were his best friend. As she got up to leave she smiled at him and, from that moment on, Onne only ever drank in that bar, hoping he would see her again. He was not to be disappointed, for she too returned, always with the same young man who he discovered, to his relief, was her brother. They got talking, and his impeccable

English led her to be incredulous, then surprised, when she discovered he was foreign – a flying Dutchman. Although he managed to charm her – as he did with everyone – it was the first time he himself had been charmed. He was so taken with her from the moment he first saw her that there was no way he would let her go.

They were married a few months later in London, soon after her nineteenth birthday, with a quiet wedding for her family and a few friends. They went on to have three children, of whom Constance's father had been the youngest, and Imogen threw herself into being a mother as much as any woman could. She never worked, never had a life outside her family, but she never had any regrets – for what she had chosen (though sometimes she wondered if she had, in fact, chosen it) she would make the best of.

Constance's father, Robert, had inherited his father's stubbornness and independence, traits that are valued in a man. He studied cognitive science at university, but went on to penetrate the banking world, soon progressing up the ranks. It was a 'work hard, play hard' mentality, and he took to his career like a bee to a busy hive. Her mother also had a career as a museum curator and Constance learned at a young age that no one should deter you from the path you wish to take. Being an only child also meant that all their hopes were pinned on her happiness, and her parents could not afford any sexist indulgences when it came to her prospects. They encouraged her to work hard and be successful at whatever she chose, as long as it was reputable. Five years ago they had both retired and moved to Rotterdam, where her father still had some cousins. It was mutually beneficial: they could be happy at Constance's success from a distance, and she would not have them enquiring after her personal life or constantly mentioning non-existent grandchildren.

In a way, she felt an obligation to dedicate her time to a career. Her grandmother had been deprived of financial independence, whether through choice or not. Her mother had

had both a job and family to contend with, which didn't give her sufficient time for one or the other. And now Constance had no family of her own, though she felt nothing was missing. She felt complete and satisfied, because she could take credit for her achievements and she had no responsibilities holding her back. It wasn't about money – it was about *control*.

But now, as she thought again of Jason's indiscretion, she realised that you never have as much control as you think you do. There are always other people to throw you off-course, intrude on your plans and – if she was honest – hurt you. Jason had been seeing another woman, a more senior colleague; he had taken advantage, manipulated, judged, played, scorned and tricked them. She was a pawn in his game, whereas once she had believed him to be a puppet on her stage.

And worst of all – worse than the faux-devotion Jason had shown her – did this mean that he had lumped the two of them together, her and Anna? Two sad, old women, desperate for a young stud, whom he could exploit and use. Did he get off on it – this power, this cunning, the ease with which he seduced them both? Did it make him feel needed, wanted, desired, different, special, adored? Did he think they would both find out and fight over him, that the cover of work would protect his dalliances and prevent them from becoming public knowledge, or did he want other people to find out? Maybe he thrived on scandal, attention and risks, maybe it made his blood rush, his heart beat faster and his life feel infinitely more exciting? And she realised then, as she asked herself that final question, that it was Jason who in many ways needed them so much more than she and Anna had needed him, and she knew what she had to do.

Chapter 12

The dinner went well, if only because Johnny was near silent throughout. He answered with 'yeses', 'nos', and 'hmms', but in such a polite way that neither of them could be irritated with him. It was clearly difficult for him, and they had agreed prior to coming that both – especially Daniel – would be as patient and understanding as possible.

As a starter, they had slices of mozzarella and tomato, piled up neatly in stacks with a cocktail stick stabbed jaggedly through each one, and drizzled with olive oil. Daniel had found the recipe in one of Flora's old cookbooks with curling pages. It was funny, he thought at the time, how Flora's things kept ageing even though she no longer could. He decided that the simpler the food the better, and was impressed to find that some of the recipes weren't as complex as he'd imagined, though they still looked sophisticated.

For their main course, they ate chicken chasseur with new potatoes, carrots, green beans and cauliflower. Daniel had recently purchased a kitchen aid whose box claimed it was the 'easiest, fastest way to prepare fresh vegetables – just microwave and enjoy!' Turned out it was nothing more than a plastic box with holes in it, and all the vegetables had to be washed, some peeled, chopped, microwaved in groups, shaken and stirred, microwaved again, left to stand and then, finally, served. The chicken itself was much simpler – frozen and left to defrost over the previous night, a sachet of seasoning and some

108

oil poured over, and one-hour-forty-minutes of oven magic.

Unfortunately, Daniel had left the main course preparation for the evening itself, which resulted in him leaving Amelia and Johnny alone for a significant amount of time while he jostled, bustled, cursed, served, drizzled, shuffled, and prayed for success in the kitchen. Daniel could hear every word spoken in the dining room through the serving hatch, which he left open precisely for this reason. Every so often, he would stick his head through as far as it would go and ask if they were alright – the answer always came from Amelia and it was always a 'yes'. Her voice resounded with false cheer. While they waited for Daniel in the kitchen's den, Amelia asked Johnny questions, attempting small talk in between sips of the wine she had brought.

"So, Johnny, your dad's told me a lot about you."

"Has he?" came the reply in a nonchalant tone that surprised Daniel; Johnny had been surprisingly perky these past few weeks and it was odd to hear him sounding so dreary again. It occurred to him that this new relationship had the potential to push things back over the edge once more.

"Of course. It's nice to finally meet you. I've…I've got two children of my own actually." Another sip – or gulp – of wine.

Daniel peered through and saw Johnny look up with slight interest at Amelia's last comment. He wished Amelia hadn't revealed this to Johnny so soon – he was only just getting used to the knowledge himself. He wondered what the antonym of 'rhetorical' was; some way of describing an answer given prematurely that dispelled all need of a question.

Amelia had made her confession a few nights previously, over dinner. She had a husband, apparently, though she no longer loved him, and two children aged seven and five. She hadn't wanted to tell Daniel earlier, she said, in case he judged her as a wife and mother, and not as the person she really was. He didn't quite understand her point-of-view – she was, after all, a wife and mother whether she liked it or not – but he understood enough to know that he did not want to walk away.

He hadn't yet had the courage to tell her about his battles with alcohol, and secretly hoped that his acceptance of her baggage would in turn lead to an increased level of tolerance on her part. He was scared to reveal his insecurities and wanted to be in the stronger position of having discussed hers before he came clean.

So far, though, her admissions had only served to increase his anxiety; ever since she had first mentioned her husband, with minimal details that he hadn't even pressed for, Daniel had been wondering nervously what he was like – whether they had anything in common, whether he had guessed she was seeing someone else (she insisted not) and whether he would be angry or aggressive – and his own insecurity was growing by the day.

After the main course, there was a unanimous vote to skip dessert, creating a wave of relief in the room, and all three bodies slumped slightly into their chairs. Johnny mumbled an excuse and scampered upstairs to his room, at which point Daniel and Amelia were left alone.

"So," she began, "how do you think it went?"

"Fine, yeah. Just fine."

"Well, do you think he liked me? Do you think he minds about us? You know him best."

"Well, I don't think he dislikes you."

"Thanks, that's helpful."

"Well, I don't know. It's early days. But we're over the first hurdle, eh?"

"It won't be the last though, will it?"

They drifted into silence as they cleared away the dishes, using the task as an excuse not to verbalise their thoughts. They shuffled around in the kitchen for a while, dodging each other's minds and movements. Eventually, Daniel took a deep breath and spoke.

"There's something I need to tell you."

"What is it?" Panic swept like a shadow across her face, and then was gone.

"I couldn't tell you before. It's just...difficult. But I suppose you should know. I mean, it's not a secret. It's just on my mind almost all the time so you should just be aware that... plus, we'll

110

be in situations in the future where I won't be able to...well, *shouldn't* is a better word I suppose-"

"Will you just tell me what it is? You're not making any sense!"

He remained silent, unsure of how to begin. But Amelia was impatient.

"Do you want to finish things? Is it because you think Johnny doesn't like me?" She put down the dishcloth she had been holding tight and stepped back through to the dining room where her comforting glass of wine beckoned. She took a large sip as Daniel watched covetously, and then returned to face him.

"You can be honest," she reassured gently, her voice slightly fragile.

"It's just that-" he began, but again she interrupted.

"I thought we got on alright. We talked a little; he's a nice boy. I understand if you need more time, more space for him, but don't end this because things aren't perfect right away."

"Sorry? What do you mean? Are you still talking about Johnny?"

"Yes – you don't think he liked me."

"No, that doesn't have anything to do with it. I was referring to your wine."

"The wine? You're finishing this because you don't like the wine I brought? I knew there was something funny going on when you wouldn't even touch it, but-"

"Exactly, though wait, just stop talking and listen to me." Almost subconsciously, she took another sip of the near-empty glass right in front of him, and he felt the salt rubbed into his wounds.

"I was an...alcoholic. That is to say, I *am* one."

There was silence. Her eyes implored him for a greater explanation, but for him everything he had been through, put his body through, was encompassed in that one term. He hadn't said it out loud to anyone before, but saying it didn't feel like an achievement. It felt surreal, intangible, like a sign that would hang above his head for the rest of his life, even if it no longer applied. He watched as she put her glass down on the table, twisting awkwardly to place it behind her, as if she suddenly thought he might leap for it.

"Actually, I stopped drinking the day after we met, slowly at first, and now I haven't touched a drop for weeks. That's why I've been insisting on us not going out to bars."

"I thought it must have been the smoke that bothered you. How long were you drinking for, before that? And how much?"

She seemed genuinely surprised, and he was alerted to her oblivion. He realised how little they knew each other outside of this realm they'd created, and he wondered what kind of bubble she lived in with her family that shielded her from anything untoward. Her husband must be a decent man, he thought.

She was still looking at him expectantly, and for a moment he thought about lying to her, but suddenly felt tired, exhausted even, with the heavy mask he'd worn for so long. "Years, actually. And I'd drink anything I could. Spirits, beer, cider, wine, on occasion even...well, things that were not for consumption. I did myself quite a bit of damage. It started when my wife died, Flora – I mentioned her before, didn't I?"

"Yes," was all she could manage, part-stunned by his confession and part-enthralled by the tale she sensed was about to unravel. She listened, wide-eyed and patient, to the stranger standing before her.

"When I first met Flora," he told her, "she worked in a local sandwich bar near to where I'd opened up my first car lot. I was twenty-six years young and full of promise – I think she liked that about me. I used to go in from time-to-time to get my lunch, and before long I was there every day and she was giving me free lunches. She almost got fired for it once, when her manager found out, but I offered to pay back a large sum in exchange for the food, and he eventually relented.

"When we got married, it was the happiest day of my life – I had no doubts. Then when Johnny was born, it felt like our family was complete. The business took off, Flora stayed at home to raise Johnny and, for a while, we were really happy. She was always so supportive, encouraging, you know? When she became ill, I couldn't handle it. For a long time I was in denial, thinking that, if I ignored it, her illness would go away, that she would go back to her old self. In a way, I almost..." He stalled, his eyes focusing on an invisible target.

"Almost what?" Amelia prompted, softly.

His eyes flicked back to her, and he spoke very quietly. "Almost resented her for destroying this idyll we'd created. Everything became disrupted. I couldn't concentrate at work and sales were down. I began to immerse myself in the business, using the decline in profit as an excuse to spend more time there, when in reality if I'd spent more time with her I might have been in a better frame of mind at work. Johnny spent as much time with her as possible of course, when she was ill. And her parents would come round – they never liked me – to criticise, as if their failure to 'protect' her from me had led to her illness. I felt more and more lost, more and more depressed, and the wife I once knew gradually slipped away from me. It sounds selfish, I know, but once I knew she was not going to get better, I gave up on her...before I was made to give her up."

Amelia stared at him blankly, attempting to process this information and add it to the catalogue through which she was getting to understand him. It was the most exciting bit, getting under someone's skin. They were silent for a minute, before he continued.

"When she died, it was like all my fears had been confirmed. The business had been going downhill and I could have salvaged it, but I simply didn't care anymore. It was as if someone had sucked everything good out of my life and spat it out in the past, where I couldn't reach or retrieve it. There was Johnny, of course, and I loved him, but I had no idea how to be a parent, how to care for him in a practical way. I told myself that the drink would help me continue, would keep me functioning so that I could look after him, but inevitably the opposite resulted. He managed amazingly well, considering."

"That's a lot for a boy to deal with," said Amelia, thinking of the comfortable life her own children led in comparison. She wondered how they would handle the absence of her or Ian, and then brushed the thought out of her mind.

"I feel like I've let him down so much," Daniel went on, "I haven't been a father to him since his mother died. The funny thing is, though, that I thought he'd be over the moon when I gave up the drink, but he hasn't been that overjoyed. In fact, he seems…preoccupied."

"Maybe he doesn't want you to raise his hopes and then let him down again. He's lost a lot in the past too. Both parents, effectively."

"Or, more likely, he's become numb to the whole thing, unfeeling. Maybe I've passed onto him the ability to emotionally shut down when things go wrong. Although, either way, I think he's ok. But, more importantly, I think I'm ok now. It's like, if I close my eyes, I can see a pin-prick of light that gets nearer and nearer, widening as it comes, until eventually I'll be able to step into it and out. But I can't ever fall backwards into this alcoholic pit; that's why I need you to understand. And to decide – can you handle all this? Because if not, it's better we just go our separate ways now."

"I don't know. It's a bit of a surprise. I mean, the first time we went out we had a few drinks, you included. I did notice that you had three or four and it seemed to have no effect on you – in fact, you seemed to relax more with each glass – whereas I had a couple and was feeling light-headed. Though I just put it down to me not drinking that often."

"That was the last time I had that much to drink. And I had nine in total that evening – including a couple before you arrived, a sneaky one when you went to the Ladies', and one when I got home, a nightcap I told myself. I always justified each drink – it was all based on a well-disguised lie that even I fell for."

"I can't believe I didn't realise. When we've been out since I've noticed you never drink, but it didn't strike me as that unusual seeing as we never went to bars – and we have been preoccupied with other things…" She grinned at him, forgetting for a minute the issue at hand. He ignored the inside joke, keen, now he'd started, to expose all of the skeletons, once and for all.

"When I finally stopped drinking, a few weeks ago, I felt relieved but bereft. I'd lost a support mechanism, something that had fundamentally become part of me even though it was destroying me. And then it occurred to me that maybe you would fill the void. Maybe something great was about to happen, something I had never envisaged, and maybe once again my past could be tossed behind me, not dragged along like a felled tree. But I don't want to place that on you – you have complications of your own."

"It's true, I do, but you've accepted those. At least I think you have. Your problem's almost in the past, but I've got a husband in the present and two children who are always going to be there. That's something you'd have to deal with on a daily basis."

"I know," was all Daniel replied, and after a weighted pause, "Maybe I should drop you home and we can both sleep on all this."

"I think that would be a good idea."

"That's one good thing about not drinking anymore – I'm free to drive as and when necessary." They both laughed awkwardly and headed outside to the car. He dropped her a couple of streets from her house so as not to arouse suspicion – she had told her husband that she was out with an old school friend who had just moved to London.

He called her the next day, anxious to hear her voice. He was afraid she'd decided not to see him anymore or to keep things casual, which he knew he couldn't agree to; he thought more of her than that. When he asked her if she'd come to a decision, she retorted with "about what?" followed by an affirmation that washed him through with relief, "There's no decision to make – it's all been decided for us. Don't you think?"

They spent the next few weeks wrapped up in each other at every available moment. With Johnny, Luke and Lydia at school most of the time, on days when Daniel didn't have to work they would check into a tasteful but inexpensive hotel (usually courtesy of the personal allowance Ian gave his wife) and spend the day in bed, making love, or eating, sleeping, talking and discovering. Each found a haven under this emotional cover and they clung to each other in their secret pupa. They experimented, coaxing, deviating and exploring the depths of each other's minds and bodies. They touched and tasted, lusted and lingered, captured, crushed and created. They made memories that only they would share, and revelled in their exclusivity.

It was one such afternoon, two months after Amelia had first come round for dinner, that she tentatively hung her idea on a hook and dangled it in front of Daniel. They were post-coital and languorous, contented in the moment. But Amelia's thoughts soon moved into the bigger picture, a melting Dalí clock.

"I know how we can be together," she stated, calmly and simply.

"Hmmm?" Daniel rolled towards her and let one hand flop over onto her arm. His eyes were half-closed.

"I know how we can be together properly. I know how to get Ian out of the picture. But I need your help."

At this, Daniel sat up and looked her straight in the eyes. "What do you mean," he asked, intrigued yet concerned. So she told him the plan, which she'd obviously been thinking about for some time.

"I met this man, once. A long time ago. It was a friend of a friend's birthday – one of those tenuous occasions where you have to make an appearance for the sake of someone your husband once knew and chat awkwardly to people you have nothing in common with. It was before we'd had the children, back when I would have done anything for Ian and I was still trying to play the perfect wife.

"We were in a small, smoky pub somewhere in the depths of the Hertfordshire countryside. Somewhere with a ridiculous name, like a string of German words all shoved together in unity – Hertingfordbury, or something like that. It was late and wintry, and I remember they had a fire going in the pub with a bored Alsatian lying in front of it. We joined a group of people, having said hello to the one person Ian knew, and they shuffled awkwardly aside to almost make room for us. Ian was soon off, chatting at the bar or moving around the group, and I was stuck in the midst of a cluster of women moaning about their workplaces – they were bankers or something. They complained about everything from the staff canteen to sexism, salaries to dress code, and then they turned to me and asked what I did. They fell silent as soon as I mentioned the word 'Housewife', which I always tried to say with a capital 'H', proudly.

"'Don't you get terribly bored?' asked one of them – I remember her name was Luciana.

"'Not really' I replied, wishing I could back it up with a long list of interesting and joyful things I had been up to, but realised that I couldn't. It was the first time I had been out, socially, that fortnight, and I didn't even want to be there. The other women barely spoke to me after that; I suppose they thought I had nothing of value to add to their conversation. I remember feeling lower than ever before and for the first time really questioning whether I had made a mistake, getting married and relinquishing my independence.

"Anyway, I slipped off to the Ladies' and on my way back passed a doorway to the car park at the back. I stepped out into the cold air, knowing that my absence would not be noticed. And there he was, this young man, blowing smoke rings into the night air. I stood next to him, hugging myself, and he smiled and offered me a cigarette, which I declined.

"'You here with that large group inside?' he asked, staring out at the cars.

"'Yes,' I answered, 'but I don't really know any of them. I had to come with my husband…though I…I don't know why I'm here.' And rather embarrassingly, I started crying.

"He glanced round at me and didn't know what to do. He didn't come any closer, but shifted his feet and turned to face me.

"'I'm sorry,' I snivelled, 'I don't know what's wrong with me. It's just...do you ever get the impression that things weren't meant to be as they are? That at some point along the way you took a wrong turning and ended up down a completely different path?'

"He didn't answer, but he looked at me as if he understood. And then, he reached into his pocket, pulled out a piece of paper and asked me for a pen. I handed him one from my bag, and he scribbled something down before offering it to me. I took it tentatively and looked down to see the letter 'J' and a phone number.

"'I'm J,' he said by way of an explanation. 'If you ever want a...distraction, give me a call.' And with a cheeky grin, he returned my pen, stubbed out his cigarette, and disappeared back inside. Surprised, I replayed the conversation in my mind before putting his number away and followed him in shortly after. I rejoined the group and looked around the pub for him, but he was gone."

Daniel was still looking at her, silently studying her face and her expressions as she talked.

"Are you trying to tell me you've had an affair before? That I'm not the first?"

"No, let me finish. To cut a long story short, I knew J for a while. Nothing happened, but he became a friend. And I eventually discovered what he did for a living. When we...lost touch, I held onto his number, in case I ever needed it. I figured that if Ian ever found it he wouldn't have a clue what it was anyway. And for a long time I forgot about it...until I met you. And then I thought – this is it. I should get back in touch with him."

"I don't understand," said Daniel. "Do you mean that you got back in touch with an old friend because of me? Why?"

"A few days ago, I realised that the only way we could really be together would be if Ian was out of the way. I can't tell him about us; he would be outraged and try to take the children away. And I don't want them to hate me either. Also, the scandal would hit his career hard, and I don't want our old friends and associates scorning me. So I wracked my brain and decided the best way to get Ian out of the way, without destroying everything we had built-up, would be if he...you know...was no longer around."

"You mean...no! You're going to kill him?" Daniel sat up straight and glared at her.

"No, not me! I could never do that. I'd be arrested, the children...and I could never bring myself to do it anyway. That's why I phoned J – that's what he does."

"You mean...?"

"Wait, yes. So I phoned the number and it wasn't connected, but I called directory enquiries and was able to get them to tell me his new number from the transfer records. He was surprised to hear from me. I told him my problem and he said he would help. But for £50,000."

"£50,000? Are you crazy? You don't...I mean, we don't have that sort of money."

"No, but Ian does."

"What? You're going to use his own money to get him killed?"

"Yes, it's perfect – he won't need it anymore."

"Have you really thought about this? Really and truly? It's so cold-blooded, it's...ruthless. He's your husband – the father of your children – and you're going to end his life?"

"It's no life! He works, comes home, we don't have a relationship anymore, he barely sees the kids. I'm doing him a favour, and us – then we can be together properly. I thought for years that the money, the prestige, the children, would make up for everything I sacrificed, I thought that this mother and wife was who I was meant to be, and now I know that it's all rubbish. It's just fake, this life, the one we go along with, the one we think we've chosen but in reality there was only ever one option; the pressures we put on ourselves to conform, to be secure, to go down the safer route – it's all meaningless.

"I love the kids, but I'm not *just their mother*. And I used to love Ian, or I thought I did. But this is so much better – this is real freedom, real passion; I'm finally doing something, taking some action, experiencing something worthwhile. I'm finally making the choice." She looked at him, forlorn but defiant, and he knew he would not be able to change her mind. He was in awe of her bravery, perhaps too much so, and he wondered if he was expected to be an accomplice or an observer.

Before they could discuss it further, she jumped up and began to get dressed, grabbing at her clothes on the floor.

"What are you doing?" he questioned, thrilled yet exasperated by her unpredictability.

"Come on, let's go outside!"

It had just got dark; it was 8pm and they should both have been getting back home. She had left her children with a friend, but Johnny would be home by now and had mentioned something about having a friend over tonight.

Daniel looked at her as if she had just announced the arrival of a UFO – a sideways glance with a slightly lopsided mouth that said, 'Are you crazy?'

"Come on!" she shouted and opened the door, waiting just outside the room until he had thrown on some clothes. They took the stairs and walked serenely out of the hotel, before she ran, knowing that he would follow, and laughing so hard it seemed like she would never stop. Her laughter echoed around the empty street and breathed life into the air. He began to jog behind her, pacing himself at first but then, seeing the increasing distance between them, let his muscles go completely and pumped his arms, speeding up so he could touch her again. She stopped a minute later, panting and still laughing, though quietly now. As he caught-up with her, she looked up at him as if he were the most important person in the world, and he melted.

It was night time in October and it was cold. She hated the cold, though in her fit of madness she had run out without a coat, whooping joyously. Now, as they stood looking at each other, the street lamp bathed their skin like a gentle remedy.

"What do we do now?" he asked. He was a little afraid of her spirit, the incredible highs and lows she brought him and her ability to draw him out of his comfort zone. He hoped he did exactly the same for her.

She slowly took two steps until she was standing right in front of him, and her breath exploded in a cloud of steam in front of his face. He wanted to grab at it, hold onto it; it was a piece of her. Instead he reached out and stroked the back of his hand across her right cheek, and she leaned into him slightly. The first time he had done that, ten weeks ago, had been wonderful, but now it was even better because there was trust. There were a lot of 'firsts' that were better the second time around, he thought.

His other hand came up until each was either side of her head and he was running his hands through her hair. She shivered, whether from the cold or otherwise, as he pulled her to him and kissed her mouth firmly. She drew back slightly, breaking the kiss, but only so she could initiate it, starting again so she was in control. He let go and instead placed his hands on her waist while she moved her body closer to his and this time kissed him.

"Let's get inside," he said. "You must be cold." His words, always true, were brought to life and they hurried back to the room, hand-in-hand. Once inside, he ran his hands up and down her arms until her body temperature mimicked the heat he was feeling, and warm blood rushed around their bodies.

He led her back to the bed without a word, not leaving her time to think. His heart beat faster and he closed his mind's eye, picturing nothing, hearing silence. He took off each item of her clothing one-by-one, kissing each part of her body as it was revealed. She stood, passively for once, clearly excited still by the newness of his touch and his attentiveness.

Once she was naked, he stood back and glanced over her, as if admiring an *objet d'art*. She appeared coy but frozen, and perhaps secretly glad. He looked up, as if satisfied with what he saw, and moved towards her again, causing her instinctively to reach out and unbutton his shirt. It dropped to the floor, followed by his trousers, and then his underwear, and he glanced at the pile of clothes as if they were already a memory, knowing that he was seeing them now, *before,* and he would see them again, *after*. *Before* and *after* were distinct existences. *Before*, you were someone – an alcoholic – and *after* you were someone else – a lover.

He looked over her naked form, and thought just how much their bodies differed, male and female. A woman's body was beautiful for its entire shape, its nature and all that it represented. A man's body was not beautiful, no, but it was equally intriguing as a woman's in its individual parts: the rough swipe of stubble on the face, the texture of hair on the chest, the strength of the arms, the robustness of the straight waist and hips, the nobility of the legs; all contrasted with the fragility, the vulnerability, of the organs. But he loved the female form – seeing it, touching it, tasting it – and nothing could compare.

He pushed her down onto the bed but, not wanting to relinquish control, she flipped over and climbed on top of him, savouring the moment before allowing him in. He groaned as she did so and clutched at her hips, keeping her in place, not letting her go.

"You're amazing," he said, but her only response was, "Shhhh." She preferred silence, never wanting to pollute their actions with words. He didn't mind – it allowed them to think, to feel, to experience. They moved and tumbled, sometimes together, sometimes not, and involved every inch of their bodies in the act.

Afterwards, he was lost for words, only able to reiterate the last he'd spoken.

"You're amazing," he said.

They lay on their backs, side-by-side, united now in a memory of something better. This is it, he thought, it's been simple all along. This is what is meant to be.

He thought she would want to be held, to be talked to, caressed and valued. But instead she smiled and turned her back to him, content in her own satisfaction. She's complete in herself, he realised. I am not completing her; I'm complementing her.

Then everything made sense, and he knew he was in love.

Chapter 13

Luke knew that there was no justice. Even before he had learned the word justice, which appeared one week on their spelling test like the stinger on a bee, he knew that life just wasn't fair. It wasn't fair that he had to argue and sulk and whine every time he really wanted something in order for there to be the slightest chance he might get it, while Lydia could shed a couple of tears and scream and would almost certainly get what she wanted immediately, because they both knew their mother would do anything to quieten her down.

It wasn't fair that he had started to get homework every day even though he spent most of the day working at school. And when he did have spare time, it wasn't fair that he didn't have a new Nintendo and, even if he did, he knew Lydia would sulk and press the buttons at the wrong time to annoy him. He wouldn't have anyone to play it with anyway, aside from his father who would have a go, lose and then give up and say he was tired. Most of his friends had brothers, or at least friends that lived nearby.

It wasn't fair that he was made to eat Brussels sprouts every Sunday, with their soggy, musty smell, just because his mother said they were good for him and he had to eat lots of different coloured vegetables, even though he knew that there were lots of other green vegetables he could eat that tasted infinitely better.

It wasn't fair that sometimes, at night, he had a recurring

dream that his parents dropped him at a shop and told him to run inside and buy some sweets, but when he came back out of the shop they were gone, and he didn't know where they were or how to get home. Each time it would be dark and he would wander a little to see if he recognised the area and, just as he saw a street that led home, a massive monster would appear that shouted and tried to chase him so he had to run in the other direction, at which point he would wake-up, sweating and shivering. He would clutch the duvet around him and lie there breathing heavily, not wanting to call to his parents because, despite the knowledge that it was a dream, something in his subconscious told him he couldn't always trust them.

Despite the unsettling injustice that plagued Luke night and day, he didn't think it was just him, because he recognised that life was not fair for any of them. It wasn't fair that his father, perhaps his favourite member of the family, had to work a lot and was never home very much, or that he had to sigh and curse when his mother spent a lot of money at the shops. It wasn't fair that Lydia worried all of the time because their mother scolded and fretted and fussed over her, and didn't seem to understand that it made Lydia anxious. And it wasn't fair that the only pet they'd ever had – a goldfish called Satsuma – had spent his (her?) life in a glass bowl and got bored, chewed away all the plants they'd put in, and then died one day and been thrown in the dustbin. It wasn't only him that didn't have fairness; it was that fairness didn't exist.

He remembered the beginning of the school year when there had been two new children, both boys. One of them was English, Jeremy, and one foreign, Nazrul (later they discovered he was from Bangladesh). Nazrul had dark skin and round, puffy cheeks, and his shoes were always scuffed. His English wasn't good then, and on the first day when they had all gathered round the 'newbies' and asked a barrage of questions, Nazrul had blinked at them slowly and said "Hello" in answer to everything. They had laughed and kept asking, for according to this boy he was from Hello, he was hello years old and his favourite game was hello. Jeremy was all but ignored.

Soon, however, the novelty of 'Hello' (as he became known) wore off and the comparatively dull Jeremy rapidly became the latest fascination. Before long, Nazrul found himself alone, then lonely, and then pushed away; he continued to talk 'funny' and one boy said the reason he was dark-skinned was because he never washed and was dirty, and on top of that he smelled. Jeremy, on the other hand, had become part of the furniture.

In this way, through his unknowing mental exploration of inequality, Luke developed some sort of empathy for other beings. Like the cat they saw everyday on their way home, lying on the front path shared by no. 56 and no. 58 Landown Road, as if it didn't know where it belonged. Perhaps it had concluded that loitering between two front doors increased the chances of one of the doors opening and a kind soul beckoning it in for a cuddle and some food (not milk: milk was bad for cats, he knew).

On the occasions they would drive past, Luke would peer out of the car window, waiting for the flash of black and white that would inevitably sweep past his eyes, and then he would crane his neck, hoping to keep it in his gaze because tomorrow it might not be there. For it was dying, this cat – that much was glaringly obvious to him. Sometimes they would walk past and Luke would stop and look intently at it, staring at its long, matted and discoloured fur, wrinkling his nose at its smell if he stepped too close. He thought it was blind, because its eyes were glazed over and when he waved it never reacted. Sometimes, if he stood right in front of it, it would raise its head slightly, regally, and sniff the air, before lowering its now heavy head and sinking back into oblivion.

"Is it blind Mummy?" he had once asked, but his mother had avoided the question, shooing him along while chiding him for going near it. It wasn't fair, he thought, that it was dying. Everything had to die, but not everything had to be dying. Luke wondered if you were born, then alive, and then dead, or if you were born, you were dying, and then you died. The first one, he decided, otherwise the word 'living' would not exist.

And with inequality came a certain feeling of imbalance, of separation – the greater the inequality between you and someone else, the greater the distance. He often tried to put this feeling into words, simpler terms that his young mind could understand. The greater the differences between you and someone else, the greater the separation of your being, because you could be in the same room, at the same time, and have completely different experiences. Luke could not understand it when his father and his mother would argue in front of them, and they would sit quietly, sometimes on the floor but more often on the sofa, and look up at them, these duelling gods. Most of the time, his father and mother would be talking and then shouting, and Luke realised that they could be having two completely separate conversations at the same time, though they both thought they were having the same one. Their conversations went like this:

M: You're back a lot later than you said you would be. What happened?

D: We got a deal signed today. It only just came through.

M: Have you been drinking?

D: We had a few to celebrate. What's for dinner?

M: I knew it! The kids have been waiting up for you.

D: It was a great day. James Chase phoned me personally to congratulate me. The deal was for his firm.

M: I suppose you forgot to bring home your other shoes again.

D: Hey Double LL [his nickname for his children when he was happy].

M: Marta phoned to arrange this Saturday…

D: I'm really hungry. I didn't have time for lunch.

M: …she said she'll pick the kids up at 10am.

D: I'm going to go and change out of these clothes.

M: Are you listening to me? You can go to work on Saturday if you want because the kids won't be here.

D: Is there food in the oven?

M: *Am I some sort of maid service that doesn't deserve your attention? I just arranged for you to work on Saturday – I thought you'd be ecstatic.*

D: *Whatever. I'm just tired – don't give me this when I walk in the door.*

M: *Give you what? I hardly see you and you won't listen to me for five minutes?*

D: *I don't want to talk to you right now, not like this. I need to go and check my emails. Laurence said he'd send through some papers that I should look over tonight.*

M: *Like what? Like we're two married people having a conversation? How else would you like to talk to me, Husband? Or talk at me, I should say.*

D: *I'm going upstairs. Bring me a drink.*

M: *You've had enough.*

D: *Yes, of you. Where are the files I left down here yesterday? I've got to drop them round to Connor.*

M: *Marta will love that. It's the first night in ages Connor said he'd be home early, and she was looking forward to it seeing as she's having the kids all weekend.*

D: *The kids all what?*

M: *They need to go to bed. Come on you two.*

D: *You should have put them to bed ages ago, why are they still up? Have they...*

M: *They waited for you, you idiot.*

D: *...eaten? Where's mine? What did you have for dinner Double LL?*

M: *I'm so tired, can you just take them upstairs when you go?*

D: *What now? I'm dropping those files off. Where are they? I need to...*

M: *...get them to sleep as soon as possible or they'll wilt in school tomorrow. You must...*

D: *...drop them off before it gets too late. They don't like it when I ring the doorbell at this time of night and the kids wake...*

M: *...up early enough, and I have enough trouble getting*

them out of bed as it is. So, can you get on with it?

D: With what? Oh, yes, ok, I'm going. Ah, there the files are. If I leave now it'll be ok, but if I leave much later it'll take me...

M: ...far too long watching television. Though if you were in charge, no doubt they'd spend...

D:... even longer because of those road works. Now, where are my keys?

M: I don't know. I can't believe you're leaving me to do...

D: Everything has to be sorted out by the morning because I've got a conference call at 9am, and Elisabeth has been pretty stressed out lately with all the pressure, so if I'm not in on time and she's arranged everything she might...

M: Just go then, fine! I'll sort the kids out; I'll stay up and wait for you; I'll do everything I always do, like the perfect wife. Not to mention your dinner, which is probably cold in the oven now. Sometimes I wish I could just...

D: ...Bye.

M: ...myself a different life, I really do.

And so it would go on, the kids' heads with staring eyes bobbing from side-to-side for a while, until they lost interest and applied the most useful skill they had both developed – the ability to tune out raised voices.

One night, having heard such a conversation drag on for half-an-hour, Luke came to the conclusion that his family was not united because they lived in different times. Not different centuries, or times of the day, but different tenses.

His father clearly lived in the present. He liked his job, which he talked about extensively, liked to know what the Double LLs had been up to today, liked to come home and have his dinner waiting, liked to get work finished now, and was happy with things as they were right then. Sometimes he would look at them and say, in an abstract manner, "Yes, good...things are good." There was another sign that told Luke his father lived in the present – he would always look you in the eyes.

Lydia, on the other hand, constantly had a dreamy expression on her face, which made her look all the more innocent; she lived in the future. She talked of becoming a newsreader, then, as she grew older, a fashion stylist because she liked the colours and fabrics she watched her mother try on. Her whole existence depended on that which might be, that which will happen, that which could happen. She started every other sentence with "When I'm an adult..." (never "When I grow up", seeing as she believed she was growing up with each second) and, for her, each moment she was on the brink of experiencing was laced with potential.

His mother was the most alienated, for she lived in the past and had a wistful, regretful air about her. Her phrases started with "You used to ..." and, "Remember when...?", and she frequently used words like 'anymore', 'before' and 'a long time ago'. She hardly ever looked them in the eyes, as if visual contact could suck her from the past and back into reality, take away her memories and force her to be who she is rather than who she was.

To Luke, she was his mother, but as he got older he began to see that she was someone else entirely, someone that had ended up acting as his mother, possibly by accident or on a whim. He thought she was a good mother – she was the only one he knew – but he saw that she was better at being this 'someone else', someone that didn't live with them, look after them, worry, fuss, protect, bathe, nourish, clean and scold. Someone stronger than this mother who caved in under pressure, argued and became easily irate, and who seemed defeated and tired and 'what if I could go back to before?'

And Luke – he didn't know which time he lived in, but he was caught up somewhere between all three, hovering above his family as if in another realm. He dipped into the other worlds: kicked a ball around with his Dad, chopped a bit of Lydia's doll's hair off when she wasn't looking, and pushed and pushed his mother to get her attention. He wondered how they were a family when none of them fitted together, why they were all living separate lives in the same location. And he merely longed for a time that didn't exist: when they might all converge to the same time.

Chapter 14

"Such a nice girl. I'm pleased for you."

These were the first words of approval Amelia had heard – or overheard – from Ian's mother the first time he had taken her to meet his parents. They were a typical middle-class, high-achieving family, and she was strangely comfortable around them from the outset – something that, at the time, she mistook for compatibility. In fact, looking back, she realised it was more a case of complacency; they were all aware a proposal was on the horizon and, on the cusp of such unending happiness, who would want to be the antagonistic villain?

After lunch that day, Ian had helped his mother clear the dishes. Not wanting to stay at the table and make yet more polite conversation with Ian's father, Harold, a retired lecturer in economics at Oxford University, Amelia had grabbed a meat-soiled dish and headed to the kitchen herself. As she approached, she became aware of Ian and his mother discussing her and paused to listen. She was both pleased and sickened by her then future mother-in-law's words.

"So, you met her at the office, dear?"

"Yes, Mother, she was my secretary for a time. She's...very clever, you know."

"Oh, I can tell dear. But you say she's stopped working now?"

"Yes, well, we're thinking of moving and she's been helping me set-up my new practice."

"Has she? And will she be working for you there as well?"

"We haven't decided yet. Anyway, why are you so concerned?"

"Well, it's never a good idea to mix business and pleasure, my darling. And you work so hard; I was pleased you had found someone to look after you."

"As it happens, she probably won't be working at the new firm, but we'll see."

"Well, it'd be for the best, dear. And, anyway, won't you be wanting children at some point?"

"Mother! Don't go jumping the gun – that's quite a way off." And then the two of them giggled, an oppressive collaboration that chilled Amelia.

Amelia's own parents had moved abroad soon after she had started her working life. Her mother was a part-time teacher at a special needs school in the small American village of Grand Marais, which they now called home, and her father worked in a medical research laboratory. He had received funding from the state university to carry out his proposed research into skin cancer and had been allowed the use of their facilities. Amelia had visited them twice; once soon after they moved and again after they had been there for three years, at which point she became disillusioned with their *Stepford Wives* resemblance and all-round efforts at Americanisation. They came back to England twice, after the births of each of their grandchildren, but never for very long. Now, phone conversations ended with one party encouraging the other to fly over, empty promises lengthening the distance between them.

Ian's parents, on the other hand, had somehow always been present, if only in spirit. Even before the children were born, they phoned frequently and indiscriminately, to speak to either of them, and visited at least twice a month. To her mother-in-law's credit, she never interfered in their marriage. She seemed content to let nature and tradition – Ian as the breadwinner and Amelia as the homemaker – take their course. Amelia knew that Ian's parents were happy with his choice of wife, as if he had selected her from a butcher's prize rack, and that they were rewarding his wisdom by leaving them in peace. Amelia was attractive, from a well-to-do family, intelligent but not ambitious, was capable of earning if necessary but willing to stay at home, and would no doubt produce lovely children. Trouble was, the more Amelia lived up to her in-laws' expectations, the more she longed to break free of them.

Just over a year into their marriage, and a week after the late-evening pub excursion when she first met J, Amelia telephoned him. She was having a bad day – she had attempted to fix a leaking pipe under the kitchen sink but had snapped off part of it instead, causing water to spray everywhere. She had phoned Ian and disturbed him in the middle of an important meeting (after pleading that it was an emergency, his secretary had finally put her through) to find out where the mains tap was, and she knew Ian would be fuming when he eventually got home. Then there had been no water in the house and so even less to do.

As a result, that afternoon Amelia decided she'd had enough of squeezing herself into a mould fashioned by those around her. She had comfortably aspired to all the things she told herself she should be, and it was driving her crazy. Her marriage – what little time she now spent with her husband – was dull, she had lost touch with most of her former friends who had climbed the career ladder, and she couldn't quite remember the point of everything, or anything. She could see who she was – which wasn't much – but she could no longer see who she *wanted* to be. She decided that the only person to give her that perspective would be an impartial outsider.

J let his phone ring an agonising five times before he picked up. His gruff voice, an early catalyst of Amelia's obsession, resonated through her the moment he said hello, and she loved it. They had a brief conversation before agreeing a time and a place to meet, and she hung up, more excited and afraid than she had ever felt.

They met, that first time, for coffee in a small place he'd

suggested. She'd realised he was younger than her, but it wasn't until they met in the daylight that she realised how much younger. Twenty-four, he'd eventually admitted, though by that point she didn't really care. He always wore light facial stubble, and dark brown hair flopped down over his face, causing him to brush it away every now and again. He reminded her of what it was to be young and single, and she wanted to steal it from him, just as she felt it had been stolen from her.

They didn't have much to say to each other. He seemed reluctant to give too much away, and she languished in this sexual enigma she had discovered for herself. She fantasised that he would be her protégé, her plaything and, ultimately, someone to adore her.

It turned out that the café was a few streets away from his flat. From that day onwards, they met approximately three times a week. She didn't dare bring him back home with her, so she always went over to his flat, thinking of their trysts as well-earned 'excursions' on her part. Their physical relationship was only as exciting as the danger that went with it and, even then, she kidded herself that Ian might find out.

J, whose full name transpired to be Jeremiah, was nonchalant in his youth – unattached, undefined and irresolute. She wasn't sure if he had a job, though he never complained about money, and his flat was a fairly smart, two-bedroom maisonette. Occasionally his phone would ring, he would speak in low tones, and then in a hurry ask her to leave. She didn't ask many questions.

Their affair continued for months and, more than her time, it occupied her thoughts. She focused on the illicit activity until everything else became a blur and her behaviour, other than that with J, was largely irrational. She thought that Ian might become concerned, but this merely spurred her on, and she began to call J night and day just to hear his voice, initiating meetings in public places, private spaces, and according to unorthodox rules. When he began to decline her invitations, she threw herself further into the game, wanting him to play hard to get. But then one day – silence.

She had been trying to call him for three days, and he wasn't answering. The phone would ring, and ring, and even his answer machine had been switched off. Her desperation became such that, despite it being a Saturday, she ditched Ian with the excuse of going shopping, and hurried over to J's flat. To her surprise, after peering through the window, he answered the door...with a black eye.

"Why aren't you answering the phone? And what happened to you?" she asked, as he hustled her in. After closing the door, he sighed, and walked through to his living room, where he flopped heavily onto the brown leather sofa.

"Nothing. I don't want to talk about it. I've just been busy."

"I've been trying to call you for three days!"

"Yeah? Whatever, look I'm busy and..."

"Whatever? That's your response? I don't know why I waste my time with-"

"Yeah, well me neither!" A hush fell over the room, and she sat down on a matching brown couch opposite him.

"Look, I don't think we should see each other anymore. I'm in some...I've got some people on my back and I need to get away for a while." He ran his hands through his hair and tilted his head upwards, his eyes closed. He looked like he was praying for small mercies.

"What kind of people? What's going on? Do you need money?"

"You really have no idea what I do, do you?"

"Of course not; you've never told me. In fact, you hardly tell me anything."

"For an intelligent lady, you're pretty stupid sometimes, do you know that?"

"Are you a drug dealer? Because I've never seen any drugs around the place. Or people coming over, for that matter."

He laughed at her, a little too loudly, and she flinched. "Is that the only thing you can think of?" And then more sternly, "I don't do drugs, buying or selling."

"Oh right. Well, what is it then? I can't help unless you tell me about it."

"You can't help anyway. I kill people Amelia. I'm paid to kill people."

"What?!"

"That is, I've only done it twice so far and I'm already in trouble. I work for this guy – I can't tell you his name – and he tells me where to be, what time to be there, and who to get rid of. Then I get a cut of the money. Except this time, the second time, it got a bit messy, and this morning he punched me and told me to lay low for a while."

"Let me get this right, you murder people for money? Ordinary people?"

"Oh, don't get all moral on me. Look at your own life before you judge mine. It's people like you I'm hired to kill – cheating spouses, idle partners, ageing scrooges, people making other people's lives a misery, people jeopardising families, friends, jobs, integrity, dignity, hope, health, happiness and honesty." His voice had been escalating, and now he stood up and began shouting at her. "People are always screwing hearts and minds for their own gain, stepping on others to get where they want to be, treading on souls, thoughts, desires, tempers, roots, unions and feelings. People ripping apart homes and relationship foundations, discarding those around them. Do you know how many people come to us? People *that* desperate to banish someone wicked from their lives – even at the price of descending into wickedness themselves? We only agree to help some of them, when we're sure it's a clean case. People will do anything to protect whatever – and whomever – they love. I'm just a means to an end."

For a few seconds, Amelia was speechless, startled. Then she felt a familiar rumbling in her stomach, her chest, and then her throat, and she leaned over the side of the armchair and threw up.

"Oh, great, just what I need." J pressed his fingers to his temple in an ayurvedic massaging gesture and applied an erratic pressure. Amelia stood up, a little shaky.

"I think I should go," she said.

"I agree. I'm going away for a while and...well, I'll see you."

'When?' she wanted to ask, despite everything, but instead turned and walked to his front door, opening and closing it behind her without turning around. She wished she could go back a few hours, blissful in her ignorance, and make her own decision not to see him again. As it stood, the decision had been made for her, painfully, and she felt control plucked heavily from her hands.

Three weeks later she found out she was pregnant with Luke and she sealed her lips.

Chapter 15

Before long Constance had planned his downfall. When she was invited to the New York office for a Development Initiatives Meeting (DIM) it was acceptable, though not necessary, that she take one of her assistants with her. Given Simon's track record, it was understandable that she should choose Jason, who was publicly delighted and privately bemused at her apparent incapacity to turn down any opportunity to stoke their affair. She added fuel to the fire by discussing private plans with him: how they would book two rooms and alternate which they would sleep in together; how they would spend their free time (the meeting was a whole day conference but they were there for four days in total); and how it was the perfect excuse to spend some real time alone together under the guise of work.

She had visited the New York Radison Head Office (as the NY constabulary was unimaginatively known) once before, but had gone on her own, leaving Jason – the sole assistant at that time – to man the fort. The fact that she had now invited him along showed their colleagues how much she valued and trusted him as an assistant, and showed Jason that he had gradually become indispensable to her, privately as well as professionally. Or so he thought.

Two days after they'd booked the trip, Constance made a point of strolling past Anna's office and, seeing that she was at her desk and not on the phone, casually popped her head around the door, as if on a whim.

"Are you attending the New York meeting in a couple of weeks, Anna?" she asked, keeping her tone as casual as possible although she already knew that Anna would not be going.

"No, I'm not required at this one. Plus, I'm going over next month to meet with Mr Hanson, the Senior Vice-President."

Constance ignored this deliberate show of seniority and continued, "Oh, right. I was just wondering, as I'm going. Actually, I'm taking Jason with me this time. He's good at keeping things in hand, and I'm sure he'll prove quite useful when I'm there." She watched Anna's back stiffen slightly as she spoke, and the way her head tilted upwards, attentive yet ever so subtle. She was pretty sure that Anna and Jason had not rekindled their affair since the argument she'd overheard, and she was also confident that Anna knew nothing of her own liaison.

"You're taking Jason?" Anna inquired, failing slightly in her attempt to hide her disapproval. If hitherto she had known nothing of the love triangle, perhaps now she would suspect something inappropriate might happen on the trip.

"Yes. He's a good assistant. I thought he deserved a…reward." She let the innuendo carry her voice, and witnessed its arrow pierce Anna's mind like an intangible realisation she could neither explain nor prove. As she turned and walked away, she knew that Jason would definitely be written off as far as Anna was concerned; Anna would not share control of any man. She would not be able to prove any impropriety between Constance and Jason, but the mere possibility would lead her to extract herself from any potential imbroglio.

The thought of Anna and Jason together made her feel queasy. It was sickening and torrid – Anna, she knew, felt nothing real for Jason save the opportunity to wield some power and control. She must have found joy in rendering him subservient and subjecting him to her desires. There could not have been an emotional element to their relations; neither of them, Constance had realised, was capable of considering anyone other than themselves. For all her drive, tenacity, and resoluteness, Constance knew that she could never exploit someone to her own end without any regard for feelings.

On the plane to New York, travelling in business class, Constance sank back into her seat and relaxed. Jason was behaving like an excited puppy next to her, being more accustomed to budget airlines and the cramped confines of economy seats. He was taking advantage of every service being offered, to the point of ridiculousness. After accepting two champagne cocktails, two newspapers, some nuts, three salmon canapés, two 'travel kits', a hot towel, a duty-free brochure, a mini-DVD-player, headphones, an in-flight telephone voucher and a coffee – all this within the first twenty minutes of the flight – Constance told him to calm down and stop acting like a child in a sweet shop. He looked down at her hand pressed firmly on his leg and accordingly quietened down, a smug look that she had come to dislike adorning his face. She knew how much he had been looking forward to the trip, but little did he know what to expect, and no one could have been more anticipant than she was.

Halfway through the eight-hour flight, she had a brainwave. Jason was watching an action film and paying little attention to anything else. She observed the couple in front of her – two elderly female friends who were clearly in the money and who must have been on holiday together. They knew the air steward and were probably regulars, as he fussed over them constantly. One of them was shifting about in her seat, trying to undo her seatbelt.

"I'm just going to the bathroom, dear," she said loudly to her friend. "If I can get this thing undone that is." She had a frail but sharp New York accent pertaining, no doubt, to the exclusive community that occupied the Upper West Side.

They both fumbled at the seatbelt for a minute and managed to get it undone. As the woman got up to leave, so did Constance, pulling Jason's headphones away from one ear as she rose.

"Meet me in the bathroom in one minute," she whispered

with a wink, gesturing towards the lavatory a few feet in front of them. Jason grinned back and nodded as Constance turned her back on him and walked through the dividing curtain. She caught the old lady just as she was entering the cubicle.

"Oh, I think the lock's broken on this one. But I'll be happy to wait outside until you're done to make sure no one else comes in."

The woman was unquestioning. "Thank you dear, very kind," she said and pulled the door shut behind her without even trying the lock. Constance immediately scurried off to the other side of the plane and peered through a gap in that curtain. She could just see Jason undoing his seatbelt and couldn't help but smile to herself. The lights in the cabin were dimmed and the other passengers were dozing or watching films. As Jason left his seat and walked forwards, she opened the curtain where she stood, turned right to go down the opposite side, and returned to her seat.

A few seconds passed before a high-pitched scream filtered through the curtain, which was suddenly whipped aside by an ashen-faced Jason who hurriedly dropped back into his seat as the air steward rushed past them.

"Where on earth were you?" he muttered through the side of his mouth.

"I was in the bathroom," she replied disconcertedly. "I assumed you weren't coming."

"Which bathroom?" he hissed, "because I just walked into that one and there was an old lady in it, bent over with her skirt pulled up to her hips and her back to the door!"

"I pointed at the one on the other side, you idiot." Constance giggled, just as the air steward appeared with his arm around the lady's shoulder. She was shaking slightly and squeaking unintelligibly as he directed her to her seat. She spotted Jason and stared at him.

"That was him! That's the one that tried to accost me in the toilet!"

"What? No…I…" Jason turned red, somewhat stupefied as

other passengers turned round and began to listen, keen for a distraction from the monotony of the flight.

"No, it was a misunderstanding – the door was open!" he protested in vain.

"The lock is broken!" she exclaimed, fortunately not recognising Constance seated there, who was trying to look inconspicuous. "He burst in and tried to get at me! You need to do something!" She turned pleadingly to the steward.

"Don't worry, madam, I'll take care of it." He helped her into her seat where she began to recount the incident to her sympathetic friend, before he turned to Jason and spoke quietly.

"It's ok, sir, I'm sure it was a misunderstanding, but I'm afraid I'm going to have to move you. Mrs Johnson is one of our regular customers and we can't afford to upset her."

"But...why me? I just got a horrible view of an old lady's arse and you're punishing me?"

"I'm sorry sir, we're not punishing you; I just think it would be best if we moved you for the consideration of the other passengers."

Jason looked at Constance, as if she would defend him, but she was still staring uninterestedly the other way. Not wanting to cause more of a scene, and with the two old ladies peering hostilely at him from the gap between their seats, Jason gathered his things and stood up.

"See you soon," was all Constance deigned to add, as he was led off. It turned out that the only spare seat they had was in economy class, where Jason spent the rest of the flight cramped, hungry, and watching a Disney film on a communal screen.

Constance, of course, spread herself out over two spacious seats, and chuckled at the thought of her plan.

The offices of Radison Consulting in New York had been a subject of great contention ever since plans for the Time Warner building had been announced. Located next to Columbus Circle, and within a five-minute walk of Central Park, the rental expense had been substantial even before the monstrous Time Warner Centre grew like a giant from dead soil. During the four years of its construction, Radison's Management Team speculated, dithered, argued, discussed, evaded, procrastinated and hesitated right until their five-year fixed rate rental agreement expired and, lo and behold, a new agreement at double the price landed on their desks, like an unwanted surprise party you knew was coming.

By that time, no one was in a position to scout for new offices. Business was booming, the client portfolio was expanding, and the Radison Head Office had the benefit of being both impressive and prestigious. The Directors decided that, despite the rent increase, it was worth staying put, and as a result the main office in London was duly informed that it could not move to a new location, despite UK office space being inadequate for the increasing number of staff. The situation became known throughout the London office as 'Atlantic Kick-back' and the UK managers were determined to get compensation, one way or another. Insisting that all DIMs were held in New York and that the US office paid for flights and accommodation for UK staff was just the beginning.

Constance felt in awe every time she flew to New York and checked in to the Oakland Hotel. Given the unwritten rule to spare none of Head Office's expense, Constance always stayed here, as it had rightly been flagged as one of the best US hotels. Prior to the trip, Jason had booked two rooms for them, exclaiming first at the hotel's website and subsequently at the price; she had emerged from her office to give a coy 'well, what did you expect?' smile that looked down upon his naivety. As they walked into the hotel lobby, Jason grinned nervously like a teenager taking his first sip of beer, and loitered by the black, leather *chaise longue*, feeling rather out of place. Constance, on the other hand, masked her usual delight and swept confidently towards the desk to check in. They rejected the offer of help with their suitcases, absorbed the hotel information proffered and retreated with anticipation to their private spaces.

They had two separate rooms on the eighth floor, a few doors away from each other. As they entered the lift and the doors closed, Jason put one hand on her waist and pulled her closer to him, kissing her forcefully. She made no attempt at resistance, for despite her anger towards him the feel of his hands on her body still overrode all rational thought. Perhaps more so, now that she knew it would imminently be just a memory. He pushed her against the cold metal wall of the lift, holding her up as her legs began to buckle, and tugged unsuccessfully at her skirt. As the lift bell tolled on the eighth floor, he let her go and turned to face the opening doors, his hands poised to drag their suitcases. She followed behind him, adjusting her clothes and wondered if it was possible for one's Achilles' heel to be someone else's body.

They reached her room first, and Jason opened the door for her, wheeling her suitcase in and leaving it just inside.

"I'll see you for dinner at eight," she said promptly.

"Are you sure? We have a few hours before then. I could-"

"No, it's fine. Come back at eight."

"Right. OK then. Um...OK. See you later." He was disappointed, she knew, and she thought to herself how their relationship had become like a storm brewing, with mutual rejection hovering on the horizon. Except Jason didn't know it yet; he could only feel it in his skin like a cold sweat. She hoped that his disappointment indicated a greater attachment to her than he'd had to Anna, though the reminder of her name brought Constance back to reality. This was his doing, not hers.

There was another reason Constance wanted to be on her own, and one that she hadn't had the chance to contemplate yet. She had pushed it out of her mind until this moment, partly to protect it from the interruptions of the daily grind, and partly through fear. As she watched Jason's back move slowly down the corridor, she felt a pang of regret at his perpetual ignorance, for now she could never share this information with him. It wasn't just his affair with Anna that had distanced her from him – the ties of desire were slowly being snipped away by her awareness of another person between them, one that had barely come into existence. And one whom she would now have to consider alone.

Chapter 16

"*Oouaais?*" mumbled Éric, having scrambled around for the phone. His eyes were half-closed and his mouth was dry. His head pounded a warning that he should still be asleep.

Suddenly, there was silence. Had the phone been ringing, or had he imagined it? He'd been dreaming: he was at the zoo, milling around other people, when a rhinoceros had broken free of its enclosure and started running towards him. Other people were screaming and running away, but Éric was frozen, stuck facing the oncoming rhino that didn't look too pleased. As it got closer to him he tried to run but couldn't and, just when he thought he was about to be flattened, it stopped right in front of him and asked for its money back. And as he'd started patting his pockets to see how much he had, he'd noticed it was wearing a green skirt...

There was a dial tone droning in his ear and, concluding he had picked it up in error, Éric reached over to the night-stand and slammed the phone back onto its cradle.

The hotel bed was comfortable, but the numerous pillows, blankets and sheets had left him in a cold sweat. Unable to get back to sleep, and slightly afraid of the lurking rhino, he got up to take a shower. The clock said it was only 8:13am. He let the lukewarm water soothe his skin, and that's when he heard the phone again. It stopped after a couple of rings, before he'd had a chance to consider stepping out to get it. It was one of those annoying high-pitched hotel phone rings, designed to wake you up from the deepest sleep. He wondered if Mr Newman had a wake-up call set-up for the room, but didn't think an alarm call would be made more than once.

When he got out of the shower, he re-entered the bedroom and glanced at the phone; it had its own voicemail function but the red light was not lit. He lifted the handset and pressed the voicemail button anyway – no new messages. He didn't know what the phone number was for the room and, even if he did, he had no one to give it to. He hoped that it wasn't the Reception desk phoning him – he was determined to avoid contact with hotel staff as much as possible, in case his game was exposed. Mr Newman must have come back to the hotel by now – after all, he had paid for the room for a week, but it didn't appear that anyone had been in the room and he hadn't been asked to check out. He'd dumped Mr Newman's large suitcase in a skip a few streets away, and had been taking his bag out with him everyday just in case anyone looked in his room. Each time he returned to the room with caution, but so far all had been well.

At 9am he decided to leave the room and hit the early-morning tourist crowd. Mr Newman's cards would have been cancelled by now, and Éric needed funds. He left the hotel and headed to the café at the end of the road for breakfast. He had a little cash left over from the £60 he had acquired yesterday by swiping the purse of a rather large lady (ah, in a green skirt – that's where it came from!) who was walking through Covent Garden talking loudly to a companion and brandishing an open handbag. That lot had paid for dinner and a few glasses of scotch, and now Éric would be on the lookout for more.

He ordered himself a continental breakfast, lamented at the weak tea he was served by a surly waitress, and looked out of the window, where he could see to the end of the road and just onto Regent Street. Tourists were already milling around, and every now and then the odd rush-hour commuter dodged the stragglers in their mission to reach their desk on time. Shops raised their shutters and buzzed expectantly at the arrival of the day's first customers. And all around him in the café, oddballs sipped, supped and slurped their various drinks, gathering up energy to face the day.

His food was taking a long time to arrive, and he wished he'd bought a newspaper on the way. Most people seated at the other tables – some surprisingly well-dressed – were alone, their heads buried in their food or in a cheap tabloid with imposing headlines such as 'TREE IN A BED – ENVIRONMENT MINISTER 'FESSES UP ON LATEST ROMPS' or 'NOT IN MY GIRL'S NAME, SAYS VICTIM'S FATHER'. Éric looked back out of the window and that's when he noticed the car.

It was a long, dark Mercedes, which he could tell from the chassis and the iconic symbol. The windows were tinted, not blackened out, and the front one was wound slightly down. Two eyes peered out, apparently in Éric's direction. It was parked on the opposite side, outside a second-hand bookstore with a neon sign (BOOKS GALORE – WE GIVE YOU MORE) and looked somewhat out of place. There were often diplomatic vehicles driving around central London, some even at this time of the morning, but why would one be parked outside a cheap shop on a dingy street off the more classy roads?

He began to feel inexplicably nervous – it was just a car, no big deal, he tried to convince himself – though once his breakfast arrived, he interspersed mouthfuls of toast, egg and tomatoes with furtive looks out of the window. The car remained, though whoever had been looking from the driver's seat had now turned, so all that was visible was a dark head of hair and the beginnings of a generous sideburn.

Éric had been investigated by the police once before. He'd been in his early-twenties with a penchant for stealing cars – the most lucrative 'work' he could find at the time. He had a deal with a friend, Rouet, whose father owned an auto-repair franchise, of which his friend managed one branch. Éric would take the cars to him, and within three hours they would be re-sprayed and have new number-plates fitted, before they were put up for auction under a false company name they had created together. They split profits 50:50 and this lasted for almost two years. Then one day, Éric unknowingly took the private car of the Chief Police Inspector, right from outside the inspector's house.

He had usually hit different neighbourhoods and sometimes would take an hour's train ride to a completely different town, although the longer drive back increased the risk of being caught. He enjoyed being able to scour an unfamiliar area, choosing the best car he could see and setting himself a real challenge. If he was feeling extremely daring, he would steal one outside a shopping centre, or some other busy area, knowing that the owner could be back any minute.

However, this one particular day he had been feeling lazy. He had taken two cars already that month and they had made a healthy profit. Rouet was becoming more greedy – the auto-repair centre was not doing too well, and his father (who was blissfully unaware of his son's extra dealings) was putting pressure on him to improve custom. Rouet needed money from the stolen cars to pump back into the business to convince his father he was a good manager. As a result, unwilling to travel far and wanting an easy job, Éric had wandered a few streets away in his own neighbourhood and checked out the cars there. He always dressed well when he went out on these forays and walked briskly when he was scanning for a vehicle – he didn't want to raise people's suspicions by loitering. And then he saw it – the brand new Citroën, dark green, leather interiors. So he waited, walked away, came back again and, to his delight, after about fifty minutes a couple exited the house behind the car, got into the other car parked in the driveway and drove off.

This was his chance. He worked swiftly and efficiently, but took extra care as the car had a sophisticated alarm system. He kept pliers and a penknife in his back pocket, and got to work on the lock. He managed to pick it with the knife – most people don't realise how easy it can be – and gingerly opened the door but, as he did so, the alarm blasted loudly. He bashed the dashboard open and was attempting to disconnect the wires when he heard a shout and saw a figure running towards him.

He grabbed his tools and ran, without looking back – he had trained himself for quick getaways.

It turned out that the car belonged to the highest-ranked police inspector, who had just retired and bought himself the vehicle as a gift. One of his neighbours had heard the alarm and 'tackled the thief', the local papers exclaimed, and the front-page article included a description of Éric that gave him a beard, a stocky build and reddish-brown hair, among other inaccuracies. Several inspectors were assigned to the investigation, an extreme reaction seeing as nothing had *actually* been stolen and a twelve-year-old girl had been murdered only two weeks previously. With her killer still at large, and Éric lying low, they apparently still had enough resources to deploy two officers in a vehicle to patrol the area and look for the would-be thief.

Éric was confident that he hadn't left any fingerprints – he always wore gloves – but to avoid being spotted, he hardly ventured out of his house for the next couple of weeks. His parents, with whom he still lived, were oblivious to his thievery and believed him to be employed on a casual basis by Rouet so they assumed he'd been laid off. Once or twice he'd noticed a police vehicle parked on his street and wondered if they had fingered him as their man. He had a small criminal record for shoplifting in his teenage years, though he'd escaped with a caution after giving a suitable 'scared child' performance and promising never to do it again. He wasn't sure if they were investigating all likely suspects his age, or if they were onto him; either way, they never even took him in for questioning. After that, he had given up stealing cars – he was bored with it anyway and it soon became evident that Rouet's business was going down, extra cash or no extra cash.

Seeing the Mercedes now, parked patiently across the road, Éric was struck with that old feeling of prey being stalked by a carnivore. He finished his breakfast, which cost him almost all his remaining cash, and approached the waitress. Handing her just over a 20% tip, he leaned in to her right ear and asked, "Do you have a back way out?"

She looked at him in surprise, but then glanced down at the money in her palm and nodded. She walked round to the counter, placed the empty glasses she had been clearing on its top and stepped through a swing door off to the side. Éric followed quickly, not looking back to see if the other staff had noticed. She pointed out a fire exit at the end of a corridor, though seemed reluctant to walk down it with a stranger in tow. He thanked her as he made his way towards it alone, trying not to breathe in the air thick with bacon fat and stale mushrooms.

Two hours later, Éric's pockets were still empty. He couldn't focus – the air was thick and felt ominous and judgmental, and it was making him nervous. He kept noticing potential victims but lacked the courage to approach anyone; the greatest risk when picking pockets was hesitation.

He had walked to Trafalgar Square, which was strangely empty. Nelson's Column was being cleaned and was covered in scaffolding, and a few pigeons shuffled around, dodging passers-by at the last moment. Éric sat on the edge of the grass verge in front of the National Gallery and looked all about him. He felt edgy and anxious, his palms sweating despite the cool breeze.

There – there he was! Éric's heartbeat picked up speed as he spotted a tall man in dark glasses and jeans loitering across the square. He had seen him earlier, soon after he left the café, and again in a shop he had passed on Charing Cross Road. And now he was there; clearly Éric was being followed. He stared straight back at the man, who returned the look before turning away. Éric was too distant to read his expression, but his unease was explained and he immediately felt better. So, the police were on to him. All he had to do now was throw them off the scent, which would involve, sadly, checking out of the Mayfair Hotel.

He got up and slipped down a small street to St. Martin's Lane, walking briskly and wondering if maybe there was more than one person following him. He hadn't seen the car again, but it must have been part of whatever investigation he was embroiled in. He had to get to work; if he was leaving his current abode, he needed money for another.

Three hours later, not having sighted his pursuer again, he was in possession of a pink teenage purse containing £10 and no cards, two mobile phones (one of which had been left on a sandwich bar counter) that he sold on to a man in Leicester Square, and £250 courtesy of a stupid guy who had allowed Éric to watch him key his pin number into a cash machine while he argued with his girlfriend, and had then left the card in the machine as he walked off. Those were the best steals – the ones that fell into your hands like gold dust.

When he got back to the Mayfair, he went up to the room and made sure everything was in order; he could leave no trace. He would take the keycard with him and simply leave, without speaking to the Reception staff. As he folded the notes of money, and left the purses and cards on one side to be disposed of later, he had a sudden sinking feeling. He checked the pile again and then his pockets. His own wallet was most definitely missing.

Elsewhere, a tall, thin man removed his dark glasses and regarded his hopeful employer.

"That was him," he said, trying to disguise his delight. It didn't pay, in this game, to display any emotion. He handed over a small, leather wallet and waited as the other man inspected the cards in them.

"Good," came the reply. "All set for Tuesday. Now leave me alone."

Chapter 17

He let her go, eventually. But not before Elisabeth had told him the full story, filled in all the missing holes he had missed in his absence and helped him understand his part in the course of events. Once he believed she had told him everything, he untied her.

And the story she told him was a criminal fairytale gone wrong, with mishaps, misapprehensions and murder. He rarely interjected; in truth they had both been waiting for this moment and they embraced it as if the re-telling was the only thing that could make the past worthwhile.

"I started working for Ian seven years ago as soon as I'd qualified as a legal secretary. I'd been actively job-seeking while studying for my final exams, and it paid off; I knew of his firm and was pleased to be offered a job as a paralegal. I was only there for about six months before Ian fired his secretary for destroying some important documents and I was asked to fill in the post for a short while. I found out as much about him as I could from others: his legal specialities, his likes and dislikes, his habits and tastes, and that helped us to get on no end. He seemed an intelligent man and, the more I got to know him, the more I enjoyed working for him. He was someone absorbed by his work; I always wondered what it would be like to socialise with him – which I never had the opportunity to do outside of working lunches – or see what he was like at home. What he lacked in generosity, he made up for in trust and loyalty, and eventually he asked me to stay on working for him.

What I hadn't envisaged being a disadvantage was his wife, Amelia. I knew that Ian was married with two young children at the time, though I didn't think too much about it at first. In a law firm, personal lives are often swept under the carpet, and it can be a surprise when the odd child or spouse rears its neglected head to request attention. I assumed Ian had the usual stay-at-home wife who was happy to spend his money and have dinner on the table when he got back, but now I know she was anything but." Elisabeth paused and asked for some water. He took the half-full glass from the desk, and brought it to her lips. She sipped, tentatively, and it seemed to give her the strength to continue.

When she had first started to work for Ian, Amelia would appear in the office perhaps twice or three times a week, heavily redolent of jasmine perfume, and laden with the two children who she would dump by Elisabeth's desk. It was infuriating, especially when she checked up on what Elisabeth was doing and told her she should do certain things differently, or start to reorganise files.

"Turned out she used to be a legal secretary herself and helped Ian set-up his business – but, as far as I was concerned, she had chosen to give all that up and her frustration should not have been imposing on my working life."

In the end, Elisabeth had a word with Ian, who was surprisingly understanding. He hadn't realised that Amelia often turned up when he wasn't there, or when he was tied-up in a meeting, and hung around with his secretary until he either returned, or the children became so whiny and hungry she had no choice but to give up and go home.

"He was a man of actions, Ian, not so much words, so once you'd asked him to do something he would get on and do it – his memory was excellent. I think he had a word with his wife, because after that she rarely came to the office, and when I answered the phone to her there was bitterness punctuating each sentence."

Elisabeth first noticed something was wrong when Amelia stopped calling the office. It was a couple of years after she had started work there, and Amelia usually rang regarding the children, or to find out about Ian's schedule that day.

"Most of the time Ian was too busy to speak to her, and it was me who filled her in; as a result, it was me, not Ian, who noticed the absence of her calls."

She wondered if they had been arguing at home – there was no change in Ian's demeanour, but then she knew that work was his escape. He was more likely to behave strangely at home if work wasn't going well than the other way round. She even asked after Amelia and the children one morning, to see what Ian would say, and distractedly he said that they were fine; from him, she detected nothing amiss.

One afternoon, late into the third week that Amelia hadn't called, Ian asked Elisabeth to phone her because he'd left some legal papers at home and needed them urgently. He wanted Amelia to bring them to the office, assuming it would be a 'nice distraction' for her. When Elisabeth phoned, it rang several times before a husky voice said "hello" and promptly cleared its throat. "Amelia?" she remembered asking, wondering if she'd dialled the wrong number. "Yes," came the reply, "is that you Elisabeth?" Her voice was clearer but she still sounded out of breath – probably running after the children, Elisabeth assumed. But no, they would have been at school. "Ian's left some papers at home. He says they're in the green binder on the dining room table and he needs them urgently – could you please bring them in for him?" She remembered Amelia uncharacteristically snapping back, causing her to recoil. "Can't it wait until tomorrow?" and Elisabeth was sure she heard a deeper voice groan in the background.

"Well, at the time, it didn't make sense, but now it does – he must have been there. She said she'd bring the papers in and promptly hung-up. An hour-and-a-half later, she appeared with them in the office, looking slightly dishevelled and severely irritated. She handed them over to me, and I barely had time to ask if she wanted to see Ian (who was in his office for once) before she barked 'No' and swept out. I remember her perfume masking a sweatier musk, and her hair untidy; I was surprised as she was usually pristine. I wondered at the time what she had been doing that was so important – after all, she had been at home without the children and she had plenty of time to herself most days. It was then that my suspicions were really set in motion and I vowed to find out more, for Ian's sake and I admit I was curious myself."

So, for a while, Elisabeth began to call the house and hang-up if Amelia answered. Most of the time she wasn't home during the day and, on the occasions she did answer, Elisabeth made sure her number was not traceable. A couple of times she put on a false voice and pretended to be a sales person, or told her she'd won a free holiday, which she knew would prompt Amelia to hang-up. And before long, Elisabeth established a pattern: on Tuesdays and Thursdays Amelia was always out all day, and on the other days she was always at home in the morning, and often out in the afternoon.

"I asked Ian leading questions about the children and he would occasionally mention them being left with a friend or relative – I don't think he kept track of them, but it became obvious to me that without the children to look after, and without a job, Amelia must have had something – or someone – else occupying her time."

The missing piece of the puzzle came on the day Amelia popped into the office to ask Ian a question about school fees and left her handbag on Elisabeth's desk. She knew she shouldn't and probably didn't have long, but she rifled through it quickly and pulled out Amelia's dark-green diary, dropping it into a drawer next to her. Amelia came out a minute later and flounced off without saying goodbye.

"With her, I never really got the impression that she didn't like me, just that she didn't like where I was. I don't think she ever had a problem with Ian and me working together, for he was always happy with my work and I'm sure she knew that. Maybe I just represented *everything she used to be*, and no one likes to be confronted by their past, of a time when life was full of promise."

Elisabeth didn't look at the diary in the office. Instead, she took a walk at lunchtime and sat by the old Second World War memorial in the park off the main road.

"Most of the days in her diary were blank – I don't think she would have been stupid enough to write anything untoward down, and she was hardly the busiest person in the world. I think a diary was just something she clung onto from her working days, something to make her feel her life was organised, or even that it was full enough to warrant organising. I looked at the back and saw a few phone numbers noted down, nothing special, but then I noticed a small, torn-edged piece of paper wedged between the last page and the cover. It was small and white, with the letter 'J' at the top, and below it were two phone numbers – one crossed out and the other replacing it. I thought I might have found the man she was seeing.

"When I got back to the office that afternoon, I phoned the second number. I didn't know what to say really. A man answered in a gruff voice and I almost hung-up, but then he said 'Hello?' again and I spluttered, 'Hello, it's Amelia,' just to see what he'd say. 'What?' he asked, and I thought at that moment that I was making a terrible mistake, but I persevered. 'Amelia Newman. I…we…' He came alive at the mention of the name 'Newman', which he obviously recognised. 'Yes,' he said, somewhat softer, and then 'why are you calling me again?' He sounded a little irritated and I wasn't sure how to respond, but then he continued, 'I got the money, I told you. It'll all be taken care of. Next Tuesday at 3pm. Don't call again.' And then, suddenly, a dial tone – he'd hung up."

Elisabeth sat pondering the conversation all afternoon. Towards the end of the day she popped her head into Ian's office and handed him the diary, saying that Amelia had taken it out of her handbag when she visited and had left it by mistake. She knew Ian wouldn't have the time or the inclination to open it and she had carefully replaced the phone number at the back – but not before she'd noted it down elsewhere, just in case.

"It wasn't until Friday afternoon when I was rechecking Ian's schedule for the following week that I spotted it. There, marked in red for the following Tuesday, in the same way as important appointments: '2:30pm, Connor, Dog and Duck'. It was one of the rare personal notes in Ian's diary and he'd asked me to make absolutely sure he didn't miss it; apparently, Connor, who was perhaps Ian's only close friend, had insisted on the meeting, specifying the time and the pub halfway between their homes. Ian had let slip that he suspected Connor, also a lawyer, was having a family crisis because he had been asking Ian how he was managing to juggle his marriage and his work. On the other hand, I suspected that Connor was going to warn Ian about Amelia's extramarital activities."

Amelia didn't often know what Ian was up to during the day, but a personal *rendez vous* with a close friend such as this was something Ian was bound to have mentioned. Especially as three weeks previously he'd had his wallet stolen and still hadn't managed to get the right cards from the bank (who had sent cards first in his wife's name and then with a misspelling) so he had been relying on Amelia to have access to the money in their joint account, which involved keeping her informed of his activities more than usual. Elisabeth put all the pieces together – the likelihood Amelia was having an affair, her increasingly erratic behaviour, the telephone number, the mention of money exchanging hands, Tuesday at 3pm, the fact Amelia would know exactly where Ian was at that time, that Ian liked to sit outside and have a drink even when it was slightly cold; the puzzle was complete – she was sure that Amelia wanted him out of the way.

"I didn't say anything to Ian of course. For a start, I would have sounded completely insane and, on top of that, I must admit I was enjoying having the upper hand. I may have just been Ian's secretary, but for the first time I really felt in control, really felt like I could make a difference to his life. I could *save* his life. And as it turned out, the situation was exactly as I had deduced."

Amelia really had planned for Ian to be killed; why and how it got that bad Elisabeth would never know, but she thought Amelia must have been, at the very least, slightly crazy. She couldn't possibly have believed it wouldn't be investigated, or that she wasn't putting her children's future at risk – she was going to get rid of their father, after all. Whether Elisabeth was a mere cog in the wheels of fate or a cunning investigator, she wasn't sure, but either way it seemed clear to her that Amelia's plan couldn't be allowed to work, for, if it did, it would ruin too much for those who really didn't deserve it.

Elisabeth spent the weekend planning what she was going to do. There was no way she would let Ian come to any harm – at the lowest level he was her employer, yet on a more complex level the potential for power she now held made her want to wield it as much as possible. She was determined to turn events around to punish Amelia, or at least to expose her ruthlessness.

"I never really *knew* her, I suppose, but I didn't like what I'd seen. And if anyone deserved some sort of chastisement, it was her, not Ian."

On the Monday afternoon, leaving it as late as possible, Elisabeth casually informed Ian that Connor had changed the venue for their meeting. He was confused – the Dog and Duck was their favourite pub, not only halfway between their houses but the watering hole that had cemented their friendship – and he was dubious of the change of plan. She assured him that Connor's secretary had called to say he had to attend a meeting in the city that morning and wouldn't make it there in time, and had suggested that they meet at the Beehive pub just past the train station instead. Ian didn't have much time to ponder it – or so Elisabeth thought. She couldn't feasibly have changed the time or day, as she knew this meeting was all-important to both busy men, but she called Connor's secretary and gave her the same story about the change of venue, making sure she would fill Connor in.

The next day, to her surprise, Amelia turned up at the office in the morning.

"I don't know if it was her way of saying goodbye, or if she just wanted to check that Ian was going to be where she thought that afternoon, but she spent a long time in his office with him, having asked me not to put any calls through. She was foolish really – I'm sure her strange behaviour that morning led to the tragic turn of events, more so for her than anyone."

After Amelia left, Ian stayed in his office a while with the door closed. Elisabeth could see him speaking on the telephone, an intense look on his face, and she became nervous. Her fears were confirmed when he hung-up and opened the door rather abruptly.

"Connor didn't change the venue. Why did you tell me he'd changed it?"

"Um…I didn't say that," she sputtered. "I said his *secretary* had – must have been a misunderstanding." She smiled apologetically, but her heart sank. She had to find another way to stop him being in the wrong place at the wrong time. For a moment she considered telling him what was going on but, from the look on his face, Connor had already given him a big shock.

"Well, I've spoken to Connor and I'm going to meet him now. I need you to cancel that conference call and the two o'clock meeting."

"No problem," she immediately replied, knowing that there was no point in disagreeing with him when he was in this sort of mood, and also relieved that he would be seeing Connor earlier than planned. He barely acknowledged her for the next ten minutes as he quickly sent a couple of emails, made a short phone call and gathered up his things. He stopped, once, to check that she'd rearranged everything, and then he was gone. Despite the change of meeting time, as he left Elisabeth couldn't help wondering if she'd ever see him again.

"Why is it that we always remember the stupid things we did? Why is it that our senses – familiar smells, sights, feelings and tastes – are more likely to rear the ugly head of bad memories than good? Looking back, I know I should have taken my instincts more seriously, risked looking a fool to stay on the safe side. I should have known they'd be there for quite a while, though I suppose I was in denial.

"Ultimately, I think my subconscious knew that it was on the brink of something exciting. As it happened, all I did was sit back and wait. You know the rest I suppose, or you wouldn't be here…we wouldn't be where we are now. I know you're angry, but you can't blame anyone else. It was your mistake."

J got up and poured himself a whisky from the bottle on the desk, knocking it back like medicine. She was almost at the end of her tale and kept on, despite her growing fear of irking him; when all was said, she would be done.

"I admired Ian a lot. He handled it so well and he had his priorities straight, collecting the children like that before doing anything else. That's why he got to keep them – because he never lost track of their needs, throughout the ensuing disarray. When Amelia fell to pieces, he kept his mind on them."

Connor did look like the French man, it emerged, though it was never proved because by the time the police found out who he was, he'd disappeared. He was a petty criminal who was an expert at disappearing they'd said at the time, in order to justify their incompetence. Both men had dark hair that curled slightly at the ends. They were the same height, the same build, and that day they claimed Connor hadn't shaved. Marta said he had been riven with angst at the task before him – telling Ian about the affair – and he hadn't slept at all the night before.

Elisabeth looked up and addressed J boldly. "You could be forgiven for mistaking them, but not for his murder." And there ends the lesson. She knew the most pertinent issue was still to be addressed.

"So where are they then?" J asked, "You know I want to find them."

"I don't know," she answered honestly. "Five years is a long time and you're not the only one that was sent away. I was made to leave my whole life behind to protect me from you. And look how successful that's been." She laughed churlishly, dismissing the deliberate lie her life had become.

He ignored her self-pity and tried again. "You must know something. You'll be here a long time if you continue to hide information from me."

She laughed again, this time peevishly, and watched the frustration seep into his face. "I can't tell you any more. They moved away, that's for sure. I really don't even know whether they're still together."

He banged his fist on the desk in desperation. "You MUST know more; you've had more access to information than I have."

"I'm sorry. I don't and I've told you everything. Now let me go; there's nothing more I can give you." Defiantly, she sat upright and looked at him squarely.

His body slumped in defeat as he duly untied her wrists and ankles. As she stood up and stretched, smoke from the consolatory cigarette J lit tickled her nose, but for once she welcomed the sensation.

She felt light-headed and liberated, not just in body. She had handled the one confrontation she had been trained to avoid, with poise and control. As Elisabeth left the building, alone and unconstrained, she felt the hand of the past slowly lose its grip on her neck, one finger at a time.

Chapter 18

"Come through," he said and she followed him back into the kitchen. She'd rolled her school skirt up at the waist to make it shorter, as all the girls did, and she could feel it unfurling awkwardly. She ran one hand across her stomach, attempting to smooth the bulge, and tugged at the bottom of her skirt to straighten it.

The kitchen was perhaps one of the most impressive rooms in the house – bright and spacious; they walked through the door and circled its main feature – a large, square breakfast bar in the middle of the room, topped with tiny blue and turquoise tiles. Sabrina ran her hands gently over it, caressing the ridges, and stopped at the corner as Johnny went over to the fridge, opened the door and buried his head inside.

"Ammph hmm inggnmm."

"What did you say?" She'd been studying the line of his body as he leaned into the fridge, the curve and arch of his hips and back, and the ruffled hair at the back of his head. Clean lines with blurred edging, she thought.

"I said, are you hungry? I can make us something if you want. I mean, we'll be having dinner later, I guess, when my dad gets home. But do you want something now?"

She looked down at her fingernails, suddenly nervous. Doing something as basic as eating in front of Johnny seemed bizarre, inappropriate even, as if it denoted a level of comfort and normality they hadn't yet reached. The side of herself she hadn't yet explored was the side she was willing to reveal, not her everyday, human self. She wanted to appear above the mundane to him, unusual, interesting, but she didn't know how to go about it. A creature of mystery, not a teenager wanting a snack.

"No, I'm fine thanks. I'll...I'll wait."

"Ok, well, I'm just going to have something." He began fetching items from the fridge and placing them on the counter, oblivious to the large sigh that escaped Sabrina's lips. She wasn't sure why she was there, but it wasn't to watch Johnny eating; she'd assumed he would pass on the food as well. She watched him put together a clumsy sandwich and take a couple of bites.

"Mind if I look round?" she asked finally, bored with spectating.

"Um...no, sure. That's fine." He wiped some crumbs from his mouth and kept his gaze on her as she slid off the high stool, her skirt lagging a little behind, and turned to leave the room. She could feel his eyes on her back and her pulse began to trot.

Back out in the corridor, she turned right into the small dining room adjacent to the kitchen. Eight chairs were huddled around the ageing mahogany table, mumbling tales of past guests and gourmands. She stroked the chairs' cold backs and watched her hand rise and fall with their cambers. Leaving the dining room, she turned into the living room and headed straight for the wooden shelves holding countless photographs. A small boy was in almost all of them, Johnny she assumed. He had a small flick of hair at the back of his head, just visible in each photo, which survived the years and crowned him as he grew. In the final picture of the row, a school picture taken three months ago, the flick had gone.

She stood back slightly and surveyed the photographs on the higher shelf. A couple on their wedding day, the lady facing the camera and smiling, the man glancing at his new bride with delight. They must be Johnny's parents, for his face echoed their features. And to the right of it, a grainy black-and-white shot of a middle-aged couple surrounded by children, none of them smiling.

"My great-grandparents apparently." Sabrina jumped and whizzed round, one hand on her chest, to find Johnny behind her.

"You scared me!" She breathed out heavily, and he stepped forward to stand in front of her. She dropped her eyes and spotted two breadcrumbs on his shirt. She wanted to reach out and brush them away, but she froze. Before she could reconsider, he stepped to the side and addressed the photograph, giving her no choice but to turn and stand next to him.

"They were my mother's grandparents, Arthur and Rose. They had eight children and they all lived on top of each other in a three-bedroom house, my mother said. She used to love going round there when she was little; I think she liked the chaos."

"I don't know why they didn't smile in the photo, isn't it strange?" she asked, thinking out loud.

"Well, apparently, you know…in those days, it took so long to set-up the camera equipment and get everyone ready that people couldn't hold a smile for that long. Plus it was much more expensive to take photographs, and they couldn't afford for it to go wrong, so the best way to guarantee a good picture was to ask people to sit as still as possible and…um…hold their pose."

His voice had dropped a tone or two, and Sabrina found herself staring at his face as he spoke. She was impressed at his knowledge; they'd never really had much of a chance for proper conversation. At least, not without the interruption of fellow pupils. It made him seem different and, as a result, she felt she could be a different person too and so this new girl reached out and took Johnny's hand.

He turned towards her and stepped closer, looking down at her small, rounded nose. She leaned up towards him and kissed him, and she felt his hands slip across her waist and her back, where they danced erratically. He tasted of tuna and mayonnaise, and warm air puffed gently from his nose onto her cheek. After a minute, she pulled away and voiced the thought that was flitting around her mind like an errant butterfly.

"I haven't seen upstairs yet."

Johnny looked at her inquisitively, hopeful yet hopeless, and waited for her to say something else. But there she was, staring back at him expectantly, just waiting for him to take the lead.

"Ok. Ummm...yeah. I'll show you upstairs."

He ushered her up the stairs first, conscious of the bulge in his trousers that grew as he watched her bottom ascend. She had a small ladder in her tights at the back of her right thigh, and he longed to run a finger down it. As the stairs veered left and they reached the top, he guided her to the right and walked slowly.

"This is the bathroom. To the left is my parents'...well, my dad's room. Opposite that is the study, with the computer and everything. And this is my room."

They stopped at the end of the corridor, in front of a door which was slightly ajar. She couldn't see into the room and she wasn't sure what to do; she felt on the brink of crossing a threshold and, although she was keen to proceed, she wanted to draw out the moment as much as possible.

"Um...can I just use the bathroom please?"

"Oh, uh...sure. I'll...um...wait in here." She dodged round him, placing one hand on his arm as she did so and felt him relax slightly. She glanced back to see him push open the door to his room and enter, and she caught a glimpse of the blue wallpaper.

Reaching the bathroom, she walked in and closed the door behind her, hearing a soft hiss as it brushed against the worn, green carpet. There was no lock on the door, and for a minute she stood with her back to it, her heart thumping. Then she moved to the mirror and looked at her image.

Lifting both hands, she smoothed back the bangs adorning her cheeks and tucked them behind her ears. She had forgotten to put on earrings that morning and berated herself for forgetting something which, in that moment, seemed so important. The lip-gloss she had applied before arriving had disappeared and her cheeks felt unclothed, though they looked the same as ever. Soon years will have passed, she thought, and this reflection will be old; this face will be just a memory. As she washed her hands brusquely, she suddenly felt exposed, like Adam and Eve in the inexplicable shame of their nudity. She removed her tights and, noticing a ladder in them, dropped them into the bathroom bin.

Taking short, shallow breaths, she made her way slowly back up the corridor and approached the door to Johnny's room. She pushed it aside with her left hand and nudged forward so her right side entered first, equalising the responsibility in a way she found comforting.

Johnny was seated at the end of his bed, reaching downwards to tidy the pile of books clustered on the floor. He looked up at her as she entered, but was silent.

She surveyed the blue walls and simple wooden desk. "Nice room," she said eventually.

"Thanks," he replied.

She wasn't sure where to sit but, having briefly considered the slightly battered black office chair that lingered by the desk, she took the plunge and sat down at the head of the bed, close to Johnny, but closer to the pillow. There was a strong scent of washing powder, as if the sheets had been saturated with it. He continued to shuffle the books around, though she knew that by now they were arranged in two neat piles. He stopped when he heard her shift and twist towards him, and he too turned.

"Will your dad be home soon?" she asked, her words laced with a naive maturity.

"I don't know. I mean...he's home at different times. I thought he'd be home by now. But I don't know where he is. He might be home soon, yes. Well, maybe not, I'm not sure."

She smiled at his verbal wavering, looking him up and down from head to waist.

"What? What is it?" he demanded, almost crudely.

"Nothing. I'm sorry, it's just...I like you. A lot, I mean. And it's weird; this is the first time we've properly been able to...you know...just us."

"Yeah. I guess."

Sabrina reached over and took his hand, edging closer to him. He took the cue and leaned over to kiss her, the two of them side-by-side, awkward. They remained thus for several minutes, neither one of them wanting to change position and end the moment. Finally, Sabrina drew back.

"Have you got any...well, you know?" she asked coyly.

"What?" He looked as if he might understand but was too embarrassed to admit it; then again, his demeanour conveyed a certain cluelessness. Sabrina found it bizarre that he might not have imagined this situation as much as she had.

"Condoms," she said outright, "have you got any?"

"No. I'm sorry, I should have thought..."

"Don't worry. I brought one with me." Something in her had hoped Johnny would be prepared, perhaps as an indication of his intention. Instead, she was feeling increasingly like the puppet-mistress. She brushed away the slight guilt of her engineering, and reached into the front pocket of her skirt, pulling out a shiny, orange square that crackled under her fingertips. She'd been too scared to buy any but, knowing there were condoms on the top shelf of her parents' bathroom cabinet, she'd sneaked in and taken one, without bringing herself to accept its significance.

Johnny was staring at her, immobile. She was slightly confounded by his ineptitude, though the princess in her enjoyed taking the lead.

"Relax, don't worry. I'll move up, look, come over here." She lay back on the bed with her head on the pillow, before reaching out for his arm, tugging him down on top of her. "Wait, shift over a bit." He was breathing heavily now, and she too felt breathless, but for different reasons.

"Have you...done this before?" he blurted, and she wished he would stay silent.

"No, of course not. I just thought we should...well, I want to, don't you?"

"I suppose so."

This isn't how it's meant to be, she thought; am I having to convince him?

The truth was that Sabrina hadn't long been thinking of losing her virginity, but once the idea and the opportunity merged, she was determined to follow it through. A couple of the other girls at school talked about having sex, but no one else really knew enough to ascertain whether they were telling the truth. She remembered being eleven-years-old, when these same girls would run around the class asking each girl in turn 'are you a virgin?' with a sneering tone. "No!" Sabrina would reply, unsure of the meaning of the term, but certain it was something undesirable. Then the questioners would giggle and skip off chanting, 'Sabrina's not a virgin, Sabrina's not a virgin!' and repeat the experiment with someone else.

Gradually, though, sex had become a taboo subject among the girls. Boys, kissing, who you were going out with, where you had been caught with them, how long you'd sneaked off with them for, which one their friends you fancied and how many people had asked you for a kiss, were all prolific topics, but sex had faded into the background of things you might well think about doing but didn't really know much about.

Sabrina, however, was a great fan of the unknown. It didn't matter if other people knew about it or not – she wanted to experience as much as possible, as soon as possible. Her father had once sat her down and asked her what she knew about sexual intercourse, barely giving her a chance to reply before launching into a speech about sperm, eggs, cycles and fertilisation. The physiological side she knew plenty about – they had been taught it at school – but she longed for someone to discuss the emotional, physical and intimate details of sex, of which she felt clueless. She'd thought about approaching her older brother, but she knew he'd be too embarrassed to tell her anything, and she no longer saw him that often anyway. And so Johnny became her experiment, her way forward out of ignorance. Though she cared for him deeply, it was more important to her that it went as planned for her own sake, rather than anything that might happen between the two of them in the future. She needed his compliance, not his inadequacies, his body, not his thoughts.

As he lay on top of her and she kissed him urgently, she moved underneath him until she could feel his crotch, but he promptly swung his hips over to the other side of her. Wondering if she was moving too quickly, she stayed where she was, but began to unbutton her shirt. She had worn her favourite bra, the only 32B she owned, filled sufficiently, and which had pink and white horizontal stripes and small bows on the straps. Johnny stared at the tops of her breasts with a lust that pleased her, and she brought his hand up to stroke them. When he moved his hand away, she slipped to one side and sat up, removing her shirt and then her bra as he watched. He remained mesmerised as she pulled his t-shirt over his head and ran one hand down his back.

"Are you ready?" she asked, not knowing if there was something else he needed to do first, wishing he would give her some indication.

"I'm....I-" but before he could finish speaking, she pulled him back down on top of her and reached for the condom.

"You'd better remove your trousers," she instructed, eager to proceed. Johnny, however, lay still.

"Johnny? You'd better take your trousers off. And, um...open this, because I'm not sure what to do."

It was the first time either of them had voiced their inexperience, and it seemed to provoke an adverse reaction in Johnny. He sat up straight and retreated back to the end of the bed.

"Johnny?" The last three letters of his name shot off her tongue with a dart of disappointment.

"I'm sorry. I just...I don't want to. I mean, I do, but...not now." He looked away.

She sat up and pulled the pillow out from behind her,

clutching it to her chest.

"What do you mean? Why not? I thought we both wanted to? Is it…is there someone else you'd rather-"

"No! No one else. It's not that. I'm…I'm sorry. Look, just get dressed, ok?" And then, as if to make matters worse, he jumped up and rushed out of the room, grabbing his t-shirt on the way.

Sabrina sat for a few minutes, thinking. She certainly felt different, but not in the way she'd anticipated. Slowly, she picked up her clothes and put them on, brushing away the silent tears that embarrassed even her.

She crept out of the room, hoping Johnny wouldn't be lurking outside, and was relieved to be met with solitude. She grabbed her bag, shoes and coat from the hallway and had one hand on the front door when it opened from the other side.

Gasping, she stepped behind it as it opened and a tall man with a crumpling, kind face strode in.

"Hello!" he exclaimed.

"Hi," she whispered timidly.

"Are you a friend of Johnny?" And then, "Johnny? Where are you?"

"Yes," she replied, "but I was just leaving."

"Oh, well you must stay for dinner! I've brought some food home!" His enthusiasm made her shrink further, and she had to get out.

"I'm sorry, but I have to get home," she declared firmly just as Johnny appeared and, before either of them could protest further, she opened the front door and slipped through it, into the cruel mockery of dusk.

Chapter 19

Fortunately for most of those around her, Lydia liked to keep secrets. She had developed the skill of when to remain quiet and when to make noise, honing it as much as possible to her advantage. She liked to lurk around corners, eavesdropping, and making mental notes of what she'd heard. If caught she would smile sweetly, toy with a strand of long brown hair and slip away in a cloud of purported innocence.

She had a pink parka jacket that she wore to school when the sky hung low, a splash of colour in the grey impression. She spent the mornings with her mother before being dropped off just after lunch, and was collected again at 5pm; the school strived to be different and experimental with the children's attention spans.

It cheered her up to wear something pink; not because she was a girl and many girls her age liked pink, but because it was bright and pleasant and it expressed how she most often felt: happy, spoilt, dreamy. She didn't just *like* pink – she *was* pink and pink was her. Her bedroom, on the other hand, was a jumble of colours: dolls of different races housed in multi-ethnic princess compounds, a yellow and red mini-kitchen placed next to the blue rotating children's vacuum cleaner in a hub of domesticity, a multicoloured mock retail village complete with greengrocers (soon to be blitzed by the large chain supermarket), beauty salon (for white-skinned, blonde-haired customers only) and bank (with limited funds, seeing as most of the plastic coins had been sucked up by the blue vacuum cleaner). Her wallpaper too was a sea of orange melting into yellows, and her bed sheet was covered with marching animals in homage to Noah's ark. Pink was not abundant, except where appropriate – in her wardrobe, on her towels and on three pairs of her shoes. It was carefully thought out, and Lydia had it as she wanted – a busy room for a busy girl, and she certainly had plans.

The school building that housed Lydia and her classmates had been specially built just a year before she'd started there. Designed to educate the youngest pupils in a friendly and non-threatening atmosphere, it had low ceilings that almost grazed the tops of the teachers' heads and narrow corridors that often extracted feelings of claustrophobia from the anxious visiting parents.

At school break times, the children in Lydia's year, along with those in the two years above her, occupied their own playground. What seemed like an expansive 2D adventure playground to the eager children embarking on their formal education was actually 200-square-metres of freshly-laid tarmac painted with bright snakes and ladders, hopscotch grids, giant segmented worms and swirls of colour.

Lydia would join the other children along the row of pegs as they hurriedly put their coats on and dashed outside into the not-so-fresh air. But Lydia – who, with the surname letter 'N', had a peg roughly in the middle of the row – would linger that little bit longer, fiddling with her pink zip and hoping to overhear some conversation or other that would give her an insight into the mind of her first proper teacher, Miss Favistowe, or even the progress (or lack thereof) of a fellow pupil who'd been made to stay behind.

Lydia did well at school, neither aiming for the top of the class nor indolent enough to slip to the bottom. She was attentive, if slightly precocious, and creative play was her forte. Her only weakness in the minds of those who taught her was her tendency, if left to her own devices, to daydream.

In the playground, groups formed like autumn puddles lurking in the road. Some spilled into others, some trickled away, and some lone drops hung around the sides, destined to evaporate. Lydia liked to dip into as many as possible, circulating as a gracious host with an air of impartiality that would trick fellow pupils into granting her their trust. Sometimes she would bring toys in from home and beguile others into her vicinity, sharing her possessions with them until they shared their thoughts. Her actions were borne not from maliciousness or deceit – for she was only five-years-old – but from a genuine curiosity about other people and their inner thoughts. In this way she soon found herself to be a friend of many and, even better, a guardian of many things.

She knew, for example, that Alan Johnston's father had just lost his job at the post office because someone had accused him of stealing a stamp (she'd heard two of the mothers discussing it, and Lydia knew that stamps cost a lot of money because of the colours on them and because Mummy was always complaining she had run out); she knew that Betty Roebeck's father was ill but better now, because he had been moved here from 'Germny' (and Mummy always said germs made you sick); she knew that Jenny's mother always made the best cakes because she put a 'special flower' into them; she knew that David Temple's mother had taken him and his older brother, Steve, to live with his grandparents because his dad had been having 'a fayre' with another woman (and Lydia agreed it was mean that he had gone with someone else and not his family, especially if there were rides and candyfloss); she knew that Lionel Atkins had problems with his spelling and concentration and he needed special medicine because he had something the teacher referred to as his 'HD', and Daddy said that meant 'High Definition', so Lydia would speak slowly and explain the meaning of words to him whenever she could (though he usually ran off quite quickly). And she also knew that Miss Favistowe had a boyfriend called Greg, because he had phoned her once at break time when she was in the classroom, and

Lydia had heard her giggling. She'll probably marry him soon, Lydia thought, though she worried that Miss Favistowe might leave and not be their teacher anymore. Lydia kept all these secrets in her head, and she told no one.

Despite her ongoing investigations and indiscriminate façade, Lydia did have a best friend, and she was called Ursula – whose favourite colour was purple. Ursula had one younger brother and lived in a big house not too far from Lydia's own. But unlike Lydia's family, both her parents worked – her father as a judge and her mother for the 'mare' – and she had a nanny that picked her up from school each day. The nanny was called Jemima, though Ursula was allowed to call her 'Jem', and she was extremely pretty.

It was Ursula herself, being the only person truly close to Lydia at school, who upset the whole balance one day. Cathy Meakin had been showing off a brand new yo-yo, which her father had bought for her on his trip to a 'Merica', which must have been some kind of big toyshop. Barely had the children arrived in the morning, when Cathy was displaying all the tricks and spins she could do with the green and blue yo-yo, which flashed bright lights and made a whizzing sound every time it spun. She would let no one else touch it, but before long the 'whizz' and 'zzzzip' of the new toy had attracted pupils from far and wide, and a small crowd had gathered around Cathy. Many begged to try it out, and all were turned down. When the bell rang for registration, Cathy pocketed the coveted trinket and ran inside with the others. Then, at first break, a cry resounded from near the coat pegs, followed by substantial sobbing. Everyone gathered round a bereft Cathy with the excitement of children too young to empathise.

Miss Favistowe had questioned them, of course, her eyes sweeping the cacophony of small children and searching among them for a flash of guilt. She had no luck; it seemed there were neither witnesses nor perpetrators among the group, though her logic begged to differ. She resorted to comforting the now sniffling Cathy and sent the others out to play, instructing them authoritatively that if anyone were to remember anything about the disappearance of the yo-yo, they must come and tell her immediately.

Towards the end of break time, Ursula, who had been missing for a while, suddenly appeared and pulled Lydia aside from her game of hopscotch.

"I just heard Ian Trellis tell Sam that he took the yo-yo!" she revealed, wide-eyed and frightened. Ian Trellis was without a doubt the fiercest bully of their year, the one that would pinch you for no reason as you walked past, the one most likely to take food off you, and the one whose mere glare could reduce a girl – and, on occasion, a boy – to tears. Lydia and Ursula generally avoided him, and his sidekick Sam, as much as possible.

"We should tell someone!" Lydia exclaimed, excited by the exclusivity of this information and the power it vested in her.

"No!" cried Ursula. "Ian will hurt us!"

"But he stole Cathy's yo-yo, and Miss Favistowe said we should tell her if we knew anything. I bet she'll punish him and he won't be able to hurt us. It'll be ok." Lydia put one arm around Ursula's shoulders and gave her an awkward squeeze. In her world of colours, Lydia's naive black-and-white morals were intact enough to sustain her belief in justice. Just then, the bell rang to signal lesson time, and the children trotted in to take their assigned places.

When everyone was seated and silent, and as Miss Favistowe shuffled some papers around, Lydia put up her hand. She sensed Ursula, seated next to her, slump down a little in her seat.

"Yes Lydia?" asked Miss Favistowe, raising her eyes to the sea of stares.

"Ian Trellis took the yo-yo Miss!" A gasp in amazment at her bravery resounded in the room, bouncing off the walls and hitting Lydia's ears. Eyes turned to Ian, who shifted angrily in his seat and bunched up his mouth.

"And what makes you think that Lydia?"

"Ursula heard him tell Sam that he took it!" There, she'd said it now, and she felt good about it – not because she wanted praise, but because there had been a mystery and because she had exposed, and therefore eradicated, the wrongdoing.

"Ursula, is this true?" Miss Favistowe turned her head towards the small soul and smiled kindly. Lydia, on the other hand, turned her body fully and beamed at Ursula, her comrade in fair play.

"Um...I don't know," replied Ursula, feeling the menacing breath of Ian creep under her collar from three rows behind.

"I bet it was Ian!" cried Cathy, defiant in her loss.

"It was not!" shouted Ian. "I wouldn't want your stupid yo-yo!"

From around the classroom came cries of both assent and disagreement that escalated until Miss Favistowe shouted "Hush!" and, on witnessing obedience, more quietly, "Hush children. This is not the way to deal with the matter. Now Ursula, did you hear Ian tell someone he had taken the yo-yo?"

"He told Sam!" added Lydia, annoyed that her teacher had forgotten this detail.

"Yes, thank you Lydia, but I'm asking Ursula."

All eyes turned to Ursula who sat with her arms folded, and silent, pearly tears slipping down her sallow cheeks. Lydia counted three on her left cheek, but only two dripped off the bottom of her chin and onto her desk.

"Um...no," she whispered eventually, and this time it was only Lydia that gasped.

"It's not true Miss; she told me!" Lydia cried, her friend's betrayal causing her stomach to contract horribly.

Miss Favistowe looked around the room, at the quiet ears and eyes of each child, stopping for an extra second only on Ian's grin and Cathy's confusion. Then her gaze fell back on the two girls who were giving conflicting stories. She almost certainly knew which was telling the truth but, in an effort to coax her pupils into the real world, she could take no action without a confirmed witness.

"Ursula, are you sure you didn't hear anything?"

"Yes," squeaked the respondent, turning her head a little to the right.

"Ian, are you saying you had nothing to do with Cathy's yo-yo going missing?"

"Yes, Miss Favistowe. I didn't take it," he sang, mocking his accuser.

"Well then Lydia, I'm afraid you are mistaken. You shouldn't accuse people without knowing the truth. Now we've all thought badly of Ian for no reason, Cathy is disappointed that her yo-yo is still missing, and you've upset Ursula." She racked her brains for the moral of the story; that was the rule: teach, teach and teach, even when she wasn't sure what she was teaching them. "I'm sure you meant well but, children, remember that you shouldn't blame someone else without having the facts, because it can lead to more trouble."

Lydia had begun to cry now – two, three, then five tears collecting in a pool of humiliation on the smooth, acetate surface of her workbook. She vowed never to reveal her findings again, unless she had gathered concrete evidence, and she had learned that even those closest to her couldn't always be trusted.

From that day on, Lydia – who was slowly learning to spell – decided to write her secrets down and keep them in a small wooden box in her room. It was a dark brown 'magic' box that her grandmother had brought back from another country. It was impossible to open unless you pulled on the opposite edges that would cause the lid to split in two and spring apart. Inside, on small pieces of paper, Lydia had used her childish scrawl to formalise the thoughts and findings to which no one else was privy. She wasn't sure if she'd spelt everything correctly, as she couldn't check her words with an adult, but as long as she could understand what she'd written, she was happy. She kept a special purple colouring pencil – not pink for, after the 'Ursula incident', purple was the colour of secrets – in the box too, its head buried among the slips of paper, and every so often she would rifle through the contents and examine a select few.

There was one secret she remembered above all others, which she placed right at the bottom of the box. She didn't understand it fully, but something at the forefront of her mind told her it was extremely important. She didn't know if it was true, if she'd misheard or if she'd misunderstood, but, whatever the case, she was going to hang onto it.

She had overheard what she could only assume to be a secret one Friday evening. Mummy had put her to bed, but she couldn't sleep – she was either hungry or thirsty and she couldn't make up her mind which. Daddy was still at work, which wasn't unusual as she rarely got to say goodnight to him during the week. She slipped out of her covers and hopped noiselessly onto the floor, squeezing her feet into the fluffy, pink rabbit slippers that she was fast outgrowing. She left her room and stuck her head round the door of Luke's room opposite, but he was sound asleep. The television was on downstairs, the low volume spreading a comforting drone through the house.

As Lydia descended the stairs and the living room rounded into view, the first thing she noticed was a half-empty bottle of wine next to an empty glass, and then her mother appeared, phone to her ear and with a flushed complexion. From her relaxed pose and the high-pitched, animated tone of her voice, Lydia could immediately tell she was talking to Aunty Marta. And these were the conversations Lydia most liked to overhear because, even though it was somewhat frightening, it was the only time she could see her mother in a totally different light. She sneaked past the living room door, unobserved, and planted herself on the floor just outside. She listened intently to the one-sided conversation, breathing quietly in the long pauses between her mother's speech.

"I don't know," Mummy sighed, "he's rarely home these days, and I wish I could make him see that that's why I..."

"Yes, I know. I wish I were more like you; it's just so hard."

"Hmmm. I still...I still feel so guilty, if he ever knew..."

Lydia pressed closer to the door, suddenly tense. Mummy

was crying quietly into the telephone now, and Lydia's ears pricked up.

"Well, promise you won't say anything? Ian's one thing, but if the children found out...I still hope they'll be close when they're older and if Lydia found out Luke wasn't her real brother she'd be devastated, let alone the effect it'd have on Luke...I can't bear thinking about it."

"Yes, I know I can trust you; it's just...can I trust myself?"

Lydia stood up slowly, pushing her back against the spine of the door. Without another thought, she ran back to the stairs and up them as quietly as she could; evidently not as discreetly as she wanted, because she suddenly heard her mother say, "Hang on...I have to go," before footsteps padded after her, making her run even faster. She ran back into her room, jumped under the covers and turned over, masking her face. She willed her eyes to stay closed and still, and to her credit she kept them squeezed tightly shut as her mother came in, inspected her, and hurriedly left the room again. Soon afterwards, she fell asleep.

The next day, Lydia opened the box, tore off a piece of paper from the stack on her desk, and wrote carefully in purple pencil, 'Luke is not my rerl bruther.'

A few months later, after witnessing a heated argument between her parents, Lydia went back to the box, determined to re-examine the buried treasure. She closed her room door, retrieved the box from her cupboard, expertly opened it on the first try, and tipped its contents out. She read each secret and put them aside, counting them as she went – she counted eleven. She picked the last one up, ready to confront the secret that belonged to her whole family. 'Luke thruw a ball at mummys pot and it brok but he sed it wasint him' she read with horror. Scrabbling around in confusion, she collected all the papers again and went through them one-by-one, each secret confirming a fear that tingled in the tips of her fingers.

Her most important secret, along with the purple pencil, was missing.

Chapter 20

On the morning of the Development Initiatives Meeting, Constance sat down at the breakfast table where Jason had already been waiting for twenty minutes. She was feeling queasy; not enough to play the sick card, but enough to make her flit in and out of the hotel room bathroom…trying to…failing to…be sick. Eventually she had given up, and taken herself and her flip-flopping stomach to breakfast, hoping that she could last the day, or at the very least position herself near a bathroom at all times.

"Are you ok?" Jason asked. "You look pale."

"I'm fine," she replied curtly, "just jet-lagged."

"I feel ok actually, managed to sleep well. Those beds are comfortable. Of course, not as cosy as if there were two of-"

"I'm going to get some food," she interrupted. "I can see you've already started."

Her chair scraped on the floor as she pushed it backwards. She stood up straight, wondering if the heels she had chosen to wear were going to prove that little bit too painful for the day. It always made her feel better to power-dress at work, to hide behind the suits, the crisp shirts, the smart shoes and handbags, and, underneath it all, the sultry underwear that only she knew was there. Except today she'd had to go for comfort with stretch black pants and matching faded bra, so she'd compensated with an extra inch of heel.

From the breakfast buffet she picked up a croissant and a

small pot of raspberry jam, a slice of bread that she had to put through an agonisingly slow toasting rack, and a glass of orange juice. The selection of hot food on offer, teeming with cholesterol, added an extra wave of nausea to what was fast becoming a high tide and she passed by the greasy food speedily.

As she sat back down at the table, she was aware of Jason surveying her selection with interest; for all the nights they'd spent together, this was the first time they'd eaten with each other in the morning. Jason, she'd observed, had already consumed a full fried breakfast, a selection of bread and cheeses, a doughnut – the remnants of which danced across the empty plates in front of him – and a strong black coffee.

"So, what time do we have to be at this DIM thing?" he asked lazily as she took a sip of her orange juice and remembered that acidic drinks were not the best choice if you felt nauseous.

"The meeting *starts* at 10am. We should get there about quarter to, which means you need to leave at 9.15."

"*I* need to leave at 9.15? What about you?"

"I have some things to do first, phone calls to make, etc. So I'll see you there."

"Ok."

"You have the directions, don't you?"

"Yes, all ready with the whole pack you gave me; relax!"

His cockiness did not elicit a response; she remained quiet with prescience, rendering Jason uneasy.

"Look, I don't get it. We come out here together, and ever since we arrived you've been distant, cold almost. I thought…" his voiced dropped several notches, "I thought we came out here to spend some time *together*. You know, just us, no one else getting in the way. Don't tell me you brought me out here just for this meeting?"

His agitation, and the way he was leaning towards her, were attracting the attention of a few of the other diners. The hotel's main restaurant, where breakfast, lunch and dinner were served, was spacious, elegant and just a little quirky. Kessler pictures adorned the pale orange walls; *Spotted Cow, Three Red Dogs with Apples* and *Cat with Purple Ball* stared amusedly at the handful of present diners.

"The meeting is important; you need to make an effort. I brought you out here because I trust you as an assistant, and because I thought you would be professional."

"But what about...us?" he hissed, his brow creased.

Constance realised she was giving too much away, being too honest and letting her guard down. She couldn't let on to him that anything had changed.

"You didn't let me finish," she continued. "I was about to say that *after* the meeting the fun can begin. I've just been preoccupied, that's all – I've had a lot to prepare. But once today is over, we'll still have two whole days – and nights – left in New York and then we can really enjoy ourselves. Ok?"

Jason visibly relaxed back into his chair. "Now that's more like what *I* had in mind," he said with a grin. "After all, great minds think like me!"

She laughed out loud at his cockiness this time, forgetting herself for a minute. Jason always had a way of being charmingly arrogant; the sort of person you found you liked even though you didn't want to. Looking at his cheeky eyes and stretched lips, she found herself slipping back into his delights – the way his ear lobes felt between her lips, the burning stubble on his chin, the curve of his shoulders, and the way his dogmatism automatically made you feel like everything was going to be ok. Except it wouldn't be this time. Not for him.

After an arduous breakfast, at which Constance had nibbled at her croissant and eventually just managed a glass of sparkling water, they retreated to their rooms where Constance gave Jason his final instructions.

"Make sure you're there on time. I have to give my presentation on behalf of the UK office at 11am. After a short welcome and coffee, you'll have about ten minutes to set-up the slides – don't mess up."

"Relax, I won't! That's why you brought me remember – your trusty right-hand man!" As he said this he slid his right hand around her waist, slipped it under her shirt and stroked her back. She could feel the blood rushing around her body, molecules fuelled by the electricity of his touch. She allowed him to lean in and kiss her then pushed back angrily until he pulled away.

"Whoa, calm down. Ow." He took his hand away from her and reached back to rub his neck. But then he smiled, taking her force as a sign of enthusiasm, and pulled her closer for another kiss. She allowed him; it was the last time he could have control.

"I guess I'll see you at the meeting then," he whispered finally, "and even more of you later on." She smiled weakly to feign complicity before Jason strode off down the corridor and she was able to unlock the door to temporary peace.

She lay down for a few minutes and thought about her plan of action. She'd never been one for revenge so much as 'comeuppance', and once she'd decided definitively that her affair with Jason had to come to an end, she knew she could no longer tolerate him being part of her professional life either. His presence was as uncomfortable to her as that of a wet glove – one she needed to peel off and discard as soon as possible.

She'd toyed with the idea of causing him to miss his flight …but he would be able to get another one – or giving him the wrong directions to the meeting...but he could hail a taxi – perhaps trying to lose him somewhere in New York…but he'd be sure to find his way back – or planting a suspicious substance on him…but it would be too risky, and in any case too severe a punishment – or firing him for incompetence…but he would be able to claim unfair dismissal, plus he was a perfectly capable assistant – or even unveiling his affair with Anna…but again, that would be too risky as he might then disclose details of both his trysts. Then one evening, seated at home in front of her laptop, she'd discovered the most inappropriate, but best, idea of all.

Constance rarely used the internet when she was at home. She was on the computer so much during the day that when she came home she liked to avoid it as much as possible. Still, occasionally she would make a few purchases online, read the news or send the odd email. That evening she had been playing around with the browser settings and came across the bookmarked sites. One of them, she noticed, was for an email service provider she recalled Jason using on her computer. She went to the webpage and started typing his name into the 'USER ID' field. She got up to 'J-A-' before his full email address appeared in a drop-down list. She selected it, and immediately the 'remember me on this computer' box was ticked. Gleeful with anticipation, she clicked 'Sign In'. Five seconds later, Jason's emails appeared on the screen in front of her, and she stared at them in wonderment.

Constance didn't advocate invasion of privacy, but under the circumstances she felt justified in perusing his online correspondence. It had never occurred to her to attempt this before, but now she saw it as the perfect opportunity to explore other options of humiliation. And, before long, she'd found it; brazenly filling the internet window were intimate photos of himself that Jason had sent to Anna two months previously. Without stopping to read his words – she had tortured herself enough already with thought of the two of them – Constance emailed five of the photos to herself (thankfully it didn't appear that Anna had sent any of herself in return), deleted these email 'forwards' from Jason's sent messages folder, and signed off from his account. She had her ammunition, and a plan slowly formed in her mind.

Now, in her hotel room, Constance thought about the extra slides she had specially produced for her presentation. She had scanned in the five images of Jason, transferred them to slides, and mixed them up with the others depicting initiatives from the London office that had resulted from a brainstorming session. From PowerPoint slides to power slides with a point, she thought nervously, hoping everything would go according to plan. Jason had all the slides, and she had instructed him not to mess up the order; as long as he opened the correct document and made sure the first one was correct, that would be enough, she'd said. She was counting on him not having enough time to run through them all.

Half-an-hour later, she sat up with a start, realising she'd fallen asleep. The television was on, a tacky talk show forming the backdrop to Constance's throbbing head. To her relief, she no longer felt sick, and drank a couple of glasses of water to ease her headache. Looking at her watch, she knew she just had time for some final ablutions before making her way to the meeting.

The annual NY DIM was usually well attended, with at least one representative from each Radison office around the world. The meeting room thrummed with the sound of different languages, a mish-mash of cultures oppressed by the American dream. Constance arrived soon after Jason and nodded at him across the room, where he had settled down to talk to other assistants grappling with files, folders and tasks in hand. Once everyone was seated with steaming cups of coffee or Lipton tea, Hank Carson, COO of Radison Worldwide, gave a welcome speech. Constance glanced over at Jason every now and then until he caught her doing so and gave her an annoying wink. She turned away and forced herself to concentrate until it was her turn.

Once Hank was finished, there was a ten-minute interval for further refreshments, and the chance for Jason to set-up Constance's presentation. She went over to inspect how it was going, and to distract him from looking through the slides.

"Everything ok here?" she asked as he untangled some wires.

"Yep, fine, all fine."

"You sure? Do you need a hand?"

"No, absolutely fine, really."

She kept her eye on him as he finished setting up the laptop, opened the PowerPoint file, checked the first slide, and aligned the projector with the screen. Then he turned and gave her the thumbs up. She mouthed 'thank you' in return and made her way to the front of the room. Once she was in place, people slowly made their way back to their seats, and she began.

"Good morning again everybody. For those of you who don't know me, my name is Constance Romijn, and I'm a Senior

Project Manager in the London office. I'm here today to give you an update on the various projects we've been working on and to reveal to you certain initiatives we've come up with. I'll be speaking for about half-an-hour, after which I'll be happy to answer any questions you might have, and hear feedback on our suggestions."

She signalled for Jason to display the first slide, at which point he reached over and pressed the necessary key. The image of some premises came into view, and Constance launched into her speech. Every so often she waved her left hand at Jason, who would move onto the next slide. The ninth time she did this, she braced herself and kept her voice in control. As she hoped, a huge gasp resounded, and she followed the gaze of the audience to the image on the screen behind her.

Jason, nude but for a bowtie, with a top hat covering his crotch, beamed down at them. Everyone was frozen until Jason jumped up and pressed the key for the next slide, which provoked another gasp. Jason, nude with his back to the camera, his head looking round over his shoulder, displaying a playful smile.

Constance stared at the screen in mock-horror, keeping one eye on the audience who were gradually matching the face looming over them to the one going bright red at the front of the room. Desperately, he pressed next...next...next, each time skipping to a different intimate image of himself. By the fifth one, many women had a hand clamped to their mouths to hide their laughter, many men were looking away in disgust, and Constance was ready with further mock-horror.

"Jason!" she cried out. "What on earth...?"

"I...I don't know...I have no idea...I-" he flicked the slides just one more time and breathed a loud sigh of relief as a photograph of Radison UK's Partners appeared, Anna seated in the middle. Constance had engineered this – what better way to humiliate him than to follow it up with a clue as to why.

Hank Carson was by now up out of his seat and making his way towards Jason.

"Young man, this is totally unacceptable. Unfortunately for us all, we seem to have identified you as the star of those images, am I right?"

"Yes, but I don't know how-"

"I think I'd better speak to you outside. Constance, please join us for a minute. Everyone else," he announced, turning back to the murmuring masses, "please be patient and we shall resume in a moment."

The three of them left the room, Jason's head hung low.

"What's your name?" Hank asked sternly.

"Jason," he answered, still in shock.

Constance was keen to interject before she could be blamed. "I'm so sorry Hank, I had no idea. I mean, he's been my assistant for a while now and I thought I could trust him. I'm deeply ashamed this could have happened."

"It's alright Constance, I dare say one day it'll be a tale of light entertainment, but for now young man," he turned back to Jason, "I can assure you that your seniors will hear about this – though I may spare them the gory details. I think you'd better leave."

"Yes, ok," he replied, not about to argue. He left without making eye contact with either of them.

"Now Constance, I think you'd better carry on your presentation *without* the use of slides, alright?"

"Yes Hank, of course; I'm *so* sorry."

"It's alright – the sad truth is that really good assistants are hard to find these days. Though I can't say I've ever had one that has…revealed so much before!" He gave a small chuckle as they made their way back into the meeting room.

The rest of the day was as tedious and successful as expected. In the absence of the supposed culprit, Constance was the one who was subject to the stares and whispers of others though it was a small price to pay for satisfaction. When she got back to her hotel room she found a note from Jason pushed under her door that merely said, 'Changed my flight. Am going to the airport now.' She crushed it up and threw it away.

Two months later, Jason was long gone, but the seeds he had planted remained. Anna had handed in her resignation – having heard about the incident in New York, and, no doubt fearing she would be uncovered as the original recipient of the emails, she had hastily found another position for herself at a rival firm. Constance struggled on with one assistant, her hopes of a promotion only dashed by her private knowledge that she was pregnant.

Sometimes in life you come to a fork in the road, she thought, that at first you scarcely recognise for what it is. It's only once you've unknowingly chosen one of the paths that you realise the prongs of the fork separate, the gap becoming wider and wider, until you can no longer envisage the path you might have taken. There was no going back.

Constance had often contemplated the idea of having children, but until now had not needed give it full consideration. Her main reason was that she had never found a man suitable enough to be the father of her children. In her twenties, when she was craving love and affection, there had been Elliot. They'd met at university, fallen in love and enjoyed the finer things of student life. Then Elliot had failed his course, started another one, dropped out of that one too, and Constance – who by this time had climbed a rung or two on the career ladder – soon realised that they weren't as well matched in real life as they had been in their student fantasy world.

Two or three informal relationships ensued in the following years: Kevin, who she was irresistibly attracted to for a few weeks until his cosmic effect wore sharply off; Jeremy, who provided her with every kind of stimulation other than the intellectual; and Terry, who she had been friends with for a while before they really connected, soon after which he decided to get back together with his ex-girlfriend.

And then there was Pedro, a Spanish would-be actor who worked as a number-cruncher for a few years in the city. They'd met through mutual friends, dated seriously for months and even thought about moving in together. Pedro was taking days off here and there to attend auditions but, despite his near-perfect English, his accent was his main hindrance.

Eventually he'd decided to move back to Spain – to

Andalucia, which was becoming increasingly popular for filming projects. He invited Constance to go with him but, being fiercely independent, she refused to sacrifice her burgeoning career to move to a country where even daily life – with the linguistic handicap – would be a challenge. Still, both of them had been regretful, both almost changed their minds in those last few weeks, and both then vowed they'd fight off the adverse distance and remain together.

If Constance was honest, Pedro was the only man she'd ever imagined as the father of her children, and had at the time even indulged in daydreams of children fluent in Spanish, English and Dutch. After a few months of denial, however, they'd drifted apart, each giving up the ghost on their relationship as kindly and gently as possible. There was no doubt in Constance's mind that if they'd remained in the same country, they'd be married by now with children. Two years ago, in a Christmas card, he had mentioned that he was engaged to someone else. Constance – not through jealousy or regret but through genuine recognition of the end of the road – had never replied.

And Jason: once she was over the initial surprise, it made her laugh to think of him as a father. A young, arrogant, playboy of an employee was hardly the man she had imagined as a teacher, role model, or caretaker of any of her potential children. He was, in many ways, a child himself, too young to take on responsibilities of this magnitude. She didn't want to place that onto him, even though some would claim she had no choice. But greater than that, she didn't want to be tied to him, in any way, for the rest of her life.

And so, when she'd come to that subtle fork in the road, Constance had taken a path that seemed like any other, and had been duped. That one night when, drunk on the illicit and ironically carefree, Jason – testing her – had refused to wear a condom, she'd silently tallied the days of her cycle, made a hasty risk assessment, and allowed him to proceed. The wise are not those devoid of stupidity, but those who keep their stupidity on a tight reign; Constance had, on that occasion, let go.

Chapter 21

On replacing the receiver, Simon looked up and about in the false belief that someone else had heard his conversation. His gaze was not met; all about him eyes were fixed on screens that flickered back in an exchange of neutrons. He leant back into his chair, momentarily taking in the odd sounds of the office (a heated telephone exchange, a desperate mouse-clicking, rapid typing, the gurgle of the water cooler, the thud-thud-thud of a tardy meeting attendee's feet on the stairs) that seemed to escalate then converge with his own feeling of shock until he felt his face would melt from the heat of it. He sat forward suddenly, his chair-back springing into action and propelling him forcefully forward with a snappy rattle to knock over the paper cup on his desk. Cursing, he watched as water slithered into his keyboard and settled between the keys, threatening to numb them. Now was not the time to grieve for technology though. He felt a familiar fear spreading through his chest; the kind of sickness you feel when afraid for someone else. No doubt about it, he would have to get to his parents' house as soon as possible.

He couldn't believe what he'd just heard. He wanted to phone his mother back and ask if this was a joke, except he'd already asked this twice during the course of the conversation and he could tell by her jilted words and gulps for air that she was distraught. Sabrina – his little sister – was pregnant. Pregnant! At fifteen! And only just fifteen at that – it had barely been a month since he had visited for her birthday to take her some gift vouchers and a t-shirt that read 'MY BITE IS WORSE THAN MY BARK' (had she known then?).

He'd managed to ascertain from his mother's garble that Sabrina had asked both her parents to sit down when she got home from school that day – their father was working from home, and their mother just back from the supermarket – and had confessed her predicament with an eerie determination.

"She didn't even look sorry, Simon," his mother had sobbed. "I can't believe it. Our little girl – how could this have happened?" ending with a feeble wail of despair. Simon had tried to soothe her, but then his father had picked up the other phone extension and shouted, "Simon? Simon is that you?"

"Yes, Dad," he virtually whispered, in a bid to counteract his father's volume – their father was rarely this angry.

"Did your mother tell you?"

"Ye-"

"Well, we know whose fault it is, don't we? That boy, whatsisname – Johnny, that's it. That boy she's been seeing for all of two minutes. We haven't even met him; I mean, this is ridiculous. We don't know what his family's like or anything, and she says he's fifteen but, who knows, he could be older! Either way, he's definitely taken advantage of her. I should call the police – she's underage; she begged me not to, but what choice to we have? We have a duty to-"

"Dad! Dad, listen to me...no...Dad, calm down. Yes, calm down; I know you're angry. Look, I'm going to come home. I'll leave soon. We'll talk about it then." And with that, he'd swiftly put down the phone.

Still reeling from the information proffered by his irate parents, Simon stood up and braced himself for the inevitable. Ever since Jason had mysteriously been dismissed, Simon had been overworked (and underpaid), taking on the majority of his former colleague's duties as well as continuing with his own. He could hardly complain though as it was his chance to prove he was up to the task and any failure would rack-up black marks faster than he could erase the ones he'd already established.

These days, he got to work on time (well, at least four days out of five), was attentive and proactive (aside from those couple of hours after lunch when he felt sleepy and often surfed the internet) and threw himself into his job with all the vigour of a lunching hippopotamus. He felt he was doing well – after all, he was the only assistant Constance had now – but he was afraid any wrong roll of the dice could send him falling back down the ladder to the snakes. And this could be it.

His hand was raised before he even got to 'Cold-Stance's' office, but he had to drop it foolishly when he realised that behind her closed door she was on the phone. He hung around outside, a sheepish schoolboy waiting to enter the headmistress's lair, and nodded briefly without eye contact at the few people who walked past, creasing their brows at his evasive manner. When he heard his boss's muffled voice cease he was just bending down to tie his shoelace and stood up hastily, turning to face her through the glass. Seeing her hang up, he rapped on her door immediately. His knock conveyed a confidence that belied the anxiety coursing through his veins. She looked up in surprise and gestured for him to come in.

"Hi, um, sorry to disturb you. I've finished typing the report for the Makowski meeting," (a lie, but an attempt to appease her) "and, well, I have a slight problem."

"Um…with the report? We uh…we went through it thoroughly Simon; I fail to see how my instructions may not have been clear." Constance stumbled uncharacteristically over her words, and for the first time Simon noticed her red eyes.

"Uh…no, actually. It's not about work, it's-"

"Well, spit it out, what's going on?" She seemed as eager to end the conversation as he was, and this mutual intolerance was somewhat comforting.

"I have a bit of a family crisis, and I have to leave early today. Right now, in fact. And I may not be back before the weekend."

"Right," she replied, clearly confused at his request, which had emerged un-Simon-like as more of a statement.

"Sorry it's short notice, but I'm really going to have to go. I'll take it out of my holiday allowance of course." He knew from the way Constance's mouth was twitching that she was hoping for more information, but he resolutely stayed silent. He seemed to have caught her in a rare display of emotion and it made him feel powerful. Still, he had no desire to take advantage more than was necessary, so after a pause he handed her back the control.

"Is that ok? I mean, I know it's not ideal, and I'm really sorry, but can I go? I need to get back to my parents' house."

"Not a…death in the family, I hope." She blinked a few times.

"No, no death."

"And no one's been taken…ill?"

"No, not as such."

"Right."

"Sorry, it's just…well, a…um…private family matter really."

"Right."

Simon wished she'd stop saying that, her steely eyes fixed vacantly on the door behind him. "Well then, I suppose you'd better get going." (Finally!) "Just…um…email me the report before you go please." (Damn!)

"Thanks, and well…um…see you…uh…next week then. Yeah," he mumbled as he shuffled backwards and out of her office. Such clumsy words of hesitation always seemed to trip off his tongue into a deep pool of inadequacy whenever he was around Constance, and he mentally kicked himself for once again losing confidence and being so inarticulate. To make matters worse, outside her door he stood on his untied shoelace with the other foot and tripped over. Blushing with embarrassment, he tied the lace and then stood up, avoiding turning back to see if she had noticed his ungainly *faux pas*.

Returning to his desk, he pondered for a moment before deciding to email Constance the half-typed-up report she had asked for. He composed a short email (avoiding the letters 'p' and 'k', which seemed to be on strike after their soaking) and sent it off. With any luck she wouldn't have time to look at it before he returned, when he could finish typing it up, delete his first email (one benefit in having access to his boss's inbox) and send it to her again. He hoped.

At the train station, noticing that he had twenty minutes before his train departed, Simon browsed in the shops. Usually when he went back to his parents' he made the token gesture of taking a present for them and something small for Sabrina, but this time it felt inappropriate. What could he take her – folic acid, vitamins, a copy of *Pregnancy and You* magazine? He didn't recall ever being acquainted with a pregnant woman, let alone a girl close to him who was pregnant. He retreated to the platform instead, and waiting patiently for the train.

His father picked him up from the station, looking haggard and older than Simon remembered. He was wearing a new pair of glasses that made the skin behind the tinted lenses look jaundiced in comparison to the rest. Sitting in the car was uncomfortable; the jerky train had caused him to spill coffee on the crotch of his grey suit and the wet patch was unpleasant. The daylight was receding as fast as Sabrina's youth, and a light drizzle graced the windscreen.

"Your mother's in a right state. I don't know what we're going to do," was the only thing his father said during the fifteen-minute drive, and Simon too sat in quiet contemplation of the predicament that would no doubt divide, but then hopefully pull together, their small family.

It was Sabrina who opened the front door when they arrived. Simon found it hard to match his parents' announcement to the younger sister in front of him, vaguely convinced that they must have been referring to someone else.

"Hi," she said with a smile, her eyes a little red from crying (so she *had* been upset, or had they upset her?)

"Hi," he replied benevolently, glazing his one word with a protective tone. He was relieved to see her, to see that she was ok, and he knew immediately that nothing terribly *bad* had happened to her, despite their parents' despair.

As he followed her into the house of their childhood it struck him that she had become an independent entity. She was no longer just his little sister, a schoolgirl, a sibling. Instead she was a young adult, a person of complex thoughts and feelings, of actions and consequences. And although he wanted to protect and understand her, at the same time he felt that in stepping into his adult world, she had become somehow alien to him. She had shattered the image he'd had of her; not by challenging his parents, having a boyfriend or even having sexual intercourse, but by transforming her life in a way he would never have expected of her. He had gained respect for her in inverse proportion to that which their parents had lost the moment they had heard her news.

As he entered the living room, his mother jumped up from the chair in the corner, an atom of scrunched-up tissues cascading from her lap splitting as it hit the floor.

"Oh Simon!" she exclaimed, hugging him tightly and burying her face in his chest. "Thank goodness you've come."

"It's ok, Mum," he soothed, simultaneously shuffling himself and her towards the three-piece suite. "Everything's going to be ok." He hated to see her in this state, vulnerable and troubled. In the natural parent-child way of things, he was used to coming home to satisfy his own needs: to be fed, nurtured, cared for and fussed over, not the other way around.

"I'll make some tea," said his father, who had appeared in the doorway. Sabrina flinched, ever so slightly, at the sound of her father's voice. Simon sensed that, having shouted his piece, now he was attempting to extricate himself from the problem, leaving the females to battle it out. He wished he could do the same.

"I don't know what to do Simon," sobbed his mother. "She said she wants to keep it!"

"I am in the room you know! And I am keeping the baby," affirmed Sabrina, who was seated opposite them, her eyes fixed on Simon. "I'm not going to change my mind." It was clear that both his mother and sister were looking for an ally, and he wasn't yet sure which side he could safely fall on.

"I knew we should have sent her to a girls' school! I told your father it was a mistake to deny her a proper education for a few extra material pleasures. And now look what's happened! Pregnant! At fifteen!"

"Well, you did always say she was baby-faced," Simon muttered, regretting the words as soon as they had slipped out. His mother looked over at him in horror, choking at his bad humour. Sabrina looked away and giggled slightly, and something in Simon felt pleased that he could still make her laugh. After a long pause, Simon resumed the painful inventory of circumstances.

"How…er…how pregnant are you? I mean…how long…?" he asked, embarrassed by the vague allusion to feminine matters.

"Not sure exactly. About ten weeks I think."

"Oh!" cried their mother, outraged all the more by her lack of precision.

"And…er, this boy wonder – Johnny is it? What does he think about it?"

"Well, neither of us planned it. But now that it's happened, he thinks the same as I do. *We* want to keep it."

Their mother burst into animation. "Oh, and how do you plan to do that, eh? Get a job will he? With no qualifications, a dead-end minimum wage job for the rest of his life? And you're going to look after the baby full-time, are you? Because I tell you what will happen – you'll be bored after five minutes and your father and I will end up looking after it."

As if on cue at her mention of him, their father entered with three mugs of tea on a tray and handed them round.

"I've put some brandy in the tea," he informed them. "Except…um…this one of course," he clarified, handing the last mug over to his daughter and ending the momentary respite they'd had from the issue at hand.

"Thanks Dad," said Simon, giving him a conciliatory smile

even though the conflict resided elsewhere. A stony silence then seeped through the room as they all sipped their tea.

In this subsequent quiet, Simon had a bizarre recollection. He remembered one evening – must have been about five years ago (yes, the summer before he went to university) – when his parents had gone out for dinner, leaving him to look after his sister. He had allowed her to stay up later than usual, and they had been watching something on TV, a comedy or sitcom that he couldn't now recall. Still, the language had been more adult than Sabrina was used to and he remembered how she'd turned to him and asked, "What's a 'con-dom'?"

He recalled how his face flushed and his limbs had wanted to curl up with awkwardness – an extreme reaction to an innocent question. Sabrina had always been quick-witted and ahead of the game, even as a child. He'd never quite been able to label her his 'annoying little sister'; she'd always had a sense of her own purpose.

"Nothing you need to know about," he'd answered, hoping to put an end to the matter. Of course, this just incited her curiosity.

"Is it rude?" she'd persevered, a glint in her eye.

"Yes! No, well not exactly. Look, just ask Mum or Dad, will you?"

"Why can't *you* tell me?"

"It's one of those 'can of worms' things."

"What does that mean?"

"It just means that it's not a simple explanation, ok? Now stop bothering me and get to bed."

Of course she hadn't asked their parents, but the next day she told Simon she'd looked it up in the dictionary and she knew "it was rude!" From time-to-time, she'd taunt him by singing, "Simon's got a condom, Simon's got a condom" just out of earshot of one of their parents, and her nonsense was enough to turn his face the colour of ripe cherries.

Now he sat opposite this same girl – the one who'd always wanted to be the first to know everything and do everything–

and he wished he'd been around to give her more advice when she needed it. As much as he'd wished she could remain his innocent sister forever, he guessed that her misguided curiosity had led her to make a huge mistake. He thought of all the things he'd done in the past eight years – things his sister would now never experience – and he felt a deep sense of disappointment on her behalf. And his parents: could their pride ever come to terms with having their first grandchild this way? He felt vaguely angry with Sabrina for being so foolish – she was fifteen now, not ten, the way he was remembering her – yet there was no air of regret about her. She looked almost...content.

They were still bound in collective silence, marred only by his mother's sniffling, when the old-fashioned clang-clang of the doorbell rang out. His mum jumped up, asking the predictable and pointless "who could that be?" before adjusting her skirt and sweeping down her frazzled hair. As Simon stood up, she noticed his trousers for the first time, and the pale brown stain on his crotch.

"Simon, what happened to your...?" The others followed her gaze until all eyes were on Simon, and he brushed at his trousers awkwardly, stating merely "coffee" by way of explanation. Their distraction was short-lived as the doorbell clanged once more. His mother grabbed her tissues from the floor before rushing off to the downstairs bathroom. Not so despairing she can't still find time for propriety, Simon thought to himself. It was almost eight o'clock and solidly dark – an unusual time for visitors in a neighbourhood that largely kept to itself after dusk.

Sabrina remained seated, one hand caressing her abdomen, as if the doorbell was a figment of their imagination. His father, on the other hand, was trying in vain to look out of the window to see who was there without moving the curtain more than a centimetre.

"Looks like...looks like...hmmm...I'm not sure..." he was saying, just as the clang-clang resounded a third time.

"I'll get it," Simon conceded, rising hurriedly. He walked down the hallway towards the front door, just as his mother emerged from the bathroom and stood anxiously behind him. She tried to peer around his shoulder impatiently as he turned then tugged the handle, and he had to ask her to step back in order to open the door. As the small kafuffle subsided, they found standing before them one man and a boy, blinking expectantly.

"Hi," said the man hopefully, "I'm Daniel Miller, and this is my uh…son, Johnny. I think we need to talk?"

Simon and his mother stepped back wordlessly, making room for these two people – who were now intrinsically linked to them – to enter their family home. As they did so, Simon stepped on his mother's foot, and she cried out at the injustice of being hurt by both her children in one day.

Chapter 22

"Thanks," says Ian as he struggles to keep the change in his right hand, which is also clutching an icy pint glass. He glares at both his hands, willing them to hold onto their contents. The barman watches as a 20p coin and then a five-pence piece slip out of Ian's palm and drop with a 'ting!' onto the floor. Ian reluctantly reverses the two paces he's taken and sets both pints down on the counter before bending with a groan and retrieving the money. He drops it into his pocket, picks up the pint glasses and continues as before, this time succeeding in his foray to the garden outside, where his oldest friend awaits.

"Here you go," he says, inappropriately jovial, as he sets the drinks down on the wooden table. "It's that extra-chilled stuff, or whatever they call it these days. Haven't tried it before myself."

"Thanks," Connor replies, raising his glass and taking a big gulp. "Aah" he gushes in appreciation, a cloud of breath seeping from his lips. The air is crisp and fresh, cold just the way the men like it. They have spent many such days supping outside in this manner, the friendly banter keeping them warm. For a while there is silence as the two of them survey the scene. They are the only ones seated outside, their privacy locked into the vast expanse. In the distance, they can hear the gleeful cries and shouts of a primary school break time, and each thinks of his own children. Then Ian speaks, "So, why are we here? You said you had to talk to me."

"I do…I…by the way, Lauren said she didn't change the time

and place. I don't know why Elisabeth said-"

"Oh, I don't know either; it doesn't matter. She's not easily confused, which is why I presumed it must have been Lauren-"

"Well, she hasn't been with me long, that's true, but I haven't had any problems with her before so-"

"Well, never mind, eh? We're here now. What's going on?"
Silence falls once more like a cloud of dust, too fine to catch. Ian can only wait as the two men look at each other's chins.

"It's a bit of a delicate matter, I'm afraid," Connor concedes diplomatically. Even though both men knew this was coming, still they feel nervous, unaccustomed to the arduous art of emotions. Usually, they talk business, staff, profits, legislation, transport, pensions, sport, certification and technology. They rarely speak of family, holidays, illness, children, leisure, spouses, shopping, music, nature, or art. They never talk of love, aches, pains and needs; that is, until now.

"It's about Amelia," Connor blurts out, each word he speaks relieving him of some unspeakable burden.

"Really?" answers Ian, his eyebrows raised. He is genuinely surprised; in his mind they are here to talk about Connor, not him. Perhaps we still are, he thinks – maybe Connor and Amelia are connected...

Connor is Ian's oldest and greatest friend. They met in secondary school approximately 25 years ago and went on to the same university and training college, finally splitting to work at rival law firms. Each has been through a lot, over the years, and each knows the other's tribulations. Aside from his family, Connor is the only person Ian would drop everything for and the feeling, he knows, is mutual. A betrayal of any kind is unthinkable. Looking at Connor now, Ian fears the worst without fully comprehending what the worst could be.

"She hasn't been..." and here Connor looks away, as if a passing bird in flight has caught his eye, "faithful to you," he concludes. When he looks back at Ian, he sees both fear and recognition rippling across his face. He glances at Ian's Adam's apple, an easier place to rest his eyes, and notices his friend swallow twice before he speaks. The words prop Connor's eyes open like splints and drag his gaze back upwards.

"Are you and Amelia having an affair?" Ian asks, trying desperately to control his voice. There, that's it. Out in the open, laid bare, cards on the table. The response is a relief.

"Nooo! Oh gosh, no, not at all, not me, no! Nothing to do with it! No!" Connor grins to reinstate solidarity, and for a moment Ian smiles before both of them realise the initial problem remains.

"Well, how do you know then?"

"I don't. Well, not directly. So whatever I say, you should talk to Amelia about it, you know, in case we've misinterpreted anything."

"We?"

"Yes, Marta and I. Amelia mentioned something to Marta about another man. It was a couple of weeks ago when they were speaking on the phone – Marta said Amelia was really chirpy and she asked why, and Amelia said something about a man doing wonders for her. When Marta pressed her she wouldn't give any further details, but Marta is pretty sure she wasn't referring to you. I'm...I'm sorry."

"Well, wait; that doesn't mean she's having an affair, does it? No disrespect to the two of you, but I can't really accuse my wife of being unfaithful based on something Marta thinks she detected, which she passed on to you and you then pass on to me." Ian's voice is raised now, his hands tugging at his hair. A sporadic breeze whips him across the face, willing him to wake-up to the underlying facts.

"The thing is mate," Connor says sharply, "this isn't the first time."

"First time for what?" Ian quips naively, looking down at his near-empty glass wistfully. It's hardly an appropriate time to point out that it's Connor's round.

"First time she's had an affair."

"What?"

"It's not the first time."

"Yes, I heard that. I meant, what do you mean? I mean, how

do you know? How is it…what the-" his words twist around each other in a muddled plait.

"I don't know how to say this, mate. I've been dreading it frankly. It's just, when Marta told me about that conversation, I knew I couldn't keep it from you anymore, even if you'd end up hating me. Marta and I talked it over and we both agreed. The thing is, mate, you have to remember, we thought we were doing the best thing, not telling you, but now things have changed." To Ian's distress, Connor drops his head into his hands and seems to sob. His springy hair nudges his glass, causing it to move a little towards Ian.

"I don't understand," confesses Ian, "what exactly *are* you saying?" He is relieved when Connor's head lifts and there are no tears. He has only ever seen Connor cry once, holding his newborn son at the hospital while waiting to hear if a haemorrhaging Marta was going to pull through. Ian does not want to be reminded of that now, and shoves the thought from his head.

"Amelia's had an affair before, mate. And that one we definitely know about. Seven or eight years ago?" Connor forms the last few words into a question, hoping in vain that he can jog Ian's mind into remembering something he has no memory of. If Ian can fill in the details for himself, Connor will be spared the job.

"Seven years ago? What are you talking about? It's all sounding very far-fetched."

"It's not, look, I promise. Seven or eight years ago Amelia was having an affair. Marta knew about it, but Amelia said she'd ended it and begged her not to tell anyone. Marta told me a few weeks after she found out, and neither of us knew what to do. But we kept our eye on Amelia and it really did seem like the affair was over. Then, of course, the kids came along and it all seemed in the past. I almost forgot about it, and then two weeks ago, when Marta mentioned this conversation, I-"

"You mean you've known for years that Amelia had an affair and you never told me? You've looked me in the eye all this time and known about it?" Ian is shouting now, his face leaning towards Connor's and his hands placed flat on the peeling table, palms downwards.

"I'm sorry, I know, I should have told you. I just – I didn't know whether to interfere, and Amelia begged Marta, who begged me, not to say anything and so I didn't."

"So that's what it comes down to, eh?" Ian says unpleasantly. "At the end of the day you'd rather obey your wife than be honest with your oldest friend. Now it makes sense."

"It's not like that and you know it. Look, don't take it out on me; you should have realised a long time ago that your marriage was a shambles!" Connor's cry rings out and flits through the air, searching for keen ears.

And that's when it happens. As if Connor's voice has upset its delicate balance, the great outdoors responds with fury. They both hear a sharp 'smash' and Ian is looking down at Connor's pint glass, which has shattered spontaneously in front of them. He looks upwards, seeing nothing but sky and no explanation. The glass lies in pieces on the table, and as Ian looks he glimpses one large shard rocking from side-to-side before it is still. He reaches for it in wonderment, his fingers carefully avoiding the edges and holding it in the middle. He vaguely hears a car speeding off, somewhere in the pub car park. Still fascinated, he raises the shard to face-level, his brow creased, and proffers it to Connor, raising his head to look at his friend. All this happens within five seconds, though Ian will later play it back, slower, in detail.

Connor too is staring at the glass, but his eyes are not focused. One hand is placed feebly across his chest, like a nonchalant American pledging allegiance, and his mouth is hanging open, his tongue protruding crudely. He struggles to speak. "Luke…Luke…Luke…he's…" he is repeating, choking on his words.

"Connor? What is it-?" Ian manages before his friend's hand falls away and his body slumps forward. Ian's own hand shoots out and shields Connor's head before it falls into the broken glass. Still supporting Connor, Ian swivels round the side of the table and then, standing behind him, pulls his friend back up, all the while shouting "Connor! Connor!"

Once he is up-sitting again, Ian sees that the table is now jewelled with blood-red shards, glittering in the winter sun. He looks at Connor, whose face is drained and pale, eyes blinded with shock, and sees the neat red trail that starts at his chest and is flowing, gently, to his navel. It is mirrored by the blood that trickles from his mouth and down his chin. Ian stops shouting and turns him around and over, lying him flat on his back on the narrow bench. He tears himself out of his jacket and uses it to press down hard with one hand on Connor's chest. The other hand is feeling for his phone, which he uses to call an ambulance.

By the time it arrives, Connor has slipped away, his vacant eyes still staring at Ian but no longer holding any sign of the deception he had been trying to confess.

Ian's second thought, after Connor's body has been taken away and the police have taken a statement, is of the children. A police car gives him a lift home, and during the silent, twenty-minute journey his frantic mind goes over and over what he should do. A young policeman is driving, every so often glancing at Ian's face in the rear-view mirror, searching for signs of guilt or distress. Ian is aware that, at this time, the conversation, the shattered pint glass, the shot and the car driving off could all be viewed as figments of his own imagination. Connor's body is the only tangible evidence to those that doubt, suspect and question him.

He is not afraid of this suspicion, but indulges in it. Because he knows he is innocent he can cast aside others' doubts and think of his children, whom he is desperate to be with. The school day is not yet over, but it occurs to Ian that he cannot collect them in a police car. And he has had a drink so instead of attempting to get in his car – which is what he'd really like to do – he asks the policeman to drop him at a taxi rank. The taxi meanders first to Luke's school, then to Lydia's, before returning home with three confused passengers bundled into the back.

Ian's state of shock is broken not by sadness, not by the

realisation of the death of his closest friend, but by the relief that swamps him when they arrive home and Amelia is not there. Adrenaline pumping, he gives the children a poor premise – that they are to accompany him on a trip while their mother visits an old aunt they've never heard of – and helps them pack their things hurriedly, like a spider rushing to build its web before the storm breaks. It would ordinarily be a whole hour before Amelia picked the children up; he does not allow himself to think about where she might be. In case she worries, he leaves a note that simply says, 'I have the children. We'll be at the Burleigh. Ian.' He leaves it in between their pillows, on their bed, because he wants his final message to her to be in an intimate place.

He packs the children and their belongings into the car, and orders a taxi with two drivers. "I'll pay double," he insists, "just send two drivers." When they arrive, he hands the keys of his car to one of them and orders him to drive his green estate to the nearby Burleigh Hotel. The other is instructed to follow. When they arrive, the car is parked, the children and the luggage taken out, and the drivers paid handsomely.

Standing in front of the Reception desk, Ian grasps each child with his cold, clammy hands and checks them into a double room.

He agonises over the note. Should he have left it? Would she try and take the children? Would she call the police? When would she phone? For three days he parks the children in front of the television, allowing them to order room service and exit the hotel for just a couple of hours a day. They become lethargic and irritable. The school is informed there is a family emergency; the police told that Ian can be reached at the hotel. Still, no one calls and no one comes.

Three days later, he drives back to the house with the children. He leaves them locked-up in the car, smearing the windows with their noses as they peer out after him. Inside the house Ian grabs a few more things and looks around. The family home feels empty, stripped of a future it once counted on. Upstairs, Ian sees that, despite his endless agonising, Amelia hasn't even seen the note. He screws it up and puts it in his pocket.

Chapter 23

It was more embarrassing than he'd imagined, at first, but he was initially consoled by the fact that he thought the world at large found it embarrassing too. But everywhere he looked there were posters using *it* as a marketing tool and people passing them by blankly; beautiful people leading exciting, sensuous lives in television adverts that weren't often watched; racy scenes in television programmes trying to cram as much as possible in before and after the watershed, causing his father to change the channel quickly or leave the room; people in general dressing and talking and acting like *it* was all they thought about. Adults talked about *it* in hushed whispers when they thought he wasn't listening; his fellow pupils discussed *it* all the time without knowing the full facts; *it* was in magazines and newspapers, catalogues and journals, books, films and documentaries; *it* was in the supermarket when he accidentally wandered down the 'family planning aisle' (anti-family planning more like, he later thought); *it* was in the news when a teacher who'd had 'relations with one of her pupils' was arrested, and *it* was even at the zoo when they'd gone on a school trip and discovered – to the horror of their teacher – that it was mating season in the lions' enclosure.

He also had to witness his father and his new 'friend', Amelia, kissing, cuddling and giggling like teenagers. Except Johnny was a teenager and he didn't act like that; mostly, around girls, he was just nervous. He was fed-up with adults assuming children his age didn't do *it*, peers asking him if he had done *it*, and Sabrina, his supposed girlfriend (whatever that meant), assuming they were going to do *it*, just like that. The main problem Johnny had was not that he didn't want to have sex, but that he couldn't get away from *it*.

The day after they'd almost done it and he'd backed away, Sabrina had refused to look him in the eyes. Both of them had been red-cheeked, evasive and sheepish, but Johnny knew it was up to him to set things right. He hadn't wanted to make her feel bad, it had just been…too much, suddenly. They'd almost been working towards an unspoken goal – to have sex – and Johnny's greatest fear was what would happen afterwards? Would they keep having sex? Or would that be it, and they'd go back to just being friends. It'd felt like having sex was the be-all-and-end-all, and he didn't want it to be so.

After many apologies, expressions of regret, promises, reassurances and gestures from him, Sabrina had agreed once again to be his girlfriend. Johnny realised she had been deeply hurt by his rejection and concluded that her reaction must mean she wanted more from him than that one experience. And once he was sure of this – that the experience itself would not fundamentally change their attitude to each other – he suggested that they try again. He even made a swift visit to the chemist on the way home from school, while Sabrina loitered outside. (Go in, locate the condoms, grab a pack, get to the counter, try not to blush, pay for them, grab the pack, make a hasty retreat.) All this was accomplished before he realised he'd purchased an unknown-brand extra-thin type but he reassured Sabrina that they'd be fine. This purchase was intended as a sign of his maturity and commitment to 'doing it'.

The first time they successfully consummated, it had been awkward and over fairly quickly. Still, both had been satisfied at the completion of the act, and both had felt closer, somehow, to the other. It can only get better, they told themselves, this can't be exactly how it's *meant* to be. Johnny felt inwardly content, whereas Sabrina felt better on the outside – the confidence she had gained as a result of her experience made her feel at once taller, more attractive, mature and poised, ready to progress in life. Johnny had looked at himself in the mirror, convinced somehow that he would grow more stubble, his voice would deepen, and – now that he was no longer a virgin – his boyish looks would fade away, revealing more manly features. He went so far as to imagine himself in five years' time, a good-looking man, a real 'catch'. He admired Sabrina all the more for taking them forward, for having courage where he had been afraid.

Over the next month or so, aside from homework and school, they made it their main task. Johnny wanted it to improve, Sabrina wanted to learn, and neither of them had any desire to discuss it with anyone else. When the subject came up at school, each of them would prick their ears up, hoping in vain to glean tips from friends in the same situation. If challenged about their activities, Sabrina would smile coyly and say she didn't want to discuss anything, while Johnny would blush, change the subject and attempt to ignore the ribbing that ensued. And often, on days when he knew his father would be back late, Johnny would invite Sabrina home after school.

It was a few weeks later that Sabrina called Johnny aside one lunchtime and told him she was 'late'.

"Late for what?" he asked innocently, wondering why she was being furtive.

"No, not late for anything! *Late*, you know."

"I don't get it."

"I didn't get my period!"

"Ooooooh," Johnny said, blushing immediately, and nodding his head like an all-knowing doctor. "So…um…are you ok?"

"Ok? Of course I'm not ok!"

"Oh…er…right. Can I do anything?" Johnny offered. Sabrina stared angrily back at him.

"You've done enough, don't you think?" She chewed her lip and looked at him imploringly. "What do you think we should do?"

"Um…well…perhaps we should just…wait?" He didn't really understand her predicament, and couldn't understand why she would want his opinion on such matters.

"Yeah, maybe you're right. It's only been a few days; it's just…well, usually I'm on time."

"Ok." He looked about them, awkwardly, willing the conversation to be over.

"Thanks," she said, hugging him. "I have to go – see you later?"

"Yeah, later," he said with a smile, and watched as she turned and jogged off towards the arts block.

Girls' bodies, in any biological sense, were a mystery to Johnny. Even when his mother was ill, he couldn't contemplate the inner workings of the lung cancer that spread around her chest, her breasts, her stomach, her womb – terms for body parts that were bandied about, clinically. Sabrina's body was like a minefield – at an age when he was barely used to his own growing physique, it was strange to him to touch, caress, hold and feel someone else's, especially in a form so alien to his own. He often prodded, pinched and poked the wrong bits of her, limbs flailing irresponsibly, extremities squashed. And as for menstrual cycles, he hadn't a clue. They'd covered the basics in sex education but Johnny, like the other boys in the class, had switched off when it came to any mention of tubes, eggs, cycles or cavities. He knew that girls got their period every month, that it involved bleeding, that it gave them cramps, that sometimes before they got them it could cause them to be moody, and that when they were pregnant they didn't have-

Oh no, he suddenly thought. That's what she meant! But…no, she couldn't be. Does she think she's-?

At the end of the school day, Johnny rushed home and pulled one of the old medical journals off the shelf in the living room. It was an ageing bible of ailments, diseases, symptoms, treatments and alarming diagrams that had fascinated Johnny as a boy. He turned the book over and headed straight for the index, noting that 'menstruation' was on pages 74, 75, 83 and on 85 in bold. He flicked straight to 85. After a bit of searching, and more information on menstrual cycles than he would ever have thought necessary, he found the section on 'Amenorrhoea' and with relief discovered a lengthy list of possible causes. To his consternation, however, this relief was short-lived. Drastic weight reduction, extreme obesity, eating disorders, over-exercising, various syndromes, cysts, anxiety, depression, endocrine problems, hormonal imbalance, stress, menopause – as far as he knew, none of these applied to Sabrina. There were only two other plausible reasons: her youth (the book said young girls often experienced an irregular cycle) or that she may have miscounted. Except Sabrina herself had said she was almost always on time, and surely her apparent concern would have led her to double-check her due date.

'Due date'. It would mean a different thing to them now. Where previously it referred to coursework, library books, dental check-ups and telephone bills, it was now linked only to one thing – a baby. He'd refused to go into the chemist when Sabrina bought a pregnancy test; it was something intimately female and he was too embarrassed. Ever since his mother had passed away, he'd been unaccustomed to daily female presence – the scents, cosmetics, hygiene, complications and *specifics* of everyday female life.

Sabrina had insisted on doing the test at her own house, needing some sort of comfort from her own environment, he supposed. It was the first time he'd been to her home, and fortunately her parents had gone out to dinner and the theatre. As she took the test and the two of them awaited their future, Johnny wandered around the corridor, studying paintings and photographs, attempting to gauge as much as he could about Sabrina's parents in case he had to face them with the news. And when the test was positive, he'd put his arm around her and squeezed her tightly as she cried, tears cradling her eyeballs like protective frogspawn. They sat, in silence, for as long as necessary, because to speak would have made it real.

Chapter 24

It was about guilt, among other things: fury, passion, escape, denial. And about lying to yourself that things weren't really the way they were or, worse, the way you had made them.

Closing her eyes intermittently as she walked down the street, Amelia headed towards the location of her first rendezvous with J. It was the back of the small café, a terrace raised on a slight plateau and surrounded with thin glass doors that rattled as the wind blew. They used to huddle in the back of the frequently empty café, relishing the change of scenery from his flat and allowing the warmth of their laughter to melt away the visible breath that carried each word.

Now, taking those familiar steps into the past, Amelia felt the sunlight on her fluttering eyelids and tried to distract herself from the inexplicable nervousness that drilled into her bones. She turned a couple of corners, barely conscious of the odd pedestrian who twisted past her, and then she was there, standing by the side of a crime scene of Biblical proportions.

She pushed open the door and immediately glanced around at the waiters, a sense of relief washing over her as she recognised not a single one. 'Why would I?' she scolded herself, 'it's been so long'. She smiled wanly at one of them as she made her way to the back and entered the terrace, thoughts of which had plagued her for the many years since she had last visited. The furniture had changed, the flooring was discoloured and the tacky hanging lights had been replaced with delicate fairy lights that graced the walls and ceiling in parody of an actor's dressing room. She grabbed a table in a corner and soaked in the familiar view of the city, overlooking office blocks and cramped housing, unkempt streets for unkempt souls.

A boyish waiter soon appeared and took her order for a coffee. When he brought it to her she wanted to grab his hand and ask him to stay, to talk to her, to listen, to laugh as you were meant to when seated here. She felt like the place had died, in her absence, as if it had been frozen from the moment she left it until the moment she returned, destined to breathe life back into it with her memories. But the waiter left her, and she was once again alone.

She sipped her coffee, and the familiar taste settled with all the other memories, creating a gritty sediment that provoked in her the most intense nostalgic sickness. She wanted to scream and cry, to run and not return, to stay, to laugh, to sing, to slam her fist on the table and reveal her thoughts to anyone that would listen. Never had a place itself – in spite of its ordinariness, drabness and mediocrity – invoked such spirit in her.

J's flat had been a couple of streets away, but she would never go back there, not even to look at the outside. This was neutral territory, where they had been equal; it belonged to neither of them and had only existed in their collusion. She had loved it for that. The two of them sat here for many hours, J's arm around her, discussing ideas, fantasising, bickering, teasing, dreaming, and stoking the lie. Sometimes, they would stare out through the glass doors in silence, a mutual vision of the unjust world going by. They participated involuntarily, adding all the while to the way of life they themselves detested, stroking their egos and embittering their hearts. They poisoned themselves, slowly, in this café, and before they knew it the café was intrinsic to their affair.

There was another reason for Amelia's return. There was an appeal to the café that she had never mentioned to J; something she had kept entirely to, and for, herself. From a vantage point at the back, when she was with him, Amelia could see across the city all the way to the statue under which Ian had proposed to her. Under that statue she had looked down at him on one knee with shock and delight; under it she had reached out and grabbed hold of the life he was offering her and closed her hand willingly around it; under it she had allowed him to slip the beautiful ring along her fourth finger, sealing her choice.

All the while she was with J in this place, throughout minutes that spun by like a whirling dervish, mounting eventually into dreadful significance, she had Ian in the back of her mind. She had glanced over now and then, unbeknownst to J, to the site of the biggest declaration of love she had ever experienced, and between the two of them – Ian and J – they filled a void in her mind.

Why is it, she thought to herself now, that she could never have been happy on her own? She thought back to an ex-colleague of hers from years ago, a girl called Cassie who had been perpetually single and full of the joys of life.

"I don't need a man to complete me!" Cassie had declared one day, in *oratio flagrante*. Her verbal enthusiasm, and indeed her volume, always reflected her general zest. "I'm perfectly capable of going out and doing everything I want to do in life on my own – I know a man would just hold me back. I feel sorry for these women who never get to do what they really want to because they're picking up after a man, doing his dirty work, having babies, giving up jobs, settling down, and all far too early because they feel they've got no other option. I just can't see the appeal."

Amelia would stay quiet whenever Cassie started on one of her diatribes. She had a manner of talking that left no room for disagreement, let alone discussion. And ultimately, at least as far as anyone else could tell, Cassie was extremely happy. She enjoyed her job, worked hard, had an aggressively full social life and plenty of stories to tell – the kind of life that seems appealing, Amelia always thought, until you dig further down and uncover the insecurities, the doubts, the low self-esteem.

Amelia had more in common with Cassie than Cassie would ever have acknowledged. She too resented the idea of conforming to a man's idea of domestic bliss; she too wanted to have it all without sacrificing herself; she too wanted to throw caution to the wind by embracing opportunities and cleansing her life of regrets. But Amelia – who appeared to be the traditional, cautious, conservative one – took the biggest risk of all by embracing the elements that women like Cassie spend so long trying to shirk, and welcomed them into her life like a beautiful bouquet whose flowers could start fading at any moment. Instead of avoiding their collective fears, she challenged them. And like a cult member whose strong faith can withstand anything but exposure to non-believers, the minute Amelia announced her engagement, Cassie ceased to be in contact, unwilling to pollute her beliefs by association. Amelia last heard that Cassie resigned from her job to go travelling in South-East Asia, and she never heard of her again.

Amelia herself – to those who previously labelled her a friend – had all but disappeared into the black hole of setting-up a family. Her friendships had deconstructed themselves in inverse proportion to the establishment of the family scene: first leaving her independent job to assist Ian, then the purchase of their large house outside London, then kissing her working life goodbye altogether, and then her first pregnancy. Finally, the demise of old friendships was sealed with her second pregnancy and buried in the cherished womb of fond memories. Old friends stopped calling, stopped arranging meetings, stopped coming to visit and – this was the definitive sign – even stopped leaving empty messages saying 'we must meet soon…' She, in turn, let them slip away and instead focused her attentions on a new world of gratification that had opened up before her.

There is something both disconcerting and refreshing about being with someone devoid of your past. Someone with whom you share no history, no memories, no previous embarrassments, disappointments and drama. No shared bitterness, sadness or regret. Someone with whom you can be whoever you want to be, and to whom you can slowly divulge yourself, unravelling bit-by-bit, editing out the pieces you wish to bury. It is disconcerting because they know nothing of you, understand nothing of you, yet refreshing because the anticipation of who you might be, who they might be, incites a chemical charge.

First, there had been Ian: he respected her immediately, valued her, adored her, deemed her worthy of being the mother of his children, and dedicated his life to her. She felt charged, empowered and strong, destined for great things simply because he thought her capable of them. Then, when that feeling lost its shine, she determined to climb out of her pit of passivity and had J: he had excited her like never before, tempted her, dragged her into his world, and spat her out thrillingly, full of life in more ways than one. And finally, Daniel had stepped gently into her world: he appreciated her, coaxed her, indulged her and had shown her that there is always room for change, always a chance to make things right – or wrong. Unlike the other two, she had no ties to him, no obligations, and no false expectations. For the first time she felt in true control of herself, though this turned out to be her misfortune.

Previously asunder in their lives, Daniel and Amelia found that the court case became ingrained in the vaults of history and bound them inextricably together in common assault. Attracted to the tale like a moth to the light, the media took the events surrounding the lovers and spun them, kneaded them, embellished them and lengthened them. The public, in faithful duty to their daily fix of scandal, devoured the broadsheets and tabloids, hungry for every real and concocted detail, each article they read abating the fear of missing out on some detail. The legal snowball thrown at the couple rolled down the media slope and continued into the public flurry until it was too big for them to surmount. Their saving grace was that no journalist managed to get a decent photograph of either of them, and they remained, stubbornly, holed up in a rented apartment.

According to the media, their intent was wholly malicious, they were two hedonists that did not care for anyone else's feelings, Amelia had never truly loved her children (accusations of lasting post-partum depression were flung around like muck), Ian's career was in ruins, Amelia had suspected Ian of having an affair with Marta...and so on. The judgemental frenzy escalated even further when one tabloid suggested Daniel may have killed his own wife ("How on earth could I have inflicted cancer upon someone?" Daniel shouted angrily at the time) and furthermore with the inevitable revelation that Daniel's 'out-of-control' son was to be a father himself at the tender age of fifteen. The press ripped them apart and refused to spit them out.

In this way, surprisingly, it was not the events themselves, but the aftermath that destroyed their relationship. Attempted murder once removed was not as real to them as the consequences; if all had gone to plan they would have felt guilt, yes, but fleeting, intangible guilt that would not have impressed upon their future together. It was the public lashing, the moral 'outing', the unsympathetic scrutiny they faced afterwards that soon became to them more unfair than anything they had done. And this twisted logic bound them endlessly to their misguided choices. Amelia silently cursed Daniel whenever the media seized upon his skeletons, and he did the same to her, unable to vent their frustrations on anyone other than their companion in misdeeds. Was Amelia more to blame – it was her idea, her husband, her friend, her lover – or was it Daniel, without whom she would never have taken things so far? Try as they might, neither one could distance themselves enough to claim compliance under duress, and they soon realised that blaming the other was akin to accusing themselves.

The case was referred to the Crown Court, and there it stayed, despite its meandering twists and turns. Ian had initially pressed charges and then retracted them, to the horror of the police. That was due to the media too – in their ruthlessness, they had hounded even the victim into silence. Ian had retracted his charges on the basis that it would be better for the children if he wasn't involved with legal proceedings and that, after all, Amelia was still their mother. He left it to the police to continue the case and, despite the media's declaration that he wasn't pressing charges due to his continued love for Amelia, Ian eventually frustrated their licentious thirst by tiptoeing backwards out of the limelight. And that was enough for him – it allowed him to put the house on the market, find a new, undisclosed abode to take the children to, and to keep things ticking over at the legal practice in his hour of need, more than ever, to work.

J – or Jeremiah Bodley as he was officially known – was arrested, somehow. Amelia and Daniel were being questioned separately at the time and were not given the details. They were eventually bailed, after handing over their passports, and used their savings to rent a flat not too far from Daniel's house. Johnny had already moved in with Sabrina's parents pending the birth of the baby, and Amelia had no idea where her children were – Ian had changed all possible contact details. In desperation, she'd even called Marta once but had been screamed at before the receiver was slammed down. The ensuing dial tone popped up disparagingly in Amelia's dreams for many months afterwards – that, and the penultimate time she'd heard Marta's voice.

The day of the shooting, she'd been out at the supermarket, determined to give herself an alibi even though she played no physical part in the crime. It would have been Daniel's day off, but she'd told him to swap shifts, go to work all day, and keep busy. In the supermarket, where she forced herself to stay for at least two hours, Amelia had an epiphany. She'd been navigating the rows and columns of goods, making sure she selected some of Ian's favourites even though she assumed he would never consume them. Presently, she found herself among the sweets and chocolates, in the aisle that her children loved, on the spot where she first met Daniel, loading her trolley with the bittersweet dark chocolate that her husband liked, and she began to shake. She trembled silently for several minutes, her mind and heart locked in the tumultuous contemplation of what was occurring, right then, elsewhere. She must have blanked out because when she came to a small crowd had gathered and a fountain of dark chocolate had slid off the shelf and scattered in between her other items.

"Are you ok?" a shop assistant asked her hesitantly.

"Sorry, yes…I'll be fine," she replied, not quite meeting anyone's eyes, and turned and left, abandoning the trolley.

Laden with knots of guilt and anxiety, she went straight to collect Luke, having killed enough time. When she got to Luke's school, she was informed that he'd already been collected by his father, and in desperate confusion she rushed to her daughter's, only to be told the same thing. Her mind raced along with the car as she made her way home, fear settling in her stomach like deep snow. She burst through the front door and found…nothing. She called out, began to cry, and then spotted the red light flashing on the answer phone. This was it: the message she'd been waiting for, the one she'd mentally practised listening to in the presence of her children, the one she imaged having to explain to them while holding and comforting them, the one that could make everything right. Except it was wrong: totally wrong, inexplicably wrong, terrifyingly wrong. For she was alone, Daniel felt more intangible than ever, her children were apparently with the father she thought they'd never see again, and the voice on the phone was…was…sobbing.

"Amelia? Amelia! It's me. It's…Marta…Amelia! Connor's dead. Connor's dead. Amelia!" it screamed, before vanishing with a beep.

The wait for the trial lasted longer than the trial itself. In the courtroom, Amelia's faced burned with the *Schadenfreude* of all those who gazed down upon her and silently condemned her to a risk they hadn't dared take. She and Daniel pleaded guilty; Jeremiah, not guilty. The guilt of all three, however, was etched in their mien – their faces, words, deportment, emotions and actions. All three were found guilty, all three were condemned. Jeremiah to a life sentence, and Amelia and Daniel, due to their compliance and Ian dropping the charges, each to a suspended sentence of seven years. The fact that the two of them were technically free, and that Jeremiah would most likely serve just five years was neither here nor there; in the eyes of the media, just desserts had been served with a generous helping of retribution.

Chapter 25

It's a funny thing, getting what you want; you can't quite believe it's real. But it's more than that – it's as if…as if you're not quite sure how you managed it, whether you engineered it or if it was commissioned by a higher being, whether you really deserved it or if it was a kiss of luck. And these doubts…these doubts sometimes convince you that it's not really what you wanted, that what you've got is great, but it would be so much better if…

Sabrina cradled her son and gently sang to him, a nameless pop song she'd heard too often on the radio. Outside, the moon beamed and, seeing that Michael was wide awake, she took him to the window and raised him up humbly for the moon's blessing. "Moon, this is Michael," she whispered. "Michael – the Moon."

And with that she returned to the bed, sitting down gently with her son so as not to wake his sleeping father. Once he'd drifted off to sleep again she placed the child into the cot at the foot of the bed and lay down herself, searching hungrily for a slice of slumber. With any luck they'd all sleep through until the morning, the three rising together as Johnny got ready for school, the two of them kissing him goodbye as he left for the day in his school uniform.

She trusted Johnny and they were united in familiarity and routine, something that she was finding far less dull than she had feared. He was finishing his last year and taking his exams before starting an apprenticeship at the estate agency on the high street. He'd already started working there on Saturdays, and they'd offered him a decent package once he left school, one that would increase steadily with time and the growth of his experience. It would allow Sabrina to go back to school next year, leaving Michael in the care of her parents, who were slowly beginning to dote on him.

She was exhausted, yes, but the hard work of a newborn baby could not dent her satisfaction. It didn't seem real, sometimes, that she had so much – a son, Johnny, a family, the chance to finish her education, and the potential to be whoever she wanted to be. Turning over, she reached back for Johnny's arm and pulled it forward, over her shoulder. She kissed his hand and he mumbled sleepily, raising his head off the pillow. "Shhh," she whispered soothingly, for her newfound motherly instincts extended to him too, "it's alright, go back to…

…where he came from. It felt comforting, despite the feeling of regret that took an unwelcome bite of his homemade pie. He hadn't been able to stay in London any longer; he'd become nervous and wary – the worst state to be in to commit any sort of crime. What's more, having his own wallet stolen made him reflect, for the first time, on his own actions – the invasion of taking other people's property and the control he'd relinquished by allowing himself to fall victim to his own game.

Éric spent days wandering around unsuccessfully, staring at a strange, cold city that he felt was baying for his blood; and so he decided to return to Paris and start again. He called an old family friend whose son worked for the government-housing department and managed to secure himself an apartment within a month.

And then he combed the city; not for lucrative pockets this time, but for building sites, volunteering here and there to help out for the day, making quick cash in a legitimate way. And eventually, one of the construction companies offered him the position of Site Compliance Advisor, a grand title for the lowest job going, but one he cherished with dedication. He was put in charge of certain equipment, uniforms, health and safety, tracking hours worked and breaks taken, and the group began to respect him. It was the first time he'd ever had a real job, and it made him feel accepted and integral to society. He was no longer …

…totally alone as she watched Simon leave her office and close the door behind him. The nausea was coming in waves now and Constance fumbled for her handbag, clutching at random items she thought she might need and dropping them into it. The pain was bearable, but the realisation was not; had her own scepticism, her own initial rejection of the most natural process in the world caused it to backfire, to fight back, to *reject her*? Or was it the hostility she'd felt towards Jason, who had trespassed within her, that seeped into her depths and pushed his likeness out?

Constance rose, slowly, and walked out of her office, across the floor, and through to the main exit. She was in line for a Partnership; the final interview was to take place the following week. She had been about to decline it, her focus gradually shifting away from work and onto impending motherhood but now, as she waited for the taxi she had ordered, her frame of mind called for her to remember all that she still had – her independence, her career, her apartment, her intelligence – instead of focusing on the imminent loss of something she never fully realised she'd had.

'It's not what I really wanted,' she told herself, over and over again. 'It wasn't ever meant to happen.' Yet, as much as she tried to convince herself, once the taxi had arrived to take her to the hospital and Constance was seated resignedly in the back, she grieved for all the things she'd never know she was missing. And as she sobbed wholeheartedly, her empathetic womb wept for want of a…

… child as astute as Luke. Both his children have adapted

Rebecca Strong

quickly to their new situation, but it is Luke in particular who amazes Ian every day. He is intuitive of moods, considerate of others, and absorbs everything around him, his knowledge and enthusiasm spilling over for his sister to drink in. Ian is constantly thankful for them.

He hires a young woman to take care of them during the week, so that he can build-up his business again. She is dark-haired and attractive, kindly and motherly – everything that the children, and Ian, need in their lives. She teaches Ian to cook, Luke to multiply fractions, and Lydia to swim. She becomes everything to the family that Amelia was not: loyal, reliable, predictable and selfless, and Ian struggles on day-by-day, this new, female presence only serving to highlight the gaping hole where Amelia once lay, next to him. Perhaps he could have done more, or less.

These thoughts only plague him at night, when the children are in bed and he is alone with a glass of wine. *Perhaps it could have been different*, but then, try as he might, he can't imagine it so. He stares at the children's photographs on the mantelpiece, his pale, fair-haired daughter and her caramel-skinned, green-eyed brother and he…

…wondered what you do when you don't know who you are. Her past had been consumed and then spat out; she could no longer use it as her hive, like a bee whose queen has died.

For a few days, which turned into a few weeks, Elisabeth moved from place-to-place, subsisting on meagre savings that belonged to someone she used to be (not the someone she *used to* used to be, the person before the last, but her penultimate identity – she had almost lost track). She made her way to London, the 'city of opportunities', and tried to start again. She got a job in a bookshop, surrounded by the vinegary smell of pages never turned, and before long became part of the furniture. It was falsely stimulating, being surrounded by all that culture that she had never experienced. Yet people asked for her advice, her opinion was valued, and her ideas were

222

welcomed. Her days were mediocre, but other people's interests brought her mind to life.

And then, one day, he came into the shop. He was wearing a suit, and caught her attention when he knocked over a large pile of books on the 'special offer' table. She hurried to his rescue and her eyes caught onto his good humour, both of them laughing at his clumsiness. He smelled of cinnamon and old pen ink – the kind she had spilled down herself years ago on a school trip to Stratford-Upon-Avon. They started talking, and she helped him find a present for his young nephew.

He came in later in the week and then again the following day when he took her out for lunch. He was a business analyst at a consultancy firm, a world she knew nothing about, but this served to make it all the more enchanting. They discussed only the present, scant details of their families and vague future plans – the past for them both was a page that had been torn out.

After lunch, unbeknownst to either at the time, they had their last-ever first kiss, laced with tea and mint. Then, like a turtle egg buried two feet into the sand, they hatched and surfaced, scurrying towards the moonlight reflected on the sea.

Before long, Elisabeth tumbled rapaciously into her new identity as Mrs Sandhurst, with all the enthusiasm of an animal born for instinctive metamorphosis. Her husband became her benchmark: *they were* and *were not* each other. She no longer had to define herself as an individual, but as one half of a whole, each part of him either mirrored or contrasted by her own characteristics. Above all, she now imagined that it is…

…so still and dark as she pulls aside the covers and slips her legs out of the bed she made that she can no longer lie in. Through the gap in the curtain, the streetlight pokes through like a voyeur, disrupting her. 'Go away', she thinks, 'leave me to do this'.

She gets dressed quietly and retrieves her travel bag, filling it with the few clothes and possessions that she's been able to hold on to. For a moment she sits and watches Daniel as he sleeps. 'Did we always know?' she asks herself, 'or is this a surprise for both of us?' She, certainly, is somewhat surprised. She's been constructing and destructing her life for years, like a cake whose ingredients she could never quite get right. There's only one letter difference between life and lie.

She thinks about the intangibility of happiness, and how her children had brought her the closest to it. And she thinks about unhappiness, how she constantly wants to be *other* than. She is disappointed, yet again, in her insatiability – but there is hope.

She fetches her coat and is about to leave when she reconsiders, and decides to leave a note. She's said so much, but it's never enough. '*Verba volant, littera scripta manet*', she reminds herself, rationalising her need to leave one last justification for her choices. But she has no means for the task. She searches the scant room haphazardly and then checks her coat pocket, where she finds a scrap of white paper and a purple coloured pencil. She unfurls the paper she'd found in her daughter's room and almost balks as she re-reads the contents, written by an innocent child's hand. But she has no time for hesitation – she has to go now, before she stays forever, locked in herself.

She crosses out the words heavily and turns the paper over, racking her brains for the best way to explain to Daniel, to make him understand the dilemma that's plagued her entire life. She writes those six finite words, the only words she has the strength for, and underlines the last one.

She lays the note on the pillow and, like a scene from a Gregory Crewdson picture, lingers just a moment, twilight splashed across her face. Then Amelia grabs her things, leaves the building and, once more, heads *there*.